FIONA RISING

KATHLEEN MORRIS

Dunraven Press

Copyright © 2023 by Kay Morris

All rights reserved.

No part of this book may be reproduced in any form or by any electronic or mechanical means, including information storage and retrieval systems, without written permission from the author, except for the use of brief quotations in a book review.

Enhanced edition, previously published as The Wind at Her Back.

Ebook Edition ISBN 979-8-9874563-1-6

Paperback Edition ISBN 979-8-9874563-2-3

Hardcover Edition ISBN 979-8-9874563-3-0

Dunraven Press May 2023

Cover Art & Design by Tabulanis

BOOKS BY KATHLEEN MORRIS

The Lily of the West

The Transformation of Chastity James

Fiona Rising

Fallen Child

Risk

Golddigger: The Legendary Nellie Cashman

May the road rise up to meet you.
May the wind always be at your back.
May the sun shine warm upon your face,
and rains fall soft upon your fields.
　　　--Old Irish Proverb

For Chris, who helped me find Ballyowen.

The old wooden chair creaked softly as she rocked the baby gently back and forth, his head lolling on her forearm, the downy red curls soft on her skin. He hardly weighed anything, this precious child, but he'd grow, she knew. He was her first, maybe her only, from what the midwife had said. She bent and kissed his forehead softly but he didn't stir. He was a very good baby.

She hadn't thought to light a candle and now it was full dark in the cottage, only the faint light of the half moon ghostly through the cracked window and the embers of the fire glowing faintly in the stone fireplace. She didn't want to disturb him, so she continued to rock, back and forth. She hummed a lullaby, one she'd heard somewhere, her throat so dry she couldn't sing the words. She rocked and the baby slept on.

"Jesus God, woman," Sean shouted, throwing open the wooden door. "Have ye no sense at all? It's cold out there. A man comes home to no fire and no light in his home, where in Jesus would that happen but here?" He was a burly man, red-faced with whiskey and the stink of him filled the cottage like graveyard dirt.

He stumbled about, crashing into what little furniture there was, finally lighting a candle stub where it sat on a saucer in the middle of a wooden table. He looked around, blinking like a rabbit caught in sunlight until he spied her in the rocking chair. He was drunk, as usual, but the sight of her stopped him cold.

"Fiona? What in God's name are you doing with that baby?"

He snatched the child from her arms, putting the bundle down on the table, backing away as though it might harm him and turned to the woman in the chair. He took a step back as she rose, her eyes wild, her black hair streaming over her shoulders.

"The babe's been dead a day and then some, in his winding sheet. Has the priest not been here?"

"He knocked, but I didn't let him in, since there was no need." Her voice was cracked, her throat so dry she thought she'd never felt water trickle down her throat before. "The child is fine, he just needs rest."

"He died yesterday," roared Sean, "ye daft bitch. He only lived two days as 'tis."

She looked at him and smiled sadly. "No, Sean. Our son will be fine. His father is always taken with the drink, but we'll be fine in spite of that."

He hit her then, with the back of his hand and she fell into the chair.

"You'll not be fine, you're crazy as a rat in the field, Fiona," Sean said, "losing the child has addled your mind and all. I'll be getting the priest meself and he can put you in the madhouse after he buries the child. I'll be well rid of you. You couldn't give birth to a turnip, skinny bitch like you, no more'n you can be a decent wife to a man. I'll be getting me a wife that allows a man a drink and poke without wailing like you never did."

He busied himself with his satchel, paying her no attention, and headed for the door. When she hit him over the head with the iron poker, he dropped like a rock onto the dirt floor. She hit him again, smiling. She stood back, breathing heavily, feeling more alive than she had in days. She took up the bundle from the table and stared at the baby's gray face.

The bastard was right. The child was dead. She kissed the cold little head one last time and smoothed the red curls, tears streaming down her face. She looked at the bloody body of her husband and put the baby down gently on the table. A funeral pyre seemed just the thing. Had the old ones not done this in the past? She wasn't sure but she took the shovel and threw the coals, load by load, around the cottage, into the barren cupboards and the mean broken furniture but they weren't catching. She smashed the kerosene lantern onto the floor beside the bloody bedcovers and coals caught the liquid as it trickled through the broken glass. At last, the fire brightened and grew, the flames orange and red, and she left through the open doorway, her feet bare, her cotton dress floating around her as she wandered out into the night, not caring where she went, only away from pain and death. Nothing else mattered.

PART I
A NEW LIFE

CHAPTER 1

Kilkenny County, Ireland
1876

"Just a sip, dearie. That's all Mary asks. Come now."

Fiona blinked. Everything was white, the walls, the ceiling, the bedcovers, the nurse's uniform. A spoon hovered near her face and she jerked back involuntarily against the pillows.

"Ah god, someone's truly been at you, haven't they?" The voice was kind. "Well, we knew that. Come on, sweetling, you need to eat. I'll not hurt you."

The spoon was there and Fiona opened her mouth. Warm broth trickled down her sore throat and it tasted like the best thing she'd ever swallowed. One spoonful followed another and soon she lay back, sated but so very tired. Her eyes closed again.

Feeble sunlight greeted her the next time she opened her eyes. She lay in a bed. A soft one in a white room, white sheets pulled to her chin. Fiona moved her hips just a little, wincing at the pain, but liking the feel of the crisp sheets beneath her. It had been a long time since she'd felt them but she'd never forgotten. In the orphanage they'd been rougher, but still clean.

She knew because her hands, among others, had been the ones plunged into hot water and strong lye soap to make them so.

Thoughts of St. Hilda's Orphanage surfaced, memories she never wanted to relive. Others lurked in the depths beside them, coming unbidden into her mind. Sean Dooley, on Adoption Day, his little piggy eyes raking over the girls standing in line in their scratchy starched uniforms and landing on her. Her heart plummeting in her stomach as they lingered on her and he turned to the headmistress, whispering in her waiting ear. She was not to be his daughter, or his servant, but his wife, she soon learned. She was fourteen but she'd bled and the sisters were eager to be rid of girls her age. There were so many more coming in, after all. Marriage to a good Catholic with a farm was the best outcome they could hope for with all the girls in their charge, one the girls would bless them for, as would God, of course.

Fiona groaned, turning her face into the pillow. The memories kept coming and she couldn't stop them, although she tried. If she could only sleep again, but they surfaced like dead fish floating on a river, she powerless to stop them.

She'd gathered what few things she had, two dresses, a hairbrush, her rosary and a cape and she'd ridden away with Sean Dooley on his wagon that February day, a fine mist cloaking them on the road. He stopped after only a few miles away and turned to her.

"Girl, you're mine now," he said, sliding his hands under her threadbare wrap and over her thin body, squeezing her breasts. He chuckled. "I've an arrangement with Father McCauley at the Abbey and he'll be marryin' us this afternoon, so you've no need to be shy. You'll be my wife afore God and all the saints."

Fiona swallowed but she couldn't think of anything to say. All she wanted was for him to put his hands on the reins instead of her and get back on the road. Surely Father McCauley, a good Catholic priest, would see she wasn't ready to be a wife and send her back to St. Hilda's. The orphanage was no haven, she knew that well, but not as bad as a life chained to a man like this.

Instead, she was married. A hasty ceremony, the rain scarcely dried on their clothes and a hasty leavetaking in Sean Dooley's wagon, arriving many soggy hours later at a sod-roofed cottage that looked as though it was trying its best to creep back into the hillside it'd been carved from. In the dim light she made out a barn with three sides whose roof was leaning precariously, covering a skinny cow and some chickens scratching in the dirt between the structures. Not such a prosperous farm after all. She was shaking from head to toe with cold and apprehension but Sean flung open the door and ordered her to make a fire, throwing her a tin of matches while he saw to the horse and wagon. Fiona crept inside, stumbling in the darkness and made out a rude hearth and set to her task, fingers fumbling with the sparse kindling and wood. A few small flames were flickering when Sean entered, bolting the door behind him.

"Can you not do better than that, for Jesus's sake?" He flung off his cloak and strode towards her, shaking his head in disgust.

"I'll make the best of it," he said. He picked her up and carried her to the bed against the wall, the coverlets smelling of sweat and dirt. "It's not every day a man gets married and to tarry 'twould be a sin, now, wouldn't it? In the eyes of God and all, fire or no fire."

When he thrust into her, throwing her dress over her head, she wanted to scream with the pain and the indignity of the assault on her body. She'd never thought anything like this was possible. Why had no one told her this was what marriage was? Surely there was something, some wonderful thing that made marriage a sacrament that the nuns and priests had not told her about. Not this. This was pain. This was horrifying. Surely she had missed something in all the teachings.

Days, weeks and months later, Fiona came to know that as Sean Dooley's wife, she hadn't missed anything. They had failed to tell her. The fine ladies she'd seen passing by in the street would not have a life like this, any more than she would ever have theirs. The wife of a crofter in Ballyowen was her lot and not one she'd been prepared for. She suspected there was many a fine lady who had to endure as she did, but at least their sheets were clean and soft.

As the days passed, she had no choice but to accept it. It might have been easier if she didn't have to share a bed with a man who sickened her, forcing himself on her night after night, beating her at the slightest offense and telling her, day after day, how stupid she was.

"Can ye not learn to cook anything right?" A blow. "This is the most shite bread I've ever eaten." Punch. "Have ye never made a stew?" The plate, when he threw it, didn't break when she caught it, but the hot stew burned her arms. She came to learn that for Sean Dooley, the only thing about her that was right was the opening between her legs. He never seemed to care that she didn't even move.

When she found herself with child, she woke up each morning with joy, touching her belly and waiting for it to move like Mrs. McGill from down the road had told her it would. Sean, on the other hand, could not decide whether he wanted a child to help with the farm, as he called the miserable three acres of potatoes he mostly ignored between trips to the pub in the village or thinking that having to feed another mouth wouldn't be worth the trouble. That he beat and raped her nearly every day didn't change at all.

Sometimes on Saturdays, market day, Sean allowed her to go to the village for supplies and Fiona usually walked with Mrs. McGill, or rode in her wagon. On Saturdays and Wednesdays,

Sean worked at the leathery, making bridles and harness. It was nice, being out with people who smiled and talked to her like she was a normal person, and not just a wife who couldn't do anything right. She braided her hair and wore the cleanest clothes she could, covering the bruises on her body and arms. She became acquainted with a few other young wives, although they seemed much happier with their husbands, mostly smiling young men who occasionally accompanied them or stopped by for a kiss and a tickle, which made them blush and laugh. Fiona hadn't laughed in a long time. She did like to hear others do so, though, just as she liked the bustling market full of goods, with buyers and sellers doing business, and young children running about between their fathers' legs and their mothers' skirts. By Saturdays, she was hungry to hear voices and be a part of a life outside the mean cottage where she passed her days.

She also met Mother Flynn, the midwife Mrs. McGill introduced her to, who gave her sound advice and promised to be at the birthing when it came. Still, as Saturday mornings were the best part of her life, Saturday nights were the worst, since Sean always came home very drunk after getting his pay and for Sean, drunk meant mean. Pleasure always had a price, Fiona learned.

Mother Flynn kept her word and delivered Fiona's baby, folding the tiny body into her arms, clucking her tongue as she did so.

"He came easy but he's got a puny cry, this one," she said, shaking her head. "Take a care, Fiona. There's nothing more I can do for either of ye. Trust him to the Virgin, you'll need her help." She'd gathered her things and left, planting a kiss on Fiona's head.

She prayed, Mother Mary, how she prayed, but the cries grew more feeble as the hours wore on and the baby wouldn't feed. Fiona couldn't remember when she'd last slept and then the baby stopped moving at all. Then she remembered all of it now and her eyes closed with the pain and guilt she'd tried to block.

"Mornin' to you, my girl." The nurse breezed in, carrying a tray. "Porridge will do you a world of good. Let's get you propped up now."

CHAPTER 2

"We've been worried about you, young woman." The doctor fingered his moustache and looked at his chart. "It was four days ago someone dropped you at the door in pretty bad shape and only today you've been awake." He frowned and peered at her over his gold-rimmed glasses.

Fiona swallowed. "I…I'm sorry, sir." She met his eyes but looked down quickly. "I've not meant to be a bother."

He waved his hand dismissively. "We are here to heal and it's never a bother. So, let's start with your name and how you came to be here," he said, his pen ready.

Fear shot through her. She'd killed Sean and they'd hang her; she knew murder was a sin against both God and men. Wives didn't kill their husbands, no matter what, and if they did, there was no mercy.

"Where am I?"

The doctor looked up at the nurse in surprise. "Have you not talked with her, Mary?"

The nurse shook her head. "No, sir, she's not been awake much but for today. A'course I thought she knew that much."

She looked at Fiona and her eyes weren't friendly. "Don't you even know you're in Cork?"

"Cork?" Fiona managed, tears slowing rolling down her cheeks. She'd never been as far as Cork in her life, a town on the water she had only heard tales about from the sisters at St. Hilda's. She'd remembered it all, or most of it: the baby, hitting Sean with the poker, the fire, and running towards the road. Then the cold, so very cold but nothing after that except a kind gruff voice and a bone-shaking journey in some sort of wagon.

The doctor sighed. "Yes, girl you're in Cork. Now what's your name?"

Fiona took a deep breath. She wasn't raised a liar but somehow she knew this was no time to tell the truth. "Why, 'tis Mary, same as yours," she said to the nurse. "Mary Flynn. From County Mayo. I was comin' to my sick aunt to be her companion, in Kilkenny. Some men robbed the man whose wagon I was travelin' on…" she shook her head slowly, fresh tears cascading down her cheeks. I think they killed him and took me off… I can't remember anything after that. Cork? How did I come to be in this place?"

The doctor stood up. "Nurse, this girl is clearly not in her right mind. After a day or two, and she's regained her strength, perhaps we should move her to the asylum or the workhouse. Hospital space is in dire need, and those bruises will heal with no further help from us. See to it."

He put his pen in his pocket, grunted and left. The nurse's face was pale, her expression shocked.

"Well, Mary Flynn," she said. "Looks to me like we've got a situation here. Can you walk?"

Fiona sat up. "I suppose I can, if I have to." She swung her legs off the side of the bed and stood up. The dizziness was instantaneous and she fell back onto the bed, her head whirling.

"That English ass," the nurse muttered, tucking Fiona's legs back under the sheet. "Poor darlin'. You've been beat within an inch of your young life and had naught but broth and porridge in days. I'll figure this out. Stay here and rest." She bustled out, full of indignation and purpose. In spite of her apprehension, Fiona lay back and closed her eyes. She dreamed no more.

Two days later, Fiona dressed herself in the clothes Mary had brought her, a brown skirt, a blouse and a jacket of the same material, only green. There were even shoes that almost fit, a bit big but they'd do.

"Hurry now, lass," Mary whispered, guiding her to the door. Fiona's steps were much surer after two days of eating as much as she could hold, thanks to Mary. They crept down the hallway, then the stairs and out a side door into the street. It was dark, but the streetlamps were lit and Mary took her hand as they walked down the cobbled streets, fog rolling in off the water, wreathing the tall stone buildings with feathery fingers.

"My brother Ewan has a pub on High Street. You'll be a barmaid and there's a room in the back you can sleep in." She glanced back at Fiona. "It's not much, but it's a start. Better than the workhouse, or God forbid it, the asylum, where his majesty would've put ye. I'll tell him you just up and left with your aunt who come to get you."

"Although, we both know there's no aunt," Mary said. "But you seem a sweet girl, and I can't leave you to the system, no matter to me what you've done. From the scars and bruises on you, lass, plenty harm has been done to yourself so I'm makin' it right. Where's the child?"

Tears pricked at Fiona's eyes and she squeezed Mary's hand. "He died before he could take many breaths."

Mary nodded. "I thought as much." She squeezed Fiona's hand in return.

"Thank you, I can't begin to thank you."

Mary snorted. "No need, girl. I was in a situation myself

once…" her voice trailed off, and it was clear that was a memory she didn't want to remember and one she wasn't partial to sharing. Fiona could certainly understand that.

They came to a low building with green shutters and a thatched roof where fiddle music poured merrily out the open half door. There were even geraniums in the green painted windowboxes. The sign read "Rose and Thistle" and Mary pulled her in. It smelled of ale, whiskey, sweat and maybe, just maybe, of hope.

Faces turned as they made their way to the bar and the man who stood behind it, polishing a tall beer glass with a spotless white towel. He grinned a hello to Mary and jerked his head towards a door behind the bar. Mary guided her through into a small office and a few minutes later, he joined them, wiping his hands on his apron. He was tall, and broad, the grin still on his face under a large red moustache that matched his ginger hair. He peered at Fiona.

"So here's your pretty little mouse that needs a hidey-home, eh Mary?"

"None o' that, Ewan," Mary said, "this is Mary Flynn, yes. Mary, this is my brother Ewan Delaney. He'll take good care of you. He may look a rogue, but he's harmless."

Ewan laughed. "To you, anyway, or you'll be ruinin' my fierce reputation." He turned to Fiona. "So, you'll stay here," he gestured towards another door, "you work hard and we'll get along fine. I'll pay you a good wage, just a bit out for board. I can always use a good barmaid and I don't put up with anyone messin' with you, they know better than that. All right with you?"

He seemed kind and she didn't have a lot of choices. Truthfully, she'd never had to make many decisions before smacking Sean with the poker but she was quickly learning she'd better make some now, and good ones. She looked at Mary who nodded in encouragement. Fiona held out her hand.

"Yes, sir. Thank you, sir."

The big man smiled at her as though indulging a child and took her small hand in his large one. "I like you, Mary Flynn. I'm thinkin' we'll get along just fine."

CHAPTER 3

Spring in Cork was beautiful and every chance she had, Fiona walked outside. Along the quay, over to the shops on High Street, loving the sea breeze so soft against her face. So unlike the bleak orphanage and the village she'd lived in with Dooley, flowers bloomed in the window boxes and the pots outside the businesses and houses and she reveled in their sweet scents and bright colors. People smiled and went about their business with enthusiasm rather than drudgery. The sun danced over the waves beside the fishing boats painted in bright blues, greens and yellows, their masts sticking up like needles into the sky with their patched sails. She liked to watch them unload their catches, the silvery fish falling into the carts and baskets and the men happy and satisfied with their day's work.

Ewan had been kind to her and the work, while sometimes tiring by night's end, wasn't anything worse than what she'd done before, in fact lighter and no one was berating her, not nuns and not Sean Dooley. Lifting trays full of tankards and dodging through tables was nothing compared to the drudgery of the filthy cottage and farm and the toil at the orphanage, and she didn't have to duck from swinging fists or try to sidestep kicks of encouragement. Ewan made sure she had enough to eat, since the cook made shepherd's pies and pasties for the pub daily, and always saved portions for her as well.

Fiona pinched her arms and smiled. They were muscled from the trays but filling out, as was the rest of her. For the first time since she could remember, she wasn't hungry and it showed in the sheen of her skin and the blush on her cheeks. True to his word, Ewan had paid her wages with no quibble, even from the first, when she was so weak she could barely manage to carry two tankards to a table, but she'd grown stronger by the day. Now she not only carried, but joked with the patrons and skipped out of the way of too eager hands with a laugh. Ewan was always on alert and she was grateful for that, but she'd learned to take care of herself.

She learned a lot more than that. The world was a big place, and Ireland not the biggest country in it, while Cork was only a tiny piece of that, and Ballyowen just a smidge. Although she couldn't remember getting to Cork from Ballyowen, she didn't think it was terribly far. Not like America, which was the place she wanted to be. Everyone talked about it endlessly, in the pubs and shops, and for years, ever since the famine and even now, so many had boarded the ships at nearby Cobh.

Fiona doubted the streets were paved with gold or that jobs were waiting to be handed out when you walked off the ship. She wasn't that much a fool. But it did sound like a country where people could start a new life and she longed for that. She'd gone to Cork's small library and read nearly every book they had, asking the lady there questions until the woman tired of her. Then she'd gone to stopping in at the newspaper office every few days. Their information was much more up to date, and told about the ships that left Cobh. This was prime sailing time, from now until November and Fiona intended to be one of the passengers that bid goodbye to Ireland forever.

She saved every penny Ewan paid her, only buying some

simple clothing and a pair of boots that fit her, but there were no ribbons or gewgaws that piqued her interest. Going to America interested her more than anything the shops could possibly offer. Every once in a while, though, she pined after a hair comb or a book in the outdoor stall at Green's Bookshop, but she passed them by. There'd be time for that. She'd gotten a second chance and she wasn't going to waste it.

The sun was high, and Fiona hastened her steps back to the Rose and Thistle. Ewan opened at noon, and closed at eleven like clockwork, seven days a week. He didn't cater to the drunks looking for whiskey at eight in the morning and kept a firm hand on all aspects of his business, including the barmaids. Besides her, there was Aisling and Siobhan who'd been in the business for a while and had taught her how things were, from the different drinks they served to managing the customers, whether they were drunk, sober, too friendly or mean.

She entered through the side door and hurried to her room, surprised to see Ewan in the hallway. She nodded and went to slip past him but he caught her arm.

"There was a man looking for you early this morning," he said, worry etched on his forehead, the ginger brows pinched together. "Well, at least a lass that sounded a lot like you, Mary."

Fiona's stomach plummeted. "What? Why would someone be looking for me?"

Ewan grunted. "Come now. We all knew you were running from something, Mary. He described you well. 'Very pretty, long dark hair, big green eyes, heart-shaped face', he says to me."

She swallowed. "Oh. Well, there's a lot of girls look like that."

Ewan stared at her. "No, there's not. Not like you. Tell me now. You've not killed anyone, have you?"

"No," Fiona said emphatically, hoping it was true and worried it was not. "Never." She swallowed nervously, hoping Ewan didn't notice.

"All right, then." Ewan peered at her in the dim hallway. "I told him I'd never seen a girl like that. But I can't promise he'll not be back. He seemed a mean little weasel to me, a countryman from the look of him. Are you ready to work today?"

"Course I am," she said. "Just let me get my apron on and fix my hair, I'll be right out." She spun around and tried to sound casual. "Did he have a name, this man?"

"Sean something," Ewan said, "can't remember the last. Familiar?"

Fiona shook her head no and hurried down the hall, her stomach heaving.

She shut the door to the little room she'd come to think of as a haven. It was small but clean and cozy, a white comforter on the bed, the china washbasin and ewer painted in pink rosebuds and even a small polished steel mirror on the wall in front of it. The trunk beside the bed held her meager clothes. Fiona sat down on the bed and tried to breathe deeply, to still her pounding heart.

Who could it be? It sounded like Sean, that somehow he'd managed to escape the fire she'd set in her rage. She'd always hoped he had, as she'd never set out to be a murderess. Still, something had snapped in her that night and she was now forever changed into another person, and not just the name she'd taken. These long months between had forged her into another person, one full of resolve and gained knowledge. She'd done more than survived, she'd grown and learned she was in charge of her own life.

How could anyone have tracked her here to Cork? It was a long way from Ballyowen. Well, at least she thought it was. Whether it was Sean or a constable using his name, it looked as though someone had. Her mind raced but she stood up, tied on her apron and smoothed her hair back into the single plait that lay across her shoulder. She had a job to do, so no one would be suspicious, even Ewan, dear as he was. If the man came back today, she'd have to deal with it.

The day and evening passed with no incident and whoever he was, the man hadn't shown up asking after her. Fiona went straight to her room after closing, shutting the door with a sigh. She'd been nervous as a twitching mouse, tired as though she'd been running from God knows what the whole shift. She splashed water on her face, peering into the small steel mirror. Shadows were dark under those green eyes and wan heart-shaped face. She fell into bed and slept dreamlessly she was so tired but woke with the dawn, staring at the ceiling in the faint light through the small window above her head.

She threw back the covers and pulled the small wooden box she kept her money in from under the bed. She counted out the coins. Today was payday and with that, maybe she had enough for the passage fare. Maybe it was fanciful, but she couldn't stop the looming sense of something dark coming for her and the urge to just pack her few things and run was nearly overpowering. She put her hands on her thighs and took a deep breath. *Stop it, Fiona. You'll be grand, don't give in to the fear,* she said to herself. She dressed and went out to the bar to get a cup of tea.

Ewan was already there, having a cup himself.

"Mornin' to you, Mary."

"And to you, Ewan." She poured herself a cup of tea from the steaming pot and added milk, stirring quickly with the small spoon.

"You're up early today."

She smiled at him. "These spring days, I only want to enjoy the sun and the flowers. It's lovely."

"Indeed." He sipped his tea and glanced at her over the rim of his cup. He slid her pay packet over the bar towards her and she put it in her pocket, trying to not seem too eager. It felt heavier than usual and Fiona looked up at him.

"He was out there this mornin' looking in the window."

Ah, there it was. "Who?"

"The same man inquirin' about you on Monday."

"After the girl with green eyes, then?"

"The very same."

She shrugged and it took every ounce of strength she had, her legs trembling. "He's mistaken, clear."

"Maybe. But just in case, there's some extra in there." Ewan nodded towards the pay packet in her pocket. "He seems a persistent sort, that one. I know you're lookin' to book passage. Today might be a good day for that, Mary."

Fiona forced herself to drink some tea. "I'll look into that, Ewan."

"The back door might be a better idea than the front, I'm thinkin'".

She wasted no time, going through the kitchen and running to the shipping office three blocks down the street.

The woman behind the counter was red-cheeked and friendly. "You're in luck, lass. There's a ship leaving Cobh tonight on the evening tide, the Adriatic, bound for New York. Let me check to see if there's room for you."

Fiona stood there, breathless, fingering the coins in her purse and silently praying to the Virgin and all the saints. Please, please, she thought, a litany running over and over in her head.

The woman beamed at her. "Yes, if you can make it, there's one berth left in steerage, my dear. Sixty shillings and that includes food and water." She held out her hand and Fiona counted out the money. Thank God for Ewan, because the money he'd put in her pay packet made up the difference, or she wouldn't have had enough. The man was a saint. She clutched her ticket as though it was a ticket to heaven and maybe it was.

"Get there before six o'clock to board. They'll leave with the tide at seven, with or without you, girl, believe me." The woman smiled at her. "Good luck. Here's a tip for free. Bring as much of your own food as you can, the provisions aren't exactly tasty."

"Thank you." She hurried outside and around the back

towards the Rose and Thistle. Hopefully Ewan could get her a ride with the whiskey man when he delivered this morning and she'd be in Cobh well before sailing time. She found Ewan at the bar, setting up.

"I bought a ticket," she said, waving it like a magic talisman. He grinned.

"Good for you, but I'm sorry to see you go, Mary. You've graced the place."

She blushed. There had been few times in her life anyone had complimented her and she wasn't sure how to handle it.

Ewan put down the glasses. "Let's go to the back. I've got a case you can use and we'll get you packed up and on your way. Patrick's already baked some pies and we'll be sure you've got food with you."

"Thanks, the ticket lady advised that, and told me she didn't think the food was very good but not as bad as it used to be. I don't know how many people I'll be sharing a room with and all. They don't really tell you anything or maybe it's because they don't know anything. They say it'll only take ten days or so as it's a steamship, so that's good but it's still a long time."

Ewan was staring at her and she realized she was talking like a madwoman. She shook her head. "Sorry."

"Don't be silly, you'd be mad to not be nervous," he said.

Ewan produced a small battered leather suitcase and Fiona packed her few clothes and toiletries, looking around the little room that had been a haven for her when she most needed it. Her hands were shaking, both from nerves and excitement and she clutched them together. Ewan returned with a canvas sack of food and some bottles of water, a woolen cloak over one arm.

"Here," he said gruffly, handing it to her. "I'm thinkin' you'll need this. It was my wife's."

Tears pooled in her eyes. "Oh Ewan, you've been so good to me, I'll never be able to thank you properly. Now I'm leavin' you when you need me and that's not right, but I haven't a choice, I think."

He pulled her into an awkward hug. "No, Mary, you do not. Write me a letter sometime and tell me your story. That man will surely be back, I know that. When he comes, it's best you're gone." He pulled back and kissed the top of her head. "Now let's get you on Seamus's cart, he's already here unloadin' and eager to be off to Cobh and those parts."

For a minute, all she wanted was to stay here, safe at the Rose and Thistle, in her little room, working for Ewan but she knew it was much too late for that.

"Please say goodbye and thanks to Mary for me, Ewan," Fiona said. "I'll miss you both so much." The tears threatened to spill over but he only nodded and took her arm, picking up the suitcase.

Seamus was the whiskey deliveryman, a father with six children and a plump wife, some of whom came along with him on his rounds, but today he was alone. He loaded her things onto the cart. "Be good to have some company on my rounds, Mary. Can you sing then?"

"Not really," she said. "I'm likely no good at that."

"Ah, well, we'll see about that," he winked. "I'm a songster myself and I'll teach you." He was a kind man and she had no qualms about leaving with him.

She waved goodbye to Ewan, where he stood outside the back door, watching as they turned the corner and set off down the cobbled street.

Goodbye, Cork, Fiona thought. *You've been good to me. I hope America will be as well.* By the time they reached the outskirts of town, Seamus taught her to sing "Molly Malone" and to her surprise, she liked it very much.

CHAPTER 4

She couldn't remember ever feeling this sick. Hurt and aching, yes, but the constant vomiting was the worst thing she'd ever experienced because it didn't stop. She wasn't alone. Near everyone else in the cramped airless room was the same and the smell alone was enough to keep them that way, even when the ship wasn't pitching like a leaf in a swift-running stream.

When she'd first seen the *Adriatic*, its sheer size dwarfed the other boats on the wharf. Walking up the gangway, Fiona thought she was walking into the mouth of a whale, one that would swallow her up and quite possibly spit her out somewhere out in the swells of the blue sea. She watched as hundreds of other people got on and only after they pulled the anchor and headed out to dark nothingness did she venture down to the quarters she'd been assigned.

Fiona raised herself up on an elbow and peered at her fellow passengers, eight other people crammed into three-tiered bunks. The Dunnes, a husband and wife and their three children, two single women like herself, Mary O'Neill and Siobhan something from Kerry, both going to join their families in New York and a pretty but aloof young man, James Ardrey, English from the few brief words he'd offered. Ardrey'd been out a great deal, the only one of them not seasick in the first three days of the crossing.

They hadn't much of an opportunity to chat, between laying flat on their bunks and using the buckets provided for their ailment, because apparently seasickness, as they called it, was common. Twice a day, the buckets were emptied, and food and water was brought in, but no one had partaken of much of it. There were privies down the hall, thank God for that, Fiona thought, but it wasn't always easy to get there when your stomach was roiling like a soup pot on the spit.

Mary O'Neill looked very bad, to Fiona's eye. She was white as Saint Patrick's ghost, as Sister Deirdre used to say, and shaking. Fiona climbed down from the second bunk and knelt beside her.

"Mary," she whispered. "How are you feeling?"

The woman's eyelids fluttered and she groaned. "Not well a'tall."

Fiona stood up and smoothed her skirts. "I'm getting the doctor. I'll be right back."

She eased open the door and found the stairway to the upper levels. There had to be a ship's doctor, or at least someone who could help. They all felt poorly, but that woman looked very bad to her. Besides, it was time she went up and got some fresh air. Perhaps James Ardrey was onto something.

Fiona trudged up the stairs, three flights, and opened the first doorway available. Cold salty air hit her face and she gasped. She pulled in lungfuls of fresh air and for the first time in days, immediately felt better. Stupid girl, she told herself. This is what you should've been doing from the first. No wonder Ardrey wasn't as sick as the rest of them.

She was on a lower deck and there were few people around,

but as she stood by the railing, a deckhand came by and she stopped him.

"Is there a doctor? We've a very sick woman in our room."

He seemed confused. "Sick? They're all sick the first days, miss. It'll pass."

"No," she said firmly. "It's more than that, I'm thinkin'. So, doctor?"

He shrugged. "Up two levels, then ask somebody."

She opened the door marked "Infirmary", immediately assaulted by the smell of carbolic acid. A dark-haired bearded man busy putting shiny instruments on a table turned to her. "What?" He seemed impatient but there was no one else in the room.

"Sir, there's a woman down on Level 5 in our room. She's very ill, not just seasick. Could you please see her?"

"Level 5?" he sniffed, as though it was something below his notice. "What's wrong with her?"

Fiona stared at him. "She's *sick*, not just the usual, I think. She's very weak."

He threw down the remaining instruments. "They're always weak, girl. This isn't an easy voyage." He seemed to deliberate and then sighed, picking up a bag. "All right, let's see to her."

When they entered the stateroom, the stench hit her like a wave and the doctor recoiled a bit as well. How had she been cooped in here for three days?

He knelt down beside Mary O'Neill and felt her pulse and shook his head. "Let's get her out of here and up to the infirmary."

Fiona looked around. No one else was ambulatory, so she had to assume he meant her. She took Mary O'Neill's legs and swung them over to the floor. The doctor grabbed her around the waist and Fiona hoisted from the other side and between the two of them, they managed to get the woman to the infirmary, a deckhand passing by on Level 3 helping. They put her in a bed and the doctor bent over her, mumbling to himself and making notes on a chart, while Fiona sat down on a nearby stool and the deckhand disappeared like wisp of smoke. Her stomach rumbled but she wasn't queasy, just hungry. She looked around. There was a scone on a plate on the desk and she grabbed it up, stuffing it into her mouth.

"Christ Jesus." The doctor came around the corner. "I can't be certain just yet, but I think the girl's got typhus. Haven't seen this on board in ten years now. We're going to have quarantine that room and everybody in it."

Fiona shot up off the stool, swallowing the last of the scone. "I feel fine, sir, just fine."

He eyed her suspiciously. "For now. How're the rest of them?"

"I can't really say," she stammered. "Mr. Ardrey's gone most of the time and he seems fine, too. I don't know about the others."

"Well, we're going to find out," he said. "I've got no help here, the last nurse quit before we sailed. What's your name, girl?"

"Tis Mary, sir, same as hers." She'd done this before.

He scowled. "You're Nurse Mary, now. You look healthy enough. At least I'll know where you are and I can keep an eye on you. Your first job is to look after that one," he gestured towards the still body in the bed, "while I go to the Captain and get some help with the rest of them."

Fiona moved her things up to a cot in the infirmary and the next six days passed in a blur. She wiped brows, bathed feverish bodies and held hands, prepared medicine and worked harder than she ever had. She fell onto her berth exhausted when she could but she never got sick again. In the end, though, eleven people died before they docked in New York, including the hapless Mary O'Neill, her friend Siobhan and two of the Dunne children, among others. They were delayed a week in harbor but no new cases surfaced and the passengers were finally going to be allowed to disembark and get on with their new lives.

The doctor, an American named Joel Prescott, stood with Fiona at the railing, watching as people walked down the onto the pier, some greeted by friends and some, most of the people from the lower levels, escorted towards another building to be processed, whatever that meant. She saw her old cabin mate, Ardrey, walk away with a man in a fancy suit, laughing. He'd seemed like a man who always landed on his feet.

"You have family here, Mary?" Joel asked, puffing on his pipe. Gruff, he was, but he'd been kind to her, and compassionate to the patients he tended. She liked him.

"No. I know not a soul."

He gazed at her. "I thought that might be the case." He fumbled in his pocket and handed her a card and an envelope. "Go see my sister. Audrey can find you something to get started. I wrote her about you, and her address is on the card. It's the least I can do, you've been a great help to me and you didn't have to. You're a sweet girl and a smart one. Without your early warning, we would've had a much worse catastrophe on our hands and you've worked hard to save lives, so I'd like to help if I can. I'll walk off with you so you don't need to go through that cattle barn," he nodded towards the mass of people lined up beside the processing building. "You're one of the crew, now."

They walked down the gangway and onto the pier. Fiona looked with amazement at the mass of immensely tall buildings and the crowds. She could've never imagined a place so big with so many people, and so much activity, like a thousand hives of bees all buzzing to get somewhere or be heard. It was another world for certain. Sean Dooley would never find her here, but then again he'd found her in Cork, so it was hard to feel safe, even with an ocean between them.

Joel hailed a cab, gave him an address and paid him, shutting the door as Fiona gathered up her skirts.

"Take care, dear Mary and thank you for all you've done." He smiled. "Oh by the way, you never did tell me your last name. Mary what?"

Sometimes you had to take advantage of circumstances, Fiona thought, when life presents an opportunity, just to be certain. Another layer between her and Sean Dooley was a good thing. After all, the woman had died with no documentation as had her friend. Many of the immigrants on the ship were the same. She smiled back. "Oh, that. It's O'Neill. Mary O'Neill."

CHAPTER 5

"Mary, I need you."

Didn't she always, Fiona thought, although with a smile. Audrey Prescott had been a godsend for her. Every time she heard Audrey call her name over the last few months, she'd become more accustomed to hearing it, even more so than at the Rose and Thistle. She'd felt a shift in her mind somehow, that this change in what anyone called her didn't change who she was. Fiona Dooley and Mary Flynn had disappeared into the heavens and Mary O'Neill had surfaced into the mind of the person she now was: a lady's maid and companion in New York City, well-fed, well-dressed and respected for her opinions and personality, at least by one Audrey Prescott.

Protected, by the Prescott wealth and position in society, she was now a person who needn't worry about what tomorrow would bring, much less any threat that could never find its way inside the elegant Fifth Avenue mansion she now lived in. Even if it was the "servants quarters", it was far nicer than anywhere she'd ever lived in her young life.

She remembered the first day she'd walked up the steps of this house, trembling as she rang the bell and ready to bolt at the scowl of the butler who answered the door. Instead, she'd handed him Joel Prescott's letter and waited outside on the steps. It had been worth it.

The room in which Audrey Prescott received her was elegant beyond Fiona's wildest imaginings. She'd never seen anything like it. The wallpaper was silk brocade, shining in the sunlight pouring through the high windows, framed by damask draperies. The furniture was beautiful, the arms of the chairs and sofas curved and the cushions they held looked as soft as the clouds of heaven. A low table was set with a china tea set and a very assured and pretty woman wearing a white silk dress gestured for her to sit, a kind smile on her face. "I am Audrey Prescott, Miss O'Neill. Please."

She poured her a cup of tea and handed it to her with a pale white hand, her buffed nails shining, almost as though Fiona was an equal.

Fiona swallowed, trying not to show her shock. She took the delicate china cup and saucer in her own hand, rough from all the scrubbing with carbolic acid and inhaled the jasmine-scented tea. She waited, any moment expecting to be shown the door when they all saw through the façade of her pretensions.

"My brother speaks fondly of you," Audrey Prescott continued, pouring a cup for herself, "and he suggests I should employ you, Mary O'Neill. You're Irish, of course, and as all New York knows, those of your heritage have had a difficult time in this city. I do not share the views of some of my fellow citizens, please know that. What skills have you, aside from my brother's praise of your wit and quickness?"

Fiona found her voice, after a moment. "Dr. Prescott is very kind and I was only happy to help with the poor unfortunates on the ship, doing what I could. I'm not sure what I may do here," she looked around the room," but I'm a hard worker and I learn fast. The nuns at . . .St. Hilda's Orphange always said so. I can read and write, as they taught me, and take direction well,

Sister Dierdre always said." Some instinct told her to leave out any mention of the Rose and Thistle. She doubted Audrey Prescott had need of a barmaid.

"Ah," Audrey Prescott said, frowning and Fiona nearly got up and left. She didn't belong here. Audrey glanced at her and quickly put down her teacup, clearly sensing Fiona's unease.

"No, no," she said. "I frown not at you, my dear, but what I have heard of some of these most . . . Christian and Catholic institutions. The children are not always, shall we say, treated gently. Taught, yes, but worked like slaves as well. Tell me, Mary, was that the case with you?"

How could she possibly know? It was as though the dark curtain of her childhood had been ripped aside and made known for what it was, the cruelty, the beatings, the bleakness and despair. Something broke loose inside her chest and she felt exposed but gratefully so for the first time in her life. Shame swiftly followed. This woman would never want a child from that sort of place to live in her home.

"Yes." Fiona blinked rapidly, to stop the tears. She'd never get a job here now but there was nothing for it. "Oh god, yes. How I hated that place." It felt so good to say it, even so.

Audrey Prescott was silent for a moment and then she rose and put a hand on Fiona's trembling shoulder. "Did you bring your things?"

"Yes, mum, my case is in the hall." Close by, which was good, as she'd be leaving very soon. Surely there were some Irish taverns in this vast place where she could find a place.

"Bentley will show you to your room, Mary," Audrey said. "Take a day and rest. I understand it was a difficult crossing, especially with the typhus and all."

She rang a small bell on the table. "He'll tell you about mealtimes and such. On Thursday, we'll decide just how I can best use you, because I think there's a lot of options when it comes to you, Mary." She smiled. "Welcome to America. I think you're going to like it here, my dear."

Fiona's legs were trembling with shock and exhaustion as she walked behind the butler down the third floor hallway, carrying her light suitcase, her footsteps inaudible on the thick carpet, even up here. When Bentley opened the door to a sunny little bedroom, she sighed with pleasure and Bentley, despite his stoic demeanor, smiled just a little. A blue comforter covered the bed, with the same color curtains on the window beside it. A nightstand, with a lamp and matches were on the other side, and a small chair sat before the fireplace, already lit and warming the room against the morning chill. A wardrobe and a washstand with a china basin and ewer atop it completed the furniture and it was more than she had ever known. Even the Rose and Thistle paled before this. She set down the case and turned to Bentley.

"Thank you, sir." She smiled at the stern butler. Right now she loved the world, him included.

Bentley's little smile turned into a grin. "You are most welcome. Bathing room and facilities are down the hall to your right. Lunch is at twelve, dinner at seven, and breakfast at six, all before the mistress, of course." He turned to go. "You'll like it here, little one. Miss Prescott is a rather extraordinary woman, you'll find. You'll get to know everyone in no time."

He closed the door gently behind him and Fiona sat down gratefully in the small chair, her muscles relaxing for the first time this day. She didn't know how long she'd be here or what she'd do, but for right now, this was a dream she was happy to live. She held her hands to the warmth of the fire.

* * *

SNOW FELL SOFTLY outside the drawing room windows. It was approaching midnight on Christmas Eve, and Fiona crept downstairs, past the glittering decorated tree in the hall and into the drawing room, the fire on the hearth giving off a glow that provided just enough light. She held the heavy drapery aside and looked out upon the street, the pools of light from the streetlights glowing like celestial beacons in the whiteness, the snow still falling like intricate pieces of starfrost. It was magical and she drank in the serenity of it, not a soul stirring on this sacred night.

She didn't know when it might be appropriate to give thanks for her good fortune, but tonight, the eve of celebrating the birth of gentle Jesus, seemed right to her and she breathed slowly, thinking of the last eight months in which she'd been so lucky and learned so very much. Oh, how she'd learned. She pressed her forehead against the cold glass.

She'd never known her parents, and her earliest memories were the hard beds and scratchy sheets of St. Hilda's. The nuns who were firm believers in punishment for any imagined sins and then just because they felt like it, from infractions in the schoolroom to not working fast enough in the laundry or the kitchens. Then Sean Dooley and her doomed unnamed child who'd never had the chance even at the poor life that she'd been granted. Now, she had more than a chance. She'd been granted a boon in the household of Audrey Prescott she could've never imagined and she'd taken full advantage of it.

Starting as an apprentice lady's maid instead of the kitchen, due to Annie's pregnancy, she'd learned very quickly the desires and ways of what it took to be a well-groomed lady of New York society, as Audrey Prescott certainly was. Fiona took note of every dress, every curl of hair, every gesture and every inflection Audrey made. She admired Audrey more than anyone she'd ever known: she was beautiful, assured, kind and gracious and Fiona longed to be just like her. Or, at least make people think she was. Kindness was a trait that only came to those who were satisfied and serene, and Fiona wasn't sure she would ever be that.

On afternoons, when Audrey was out making her calls or at social functions, Fiona practiced in front of her mirror, even sometimes wearing Audrey's clothes, which she carefully hung back in the closets before tiptoeing quietly out of the room. She learned the intricacies of silk stockings, corsets, scarves, hats, the vast variety of choices of fabric, color, style of everything from morning jackets to ball gowns and even the wonders of delicate slippers, heeled shoes, and wonder of wonders, soft white leather boots with fifty hooks and laces.

Fiona listened carefully to every word Audrey spoke and now she herself could speak with the same accent, foregoing the country Irish one which was all she'd always known. She watched surreptitiously as tea was poured, dinner was eaten, forks were poised, parties given, and waltzes danced. Fiona didn't want to be Audrey, but she wanted to glean every tidbit she could to make herself into someone like her. Someone who would be well-spoken, well-mannered and well thought of in the world in which she'd found herself, and she was indeed, a quick learner, although one who had learned to hide her inner transformation well from the other servants as well as her mistress.

While grateful, she knew there was a whole world out there, especially after listening to the guests who frequented the Prescott dinner parties and she wanted to prepare herself not only to explore it, but succeed, no matter where life might take her. Because in the end, deep inside, Fiona knew 515 Fifth Avenue was only the beginning of her life in America. She discovered ambition, not an attribute they taught at St. Hilda's but perhaps her rebellion against personal tyranny had begun the day they'd sold her to Sean Dooley. Subservience and submission were not traits Fiona ever wanted to exhibit again, even though that was now her lot, kind and comforting as it was.

"Merry Christmas, Fiona. May you have the gift of grace on this night," she whispered to her reflection. "Take me in your care, what angels there may be. I think I may be on a long journey and I don't know where the road leads." She looked one more time at the snowflakes on the other side of the glass, gathering her nightgown close and climbing up the stairs to her warm bed. It was the best Christmas she'd ever known.

CHAPTER 6

"They do this every year?"

Audrey Prescott laughed merrily and adjusted the outrageous hat on her head, pink ostrich feathers towering skywards and the brim nearly hiding the left side of her face. Her outfit matched, a pink silk jacket and skirt with its pleated back, the toes of her white kid boots peeking out below the hem. "Absolutely. The Easter Parade marks the beginning of spring in New York and mustn't be missed, Mary."

Audrey pulled on her white gloves and placed her hand on her brother's arm. Joel had shown up two days ago from a voyage he'd been on, as he did now and then. Audrey delighted in his visits, as did Fiona since the man was her savior. "Don't worry about us, we'll be fine in this chaos." He winked at Fiona. "There hasn't been any fatalities yet, but as a doctor, I'll be there in case of any injuries."

He was elegant in a black suit, white spats covering his polished shoes, top hat gleaming. Even with his profession, he was as much of an aristocrat of New York as his sister.

Fiona smiled. Joel always made her smile, since she'd learned to appreciate his dry humor. He opened the door and the refined Prescotts joined the throng on the sidewalk. It was truly a parade of the wealthy and well-dressed, a riot of color and more outrageous hats than Fiona'd ever seen before. While the rich paraded, those not so well off watched from the sidelines, wonder on their faces. She watched for a while until she grew bored and went back to the kitchens. At first dazzled, she'd found herself resenting the huge class distinction, something else she'd learned a lot about in the last few months. The Irish were treated worse than she could've imagined, but not in this household. Anywhere else in the city, it was a very different story.

Cook's hot cross buns were still warm, sitting on the wooden counter and Fiona took one, sitting down at the big kitchen table, licking the sweet frosting off her fingers. She loved this kitchen, so warm and cozy, as did all the servants. There was Annie, Irish as well and Laura, the maids, Henry the footman, John the carriage driver, and of course Bentley, who was a little more elevated than the rest of them, along with Fiona herself as Audrey's lady's maid. The gardener Paul came and went, as did the two kitchen lads and she could never remember their names. Susie, Cook's assistant, sat down beside her with a smile.

"Didn't she look beautiful?"

"She certainly did," Fiona said. "Took me forever to get her ready, but she looked very fine indeed."

"I wish someday I could have a hat like that," Susie said dreamily. "Just think of it." She cast her eyes to the ceiling, as though watching a vision of what she wished for.

Cook huffed. "Someday mayhap you will, girl, but today you've got an Easter ham needs bastin' so quit your moonin' over a hat." She tempered her words with a smile and waved a spoon in Susie's direction.

Fiona finished her bun and brushed the crumbs from her hands. She needed to straighten Audrey's rooms but after that, she'd have a couple of hours free to spend in the library and she didn't want to waste a minute more.

She hadn't wasted a minute of winter or the "season" as the New Yorkers called it, or a single day since she'd been there in the last year. She'd spent untold hours in the library, learning about everything from Shakespeare to the vast country she now lived in, entertaining dreams of traveling to those faraway places that were still America, so different from the small land she'd come from it never ceased to amaze her.

Aside from the library, she'd observed and learned to mimic the accents of all the dinner and party guests that came to Prescott House, practicing in front her mirror and usually dissolving in giggles at herself. Still, she'd learned and not just the way they talked, with no give-away Irish accent. She'd carefully watched the dinners and the way they used the silver, which course went with each chosen wine, and each movement, from napkin to salad fork. It had been a revelation to her, she who'd only known one utensil and a bowl to keep hunger at bay. Even at the servants' tables, she marked who used proper manners. Bentley, of course, but Annie, the upstairs maid, had been a curious discovery, Irish but knowing enough to transform. Most of the servants copied them after a time, Fiona included. Cook and her marvelous food had been a gift not only for her body but her mind, finding that food could be not just sustaining, but delectable in so many ways.

Ah, yes, she thought to herself, she'd learned. Prescott House hadn't just been a haven, but her own special academy of higher learning.

Then there were the clothes. Audrey tired quickly of hers, tossing them aside in favor of the latest fashion with a quick dismissal. "Put that in the poor basket, Mary, or if you like, alter it for yourself."

She'd quickly taken advantage of that and with her nimble sewing skills, had amassed a closet of clothing that, while out of fashion with New York's most stylish, was beyond anything she'd ever seen, let alone worn. Careful to never show off the loveliest of her altered creations in the house, on her Sunday afternoons and Wednesdays off, Fiona took full advantage of her new wardrobe.

Those days off had become her lifeblood. Venturing out, as she'd done even before she'd had new clothing, Fiona discovered New York. At first she went to the streets and avenues she'd become familiar with, because the sheer size of the city and the tall buildings intimidated her. Occasionally she felt as though she was in a tunnel where the high walls would come crashing down on her but the feeling had eased. There were many streets she'd become familiar with trailing behind Audrey as she went to her dressmaker's, the jeweler's, the department stores, the shoemaker's and the myriad of other specialty shops and restaurants where Fiona was relegated to her own table near the kitchens while Audrey met and hosted her friends. She didn't mind, the food was the same and silence preferable to the mindless prattle of the society women.

Gradually, she'd taken notice of other streets, other shops and places that called to her and before long, she explored where and when she would. The cathedrals that she never set foot in, the parks, museums, the library, the Jewish and Italian neighborhoods and their savory food and wonder of wonders, Broadway and its bright theaters. She'd never been to a show of any kind, but she loved wandering down the street, watching the people and actors who were part of this magical experience, daydreaming as she went. She loved the gaiety of it all, the people, the signs and the theaters themselves, quiet now during the day. She could only imagine how lovely it would be in the nighttime. Even during the daylight hours, she was thrilled.

One afternoon, she'd even ventured into the Irish neighborhoods, just for curiosity's sake, she told herself. She wasn't ashamed of her nationality, but she was in a city where it wasn't wise to flaunt it, she'd learned from her first step onto American soil. As she'd gone further into the Lower East Side, her uneasiness expanded with each step she took until she found herself standing on the sidewalk in front of a large building where people were busily going in and out, the building like so many others that lined the streets she'd just come down. They were crammed with occupants, washing strung from lines between the windows, reaching overhead to the top floors. Women yelled, babies shrieked, and the smell of boiled cabbage was everywhere that the smell of the trash that had collected in the alleys was not. When a rat ran by her foot, Fiona turned and fled. Had the typhus not visited the *Adriatic*, she could very well be living on Orchard Street too. No matter what, she vowed, that would never happen.

In early May, she ventured out as usual and found herself drawn to Broadway first, rather than her first stop at the Goldbergs' delicatessen for the bagels and pastries she'd come to love. It was a fine day for walking, she thought. It was a beautiful spring day and she wore the green-striped skirt and white jacket she'd altered when Audrey had tired of it. Fiona had refashioned a hat with a green feather and it perched atop her glossy dark curls. Many a gentleman and even a few ladies had smiled at her in appreciation and she knew she looked quite fine indeed. She nearly laughed out loud at the thought of how pathetic she must've looked on arriving here, dirty and disheveled in her rough clothing, so ignorant in comparison. Still, while this was fine, she knew there was a great deal more to learn and she couldn't wait to step up to whatever challenges presented themselves. Nothing had for some time now, and she was becoming impatient. Perhaps she would have to search them out for herself rather than waiting for fate to take a hand. She was only wondering where exactly to start.

"Mary?"

She turned her head. Surely it was some other Mary the voice called to. She knew no one in the theater district.

"Mary!" Closer now. A man pushed his way through the other people on the sidewalk and touched her arm. She recoiled and then stopped.

"Mr. Ardrey? James Ardrey?"

His handsome face split into a wide grin. "The very same." He took her arm again and she let him. "Your old cabin-mate on the *Adriatic*." He peered closely at her and took a step back, running his eyes up and down but not in a way that made her feel uncomfortable. He cocked his head appraisingly. "My girl, you look wonderful. New York agrees with you, certainly. You were a pretty thing, how could I forget. But now, my dear, you have some style and a bit of polish. My, my."

Fiona blushed. No one had ever said that, but then, she didn't know anyone outside of Prescott House and hadn't made any real friends on her explorations.

"Thank you. You look very fine yourself, James." It was true. The handsome young Englishman who'd kept to himself and had made himself scarce had turned into quite a peacock. He wore a waistcoat in dove grey with pants to match, and his vest was an embroidered wonder in greens, blues and purples.

"Thank you, madam," he smiled, doffing his modish beaver hat and quickly setting it back on his head. "I try."

They strolled slowly down Broadway, glancing at the theaters and marquees, James chattering away. "Thank god we made it off that tub in one piece, Mary. How many died in the end, anyway?"

"Eleven," she said, remembering the horror of it all from bathing the feverish bodies and sewing them into the shrouds that were their last outer garments on earth, but he went on after a second as though it was of no consequence. And, she thought, for him it would not have been, really.

"Christ almighty. We should've never boarded that plague ship. Oh well, we're here now, aren't we, my girl?"

"Well, we are 'tis sure," she started and he put his arm through hers and dragged her to a stop in front of a marquee.

"Look at that, Mary," he crowed. "Love's Labours Lost" and right there," he jabbed his finger at the placard on the side, 'James Ardrey'. I was meant to be here and nothing could stop me. Five evenings a week and a matinee on Sundays."

He was grinning like a jackanapes and she couldn't help but smile, sharing in his good fortune. "James, I had no idea you were an actor."

He performed an elaborate bow. "At your service, my dear, any stage, anywhere."

He propelled her on down the street, pointing out this theater and that. "My first part a week after we landed, right there at Niblo's Garden. And then, over to the Fifth Avenue," he gestured across the street. "The Duke in Twelfth Night. Augustin has been taking good care of me."

"Who's Augustin?" Fiona said, trying to not sound as naïve as she felt.

"Only the greatest theater man in New York, of course."

"Oh."

"Well, you couldn't possibly know that, Mary," James said, patting her arm. "I'm sorry if I sound like a conceited ass. It's just been so, well, so great for me. Leaving England was the best thing I ever did." He actually looked contrite. "Come and tell me about what you've been up to, love. I'm all ears."

The restaurant was nice, dark wood and paneled with theater advertisements. The waitress took their orders and Fiona fidgeted, her hands under the table. She hardly knew this man, and yet here she was, sitting at a table with him. She peered up at him under her lashes. He was so handsome, beautiful even, and she could see why he was an actor. On board the ship, he'd seemed pale and haunted but here, now, it was as though he'd come to life, his eyes snapping and his cheeks flush with life. She smiled at him and he leaned back in his chair.

"So, tell me, Mary."

She took a breath. He wasn't going to be impressed, not this young man who'd conquered the theater, but she could only offer the truth.

"I'm a lady's maid. To Audrey Prescott, the sister of the ship's doctor from the *Adriatic*. It's fine, for now. It's a good house, the people are kind and I'm learning about New York." She smiled again, feeling defensive.

He nodded. "Good for you, dear. Many Irish girls end up in the kitchens, brothels, the streets, the factories or far worse, if you can imagine, from what I've heard. Clearly you've avoided those fates." He stared at her for a few seconds. "What's next?"

"What's next?" She parroted his words, feeling like an idiot.

He laughed. "With a face like that, there has to be a next and you have to take advantage, Mary. Of course there will be a next for you. You aren't destined to be picking up after some society woman for the rest of your life."

Mary could feel the color rising in her cheeks and she truly didn't know what to say to that.

Luckily, the waitress arrived with their food and tea and she busied herself with lemon, sugar and taking a bite of her chicken sandwich, delicious and elegantly crustless.

James polished off half his sandwich and leaned back, dabbing his mouth with a napkin. "Forgive me. I just see a face like yours and I think, she should be on the stage."

Of all the things he could've said, she hadn't expected this one. She blinked and looked up at him, dropping her hands to her lap.

"Me? On a stage? That's ridiculous, I couldn't possibly."

He laughed and took her hand. "No, Mary, it's not. Have you not looked in a mirror lately, girl?"

She felt the heat rising in her cheeks again and stared at him regardless.

"I'm serious. Tell me, can you sing, dance, any experience at all?" He sipped his tea. "Not that it matters, because you can learn. It's not all that difficult, believe me."

She shook her head. "No, James, no, no. People would laugh at me, a girl from an Irish village an actress, dancer or performer on the New York stage? I'm not such a fool as that."

Fiona's stomach was doing tumbles. Surely he was having fun at her expense. Plenty of men at the Rose and Crown had done the same and she wasn't all that green anymore, even if life at Prescott House had been a buffer from the past as well as the frightening future. Even so, she felt a tightening in her stomach and lifted her eyes to his.

He was smiling at her, shaking his head. "I hardly know you, but Mary, there's something about you that draws people, and that's me included, darling. I don't know what you want from your life, but I know just from looking at you that if you want this," he flung out his arm, as though encompassing Broadway and its minions, "you have the start of a career, just because you're breathing. The rest of it will come."

"James, stop." Fiona stood up, her hands shaking. "Thank you for lunch. I have to get back. As for the rest of it, I can't think about that now. I'm glad you're well and wish you success with your acting. Perhaps we'll see each other again."

He took it well. He stood up and bowed from across the table. "I'll send you tickets to the play, Mary. Everyone knows where Prescott House is." His smile was part sincere, part rueful. "I'm delighted to have met up with you again. I know you don't believe me right this instant, but I know you have a future in the theater."

She fled. There was no other word for it. Graceless, frightened and unsure, she cut short her afternoon foray and entered the kitchen at Prescott House breathless, happy there was no one at the cold hearth as she stumbled up the back stairs. She went to her room and tore off the clothes she'd worn, pulling on her old gown and robe, sitting morosely on the side of her bed as darkness fell, greying the white walls as each minute passed.

She'd acted like a witless clod, and she flushed with embarrassment every time she thought back on their conversation. What did she want? The future was pulling on her with a relentless tug. Decisions had been made for her all her life, even though they weren't ones she would've chosen even if she'd had any choice. Even coming to America hadn't been a choice, but the only avenue open in pure desperation. James Ardrey had just shown her a door she was both excited to enter and one that could lead to disaster, one she was mortally afraid to step into.

An actress? The man was daft if he thought she could do that. She'd never seen a play, or been to a theater in her short life. The closest she'd come to entertainment was listening to blind Padraic Gallagher play his fiddle on Ballyowen market days while some drunken farmer warbled a tune to go with it.

She fell back onto the bed and closed her eyes. Unbidden, James Ardrey's handsome face swam into view, his eyes sparkling, looking at her like she was something special. "I know you have a future in the theater," he'd said. Could he possibly be right?

CHAPTER 7

"Have anything special planned for tomorrow afternoon?" Audrey Prescott sat at her dressing table, patting her hair here and there. It was an elaborate coiffure, piled atop her head, with thin braids as well as many pins holding it in place. Fiona had spent two hours on it and it looked lovely, even she had to admit.

She smiled at Audrey in the mirror. "No, ma'am, not really. I just enjoy seeing the city and the shops." She could feel the theater ticket in her pocket like it was burning a hole through the muslin of her skirt, as though the lie was betraying her. A messenger had brought the envelope yesterday, just the ticket and a note that said, "Don't disappoint me, pretty Mary. See you after the show."

It had been three weeks since she'd run into James Ardrey and she hadn't ventured back to Broadway. Some part of her wanted to do just that, while another never wanted to see a theater again. There had been many a sleepless night and she'd gone quietly down to the library, reading more Shakespeare plays. She started with Love's Labours Lost, of course, and then moved on to Romeo and Juliet, As You Like It, and was currently on MacBeth. It had been daunting at first, the unfamiliar words and cadences, but once she began to read it out loud, whispering, it came to make sense. The thought of hearing and seeing actors say those lines would be wonderful and now that chance had come. She wasn't going to pass that up, the excitement greatly outweighing her apprehension.

"That's nice," Audrey said, peering closely at her chin in the mirror. Satisfied, she stood up, the blue silk dress unfurling around her. "Don't wait up, dear. I'll be very late. First the theater and then an after-dinner. I can manage."

She swept out. Fiona looked around at the carnage in the room, clothes, shoes and undergarments everywhere and started anew the endless folding, storing and sorting, the endless job of a lady's maid. She was beginning to resent it. To have to tend to all these lovely things that would always belong to someone else was beginning to nettle her.

Sunday afternoon just before two, she stood outside the Fifth Avenue Theater, the ticket clutched in her hand. The placards announcing the play were posted outside and the theater itself looked as though as it was a gateway into another world, one she was both excited and terrified to enter. Fiona had dressed carefully: a white blouse, navy blue jacket and skirt and Audrey's cast-off French boots which she had polished to look like new. She watched everyone file in, laughing and happy, in groups, couples and one by one. She took a deep breath and went through the door.

It was just as magnificent as she'd imagined. The carpets were a deep burgundy, as was the wallpaper in the lobby, the ceiling rising so high above her, the chandeliers glittering. It was already quite amazing and she breathed softly, creeping forward and handing her ticket to an usher beside the two wide bombazine doors.

"We'll have to hurry, miss, you're in the second row. Follow me." So she did, her footsteps soundless on the thick carpet. He led her nearly to the front, and gestured towards the empty seat in the row, walking silently away after handing her a program. She murmured her apologies to the people she shifted by and sank gratefully into her seat, and not a moment too soon. The lights flickered and dimmed in the theater, while a white light centered upon the stage in front of her in a perfect circle, bright against the drawn dark maroon curtains.

A man stepped out and the audience hushed expectantly. He held out his arms and bowed. He was magnificent, his long brown hair brushing his shoulders, and his handsome face and dark eyes seemed to pull every person in the audience in like a magic trick, Fiona included.

"Good afternoon, ladies and gentlemen. It is my privilege and pleasure to present to you "Love's Labours Lost", the Fifth Avenue Theater's current production. I am Augustin Drewry," a sigh rippled through the audience as though royalty had been announced, "and welcome. It is my fondest hope you enjoy our endeavors."

He bowed again and left the stage, the circle of light disappearing with him. It was very dark and Fiona wasn't sure what was going to happen next. Then, the curtains opened.

It was indeed magical. A magnificent castle rose behind other scenes painted as a forest, complete with trees, flowering bushes and benches and Fiona gasped in delight. Men strode onto the stage, one wearing a crown, the others dressed in medieval costumes, tights on their legs, and she spied James Ardrey among them. She sat back, enchanted before anyone had spoken a word and watched as the play was brought to life before her eyes.

Two hours later, she stood up with the rest of the theatergoers and made her way to the lobby, dazed, words ringing in her head. As most of them departed, she finally stood alone, humming the final song. "And greasy Joan stirred the pot..."

A hand fell on her shoulder and she whirled around. James

Ardrey stood before her, still dressed in his costume as Lord Biron.

"You came." He smiled and took her arm. "Come backstage with me, love."

Her heart skipped a beat. Backstage? She put her hand on his arm and realized she would have followed him to hell at that point. She'd been in wonder just walking down Broadway, but after this afternoon, she was entranced, in fact, ensnared. She knew it, and she didn't care.

He led her down the theater aisle, then into a side doorway hung with curtains, and backstage erupted on her senses, a whirlwind of life and color. The same people she'd seen on stage only moments before were all there, running in and out of doors into small rooms, laughing and holding glasses of wine and whiskey, some still in costume, some in much less and others already in street clothes like her.

"James," called one lovely woman she recognized as Lady Katherine from the play, clad now only in her shift and gesturing towards her room, "come in and have a glass, darling."

"In a minute, love," he answered with a smile and whispered in Fiona's ear, "she's so needy, that one. Come on."

They went further down into the warren of rooms and people. "Did you like the play?"

"Oh, my. Yes, so much."

"How about me?"

She felt stupid. The first thing she should've done was tell him how much she liked his performance, but she'd been so dazed by all of it her head was aswirl.

"Oh, James," Fiona stopped dead. "You were wonderful. I'm sorry I didn't say that right off, but the entire thing left me with such a. . . .I don't know, daydream. I loved it and you most of all." She meant every word.

He grinned. "Not to worry, sweetling." He gazed at her, up and down. "My god, you are adorable. So innocent and yet, so, I don't know, I sense something in you. Have from the first, even on the ship."

Fiona nearly choked. He was way too perceptive, Ardrey was. She knew she was naïve, in New York and especially in this arena, but even so. She looked up at him, her eyes sincere.

"I'm not sure if that's a compliment, James. I am what you see, nothing more."

He burst into laughter. "Oh, girl, you are so much more. Come on, you've got to meet Augustin. He's going to love you, Mary Flynn."

She froze. "What? My name's Mary O'Neill, James. Have you forgotten?"

He looked at her quizzically. "Do I have it wrong, then? I'm sorry. I thought she was the one that died, from that village in County Mayo or somewhere. Usually I have a good memory for names. My apologies."

"Yes, but it was Mary Flynn that passed. You mixed up the names, I suppose. So many Irish girls, so many Marys, it's hard to keep track. I'm the O'Neill, from Leinster."

He blinked once and the smile returned. "Of course, how stupid of me." He barked a quick laugh. "We English. Have a difficult time of it, not so familiar with the Irish names and all. Still, the *Adriatic* was the only ship out that week, and I landed in Cobh just in time. Served me well, didn't it?"

Fiona nodded. "Indeed it did." She didn't dare say a word more. She smoothed her skirts and they resumed their passage through the actors until they came to a closed door. James knocked and a voice within answered: "Come in, then, if you dare."

They dared. James gave her hand a reassuring pat and in they went, and he softly closed the door behind them.

Augustin Drewry's room was quite different from the ones she'd glimpsed on their way down the narrow hallway. Not only larger, but furnished luxuriously and a Turkish carpet on the floor. The man himself sat on a chair that nearly resembled a throne, its ornate back rising over his head. James had no hesitation and stepped close to the man seated on its velvet cushion. He was truly like no one she'd ever seen. It wasn't just the clothes – the velvet waistcoat, the elegant cravat he wore, but the man himself. Brown hair gleamed, brushed away from his chiseled face in waves, his eyes piercing in a face so chiseled he scarcely looked mortal. Power radiated from him and Fiona drew in a deep breath, both awed and frightened at the same time.

"Augustin. Another exemplary evening, thanks to you," James said. "I brought along a friend, the one I mentioned last week, for you to meet." He gestured towards Fiona and she stood there like a stone, feeling almost like she should curtsey but not wanting to do so. She'd never curtsey to anyone ever again.

"This is Mary . . .O'Neill," he finished, taking her hand and pulled her forward. She wasn't sure what to do or say, so she made it simple. She bobbed her head and hated herself for even that, staring at the man, trying not to be entranced.

"Pleased to meet you, sir," she said and even as the words passed her lips, she felt like she'd given something away.

"Well." His voice matched the rest of him with just that one word: elegant, sure and a touch acerbic. He looked her up and down and laughed softly.

"James, where did you say you found her?"

James coughed and squeezed her hand. "We were shipmates on the *Adriatic*, coming across. She was a stalwart companion and we met up again just a short time ago, here on Broadway one afternoon and I was delighted. She's lovely, isn't she?"

"Indeed," Augustin Drewry said. "Possibilities, eh?"

Fiona tore her hand from James's. She might only be a lady's maid, but she was a person, not a figurine to be discussed. She had a horrible moment thinking that they were no different from Sean Dooley and men like him.

"I'm right here. Don't talk about me like I'm a choice piece of beef from the butcher. Who do you think you are?" She glared at James and at Drewry as well. "Good afternoon." She whirled around, throwing open the damask-covered door and stomped into the hallway. *Christ, the nerve of these men.* She'd had enough of that to last her a lifetime, theater or no. She was nearly choking with regret. She walked down the hallway, tears blinding her. How silly she'd been.

"Mary, please." James was pulling on her arm. "I'm so sorry, please stop." She did so, her feet poised to flee. Then again, she'd done that once before at the thought of the theater, so she listened, if only for a moment, her desire and her anger warring within her.

He pushed her gently to the side of the hallway. "We handled that badly, both me and Augustin. Would you please give us another chance?" He seemed contrite but she wasn't convinced. "I think you have a future here, Mary, I really do and so does Augustin, even after seeing you for a few moments. I knew he'd be impressed, as I am. Please?"

She stared at him. He seemed sincere, but she'd learned that sincerity could be false, many times. Still, what could it hurt? She could always leave, no one could stop her.

"All right," she said, knowing instinctively this decision could change her life forever, but wasn't that what she wanted? She took his arm, following him down the hallway, and entered Augustin Drewry's sanctuary once again.

CHAPTER 8

"Mary!"

She started, her eyes flying open. Oh god no, had she actually dozed off while Audrey was primping at her dressing table? "Yes, ma'am?"

Audrey stared at her, hairpins in hand. "Are you ill, Mary? For the last week, you've not been yourself. Perhaps we should have Joel take a look at you when he gets here."

"I'm sure that won't be necessary," Fiona said, panic scurrying down her spine. "I think it was something I ate at the pier last week, likely the fish. I'm sorry."

"Hmm." Audrey eyed her suspiciously. "We'll see how you feel tomorrow, then." She held out the hairpins. "I think the curl on the left should go atop as well, don't you?"

"I surely do, ma'am. Let me fix that."

By the time she finished tidying up and Audrey had left for the dinner party at the mayor's, Fiona was exhausted. She'd been sneaking out for rehearsals every night for the past two weeks and studying her lines at any opportune moment during the day, all the while catering to Audrey's every need, as usual. While Audrey was not a demanding mistress, Fiona spent most of her day and early evenings making sure Audrey looked and felt as well as humanly possible, as that was her job and her livelihood, at least for now, and it took a lot of time.

She took one last look around Audrey's room and left for her own, yawning as she opened the door. She fell back on the bed, thinking of the impossible whirlwind that had been her last few weeks and before she knew it, fell fast asleep. Her last thought was of that first afternoon in Augustin's office and her first step into the theater.

She and James entered and Augustin stood up, came forward and took her hand. "My dear Miss O'Neill, forgive me. You were absolutely right in your annoyance at my high-handedness. Please?" He gestured towards the armchairs beside his and they sat down. She nearly launched herself up again when he sat down and perused her with the same earnestness he'd displayed earlier. He sensed it and shook his head, chuckling softly. He patted her hand.

"Again, forgive me, but you are quite naturally lovely, not something I see every day. James was correct in everything he said." He sat back in his chair.

Fiona glared at James, sitting nonchalantly beside her and he shifted uncomfortably under her gaze, not meeting her eyes.

"And just what would that have been?" she said to Augustin.

"That you were something special and could have a future in the theater, Mary, that is all. I believe he is right in that assumption. What do you think?"

This was news to her, or had been until a few minutes ago. She knew she was pretty enough and so far that hadn't served her well. First catching the notice of Sean Dooley, then the men at the Rose and Crown, the annoying men on the street when she strolled by and now this, but somehow "this" might be different. Ever since she'd stepped off that boat on Joel Prescott's arm, she knew this new country was a new beginning, scared as she'd been. Prescott House had provided the haven she'd needed to feel safe and learn who she could become. She'd been waiting for something, for a chance, an opportunity or fate to take a hand and maybe this was it. *I make the rules this time,* she thought, *and this time it's going to be different.*

"I think I would like to hear exactly what you have in mind," she smiled at Augustin Drewry. "Sir, remember I'm from a small village in Ireland and not familiar with the ways of the theater, or what skills I might put to use." In a way, she meant it, too.

He smiled back. "Nor am I, truthfully, Miss O'Neill, but we shall discover those together."

So they did. She could sing, she'd discovered that on the whiskey wagon, with a high clear voice, and all those snowy afternoons reading Shakespeare had given her some basics, and her memory was sharp, amazingly so. She could thank the nuns at St. Hilda's for that, the drilling and the rulers, horrid at the time but good training now. But it was her speaking voice that captured him and everyone else that heard her. A low-pitched alto but sweet and resonating, reciting lines as though she'd always known them, and she became the darling ingénue of the theater troupe quickly. She surprised herself, practicing in front of her mirror when everyone was asleep, and smiled at her reflection.

"My god, you're a natural," Augustin said. "I've never seen anything quite like it."

High praise, and praise she savored. Then, he cast her as Juliet and she'd gasped with surprise and fright. How could she possibly learn all those lines in the four weeks before he'd planned the opening? But she had, rehearsing at night with the troupe, and practicing in every spare minute in her room. She was exhausted, but exhilarated. Now, they were due to open in two days. She knew she couldn't keep up this pace and something would have to give. First, though, let the play open and see what the public thought. Whether she was truly an actress, or just some ignorant orphan girl from Ballyowen whose face alone had put her on a stage. She needed confirmation and credibility, beyond that of Augustin, James and the rest of them. She needed New York to know who she was and what she could do. Only then would she have the determination to leave Prescott House and throw herself onto the none-too-tender mercies of the theater world. She'd eaten too many green potatoes, field-snared rabbits and little else to chance that she might have to ever again.

Dress rehearsal night loomed, thankfully on a Wednesday night and Fiona was surprised she didn't have the nerves she'd been warned about. It went off well. She had just finished changing out of her costume when Augustin came into her dressing room.

"You were perfect tonight," he said, sitting down on the armchair he'd had brought in the week before. "This Romeo and Juliet is going to be quite a success, I think."

He lit a cigarillo and peered at her through the smoke curling upwards in the small room. He lounged in the chair as though her dressing room was his own personal fiefdom and Fiona couldn't help but think it probably was, but she wasn't part of his ownership, much as he'd like to think so, she and every other actor in his troupe.

"I hope so." She wiped the makeup off her face with cold cream and a hand towel, watching him in the mirror.

"We need to think about what comes next," he said and her heart jumped a bit in her chest. "Always follow a success with another."

"Providing it really is a success," she said, turning around and facing him.

He laughed softly. "Trust me, sweetheart, I've been in this business a long time. You're something special. Maybe next time we'll do something more modern. Let me think about just the vehicle for you."

His confidence made Fiona nervous now like she'd never

been before tonight. What would happen if she fell on her face opening night? So far, he'd not paid her a penny and her future with Audrey was in jeopardy, thanks to the late nights and her sleeplessness. It *had* to work, if only for the revenue from ticket sales which was when she'd get paid as well. She had no wish to be looking for a job as a maid or anything else, after this. The theater bug had bitten and she knew it. If not Juliet, she'd find a way to do something—sing, dance, costumes, whatever, but working for Augustin or some other theater producer was where she wanted to be. She knew, though, even in the little time she'd been in this business, that Augustin Drewry was the leading producer in New York and it was his genius that led the field.

He seemed to read her mind. He rose from the chair and patted her on the shoulder. "Go get some sleep, little one. You and the theater are a match for all time, and you can believe me when I say that. I've seen them come and go, but you're different."

He closed the door behind him and Fiona sat at the mirror, staring at her reflection, praying he was right.

It was touch and go, getting Audrey ready for a night on the town. Fiona didn't ask where she was going and she didn't really care, as long as it was early enough to get to the theater on time. When she heard the front door close, she was already throwing on her cloak and hurrying out behind the carriage that took Audrey away. She arrived at the theater breathless and threw on her costume. Annie the makeup girl was tapping her foot impatiently.

"Would've been nice you got here sooner, Mary," she said, dabbing on the greasepaint. "At least I don't have to do that much, you being so fresh and Juliet the same. Still, the gaslights make everyone look like a ghost and we can't be havin' that." She frowned and bent to her work, clearly displeased. Fiona couldn't have cared less but she murmured apologies to appease her.

James, who was playing Romeo to her Juliet, poked his head into the dressing room. "Ten minutes, girl." He was resplendent in his scarlet doublet and tights, feathered cap on his head. He grinned at her and left. If he had stage nerves, they certainly didn't show. Annie departed and Fiona stared at her reflection. It wasn't her face, but that of Juliet that stared back at her, some of her hair braided into a crown while the rest tumbled virginally onto her shoulders. Her dress was white and filmy, falling in waves to her feet, clad in white kid slippers. She smiled, satisfied and went out to the wings. Verona called and she would answer.

And answer she did. It was as though she'd always known this: the lines, the pacing, the rush of excitement followed by the surety of what she'd known and rehearsed so many times before. It was as though she was in a different place from the reality of New York, transported to Verona and becoming Juliet, her passions and her fears those of this young girl, so in love and so doomed.

Fiona stood in the wings, watching the others. When the lights briefly dimmed and Scene III opened, there she was, with Nurse.

"How now, who calls?"

"Your mother," said Nurse.

"Madam, I am here," said Fiona, "What is your will?"

The rest of the performance passed in the secret place she'd created for herself but she'd never missed a line from the first to "there rest and let me die."

The curtain came down and the applause was tremendous. It swept open again and they took their bows, which seemed to go on for inordinately long time, and then Fiona and James took a bow to more clapping and shouts of "Bravo!" but Fiona had no measure to guide by, except the huge grin on Augustin Drewry's face and the numbing grip James had on her hand.

"So, it went well?"

They laughed, as did nearly everyone else, from actors to stagehands.

"Oh, yes, my dear. It went very well indeed," Drewry said, hugging her unexpectedly and setting her down with a thump. "Get used to Juliet, you're going to be living with her for some time."

Fiona was elated and at the same time, tired down to her bones. She had to make a choice, now. Take the leap and hope life in the theater was her future. James followed her back to her dressing room and lolled in the armchair while she changed behind the little privacy screen.

"We're going to Antonelli's for the after party, Mary. Don't dawdle, you'll love it. The theater critics will be putting out the late editions and we can't miss those. Tonight will be legendary. 'Mary O'Neill, the sensation of the year'. Just wait. I only hope I'm just as touted as your faithful Romeo, darling."

She came around the screen, buttoning up her jacket. "I can't do it, James. I've got to get back to Prescott House before anyone finds me gone. It's a miracle I've not been discovered before now."

He gaped at her. "You mean you've been working there this whole time?"

"Where do you think I live? I've got nowhere else. And now, if this play is popular, I don't know what to do."

He put his arms around her and she laid her head on his shoulder. It felt good and she was so tired.

"Oh my darling, we'll figure this out. First, quit that job. You can come stay with me. It'll be a bit cramped but that's no matter. You're going to be a star and we can't have you exhausted from picking up after Lady Society Audrey Prescott and having your stagework suffer for it."

Relief flooded through her. "Really? Are you sure?"

He pulled back, his hands on her shoulders. "Of course I'm sure. I got you into this, didn't I? Besides, Augustin will have my head if anything happens to you, so I've a vested interest, you might say." He smiled. "Come, fair Juliet. I'll walk you home and join the others later."

CHAPTER 9

Audrey had not been pleased. Every time Fiona thought back on that morning, she cringed a little. It seemed Audrey had been at the opening performance and had never for one minute suspected that her meek Irish maid was playing Juliet. It might not have been as bad, except for that. Audrey Prescott did not like being played for a fool.

They were in the library, where every morning after breakfast Audrey sat at her French writing desk, doing her daily correspondence–responding to invitations, sending some herself, messages to her bankers and accountants, tallying accounts and paying bills, and even attending to letters to old friends in faraway places. Fiona thought this would be an ideal time to discuss her plans to leave and her reasons why, an oasis in the busy day of Audrey Prescott. The sunlight streamed into the room through the high windows, dust motes floating in the air, bathing the room in golden serenity. Fiona stood just inside the doors.

"Ma'am, may I speak with you for a moment?"

Audrey put down her pen with only a slight sigh. "Of course, Mary. What is it?"

"I'm very sorry, but I'm giving my notice," Fiona said. "You've been very kind to me and that has allowed me to learn so much. I've a new job, well, some would call it a profession. I'm an actress now for Mr. Augustin Drewry, in his troupe. I would have liked to stay on with you, but the demands on my time have made that impossible for me, what with rehearsals and all, and I've not the strength to keep on. I know it's not fair to you, the benefactress you've been to me and all."

"Come closer, Mary," Audrey commanded and Fiona took a few steps toward the desk.

"Ma'am?"

"I'm very disappointed, to say the least." Audrey peered closely at Fiona's face.

"Yes, ma'am." She couldn't help herself, regret and a little shame mixed in with the exhilaration of her life waiting to be lived outside this house. She kept her eyes downcast. If nothing else, she'd learned to play a role well.

Another sigh. "Honesty is something I value above all else."

As do I, Fiona thought, *but lady, you've never had nothing but porridge to eat for days on end and sometimes that was what honesty got you.* What she said was, "Yes, ma'am."

"That said, I saw the performance last evening," Audrey said. "Now that I know, I can see you were Juliet, weren't you? You were really very good, the best Juliet I can recall."

Fiona stared at her. She should've known never to underestimate this woman. "Yes, I was Juliet. I had no idea you were going to the theater last night."

"I'm sure that, at least, is true," Audrey said with a humorless laugh. "Oh Mary, what am I to think? I don't appreciate you not telling me the truth, but I must admit, I likely would not have been supportive of your after hours pursuits, so I understand your secrecy. However, leaving me with no lady's maid at the height of season is a terrible thing to do, my girl, after the kindnesses I've shown you."

Fiona felt that rush of shame again, but she knew this couldn't have gone any other way, in truth. She couldn't have taken that chance. Leaving someone without a hairdresser wasn't quite the same as having no place to live, but things were never equal in life, as she had found long before now. She could feel the heat rising in her cheeks, blushing them rosy as well as telltale.

"I wanted to tell you," Fiona said. "I apologize that I didn't. I want to thank you for all you've done for me. You gave me a place when likely no one else would have soon as I landed on these shores, and I had the opportunity to learn a great deal. I will always remember your generosity and your many kindnesses to me. There's not many would've done what you have, and your brother as well."

Audrey stared at her for a long minute and waved her hand with a regretful smile. "Gather your things, Mary. We will have no hard feelings. From what I saw last night, you will be a success in your new endeavor. I'm certain Joel will be eager to hear this news when he comes into port next."

"Thank you, ma'am." Fiona curtsied and couldn't wait to get past the door. Audrey's voice stopped her as she put her hand on the knob.

"My dear Juliet. The theater can be a fickle mistress. If you ever need help, I'm here. I believe there's a volume of Shakespeare plays in the library that no one but you has ever opened, so please take it along with you on your journey. I wish you only the best of luck in your life."

Fiona's throat was clogged with unshed tears but she managed a smile and a nod. She closed the library door and stood with her back against the painted wood. That was a scenario she never wanted to have to repeat under any circumstance. After a year in New York, seeing the signs "No Irish Need Apply" for all work, even the most menial, she knew full well how incredibly lucky she had been to have met and been sponsored by Joel Prescott and his sister. She would always be grateful to them, but gratitude wasn't something she could base a life on, nor a reason to stay when she had an opportunity like this. She took a deep breath and climbed the stairs to pack her things. In the end, she said goodbyes to no one else, because no one else mattered to her, not really.

* * *

JAMES WAS RIGHT. His place was indeed a bit cramped. On the other hand, Fiona thought, it was larger than Sean Dooley's cottage or her room behind the bar or even the servants' quarters at Prescott House. It was two rooms above a bar not far from the theater but with windows that faced the street, so it had plenty of light and even with a bachelor's idea of décor, the bachelor was James, who really did have exquisite taste, if his clothing was a judge, and Fiona thought it could be. It smelled a little of James's hair oil and smoke but she didn't mind. With a bit of re-arranging and fresh flowers it would do for a short time.

Except for the bed. There was only one, a large one for all that he was a single man. It did look quite clean and comfortable, but she didn't want to think about that now.

James flew about, putting things here and there and showing her where to stow her meager belongings, and finally flinging himself down on the small couch, grinning.

"See? What did I tell you, Mary? This is going to work out just fine. We can even rehearse right here without having to go to the theater." He put his booted feet up on the small table in front of the couch.

"Ah, Romeo," Fiona said, sitting down beside him. "Wherever would I be without thee?" In a way, she meant it, too. Running into James had been another turning point in her life.

"Blissless," replied James. "You belong in the theater, Mary, and you can thank me for pointing that out."

"I know it," she said. "Thank you once again, fair Romeo." She fell silent, looking around the room and pointedly avoiding the bedroom door.

He studied her face for a minute and smiled knowingly. "We can share the bed, Juliet, with no expectations, if you're wondering. It's a big bed. I'm not inclined that way and you'll be safe as a nun. Besides, I'm way past sacrifice and couches are not conducive to proper sleeping. I have my appearance to think of, after all, since it's my livelihood, and you do as well."

Fiona blinked, her thoughts whirling. "What?"

"Darling, I adore you, but women are not my first predilection, if you need me to spell that out for you, which I can see from the look on your face that you do. So, you are safe as houses against my lustful predations, I assure you. You must think of me as your brother, no matter that I'm cute as a button, so I hear." He laughed, looking at her face. "They don't do this in Bally whatever, do they, pet?"

She swallowed. "Ah…no." Or at least if they did, she'd never been privy to it. Holy mother of god. She just kept learning new things but she'd had no experience of this one. There'd been occasional jokes among the boys at St. Hilda's but she'd never understood them 'til now. She could feel herself blushing and she felt like a fool.

James laughed softly and kissed her cheek. "Oh sweet Mary, you are adorable. I have my work cut out for me, I can see that. Not just the theater world, but so much more that I must introduce you to."

She jumped up. "No, I can't. I mean, that's not who I am."

James pulled her back down beside him. "Don't be a ninny, Mary. It's not for you, clearly, but just a wider experience of the world, which obviously hasn't presented itself for you until now. Girl, you've not only been raised in an ignorant country bubble but then a very confined and proper one over on Fifth Avenue. The world, not just the theater, is a much bigger place and one you'll soon get to know, I promise."

She sat next to him, his warmth comforting, and after a while as he chattered on, she allowed herself to lean into him and felt better. She did have a lot to learn, and it was not always going to be about things she was familiar with or wanted to know. It was, however, going to be what she needed to survive and prosper in the world. Not just the theater, but anywhere. This was just the beginning.

That first night, when he'd lain down beside her, she'd trembled with anxiety, but he clasped her hand, wished her good night and rolled over. Within minutes, she heard his soft snore. It had been the same or close to it, ever since and he'd never once done or said a thing that unsettled her. She did think of him as a brother, although one she was fond of watching and every once in a while, wondered what it would be like to be kissed by James Ardrey. Not that she was ever going to find out.

She settled into her role. Romeo and Juliet drew record crowds and Augustin was happy, in fact delighted, hugging her enthusiastically after nearly every performance, calling her "my little star" and offering her champagne in her dressing room. The critics from the New York Tribune, the Times and the Evening Post had given the show rave reviews, especially for its radiant Juliet. "Fresh and lovely," the Times reviewer gushed, "Mary O'Neill is the girl Broadway's been waiting for, an actress with such natural talent she can generously share the stage to make everyone shine with her."

Every time a reviewer praised her, Augustin made certain she knew of it, leaving the papers in her dressing room or shoving them in front of her face when she returned. "See, my dear? You and James are the perfect match. I'd been nearly ready to give up on Mr. Just a Pretty Face, but then you came along and proved he could act, after all. Delightful!"

It made her unhappy when Augustin said things like that about James, since he'd been so kind and helpful in tutoring her, and she knew once or twice James had overheard some of those remarks, although he never admitted it or said a word.

Augustin had an artist draw her and James in costume for the playbills and the posters outside the theater, and that had ramped up ticket sales even more than the reviews. The play was originally scheduled for a four-week run, then extended for another three, but he was already planning his next production five days after opening night. She supposed that was the smart thing to do and Augustin was nothing if not clever in the ways of the theater. His reputation grew by the day and she was grateful that her initial foray into New York theater had been at his hands, thanks to James.

They sat in his office while he ran through his ideas, thinking out loud.

"So I was going to go with something more contemporary, give some new playwrights an opportunity, like Purcell or that Goodman but the audiences seem to be delighted with Shakespeare at the moment, and never say the bard can't entice. What do you think, James?"

Ardey nodded. "I agree. They clearly seem to have a taste for it, so let's give them more of it, for now. I'd steer clear of MacBeth or Lear, but something lighter. Midsummer, perhaps?"

Drewry seemed to consider but Fiona, even novice as she was, had seen that ploy before. He already knew exactly what he wanted to do. He snapped his fingers as though an idea had just occurred to him.

"I know. 'As You Like It'", Drewry said. "How perfect. I have my sweet Rosalind and charming Orlando right here in front of me. And," he grinned, "I've a yearning to play Jacques once again. To 'suck melancholy out of a song the way a weasel sucks eggs.'"

James clapped his hands, clearly delighted, and Fiona was

momentarily stuck in limbo. She hadn't read that play yet and had no idea who Rosalind was, although it looked as though she'd better learn quickly.

"What do you think, Mary?"

She smiled at Drewry. "Sounds lovely." He quirked an eyebrow and she knew she hadn't fooled him for a second.

"Excellent. I'll have scripts out in a day or so. In the meanwhile, keep on doing what you do, my darlings. See you tonight."

They both knew when they were being dismissed, even James. Outside in the hallway he grabbed her hand. "Don't worry, Mary. It's an easy play, as Shakespeare goes and you'll be a perfect Rosalind."

When they reached the lobby and opened the door to the outside, they both blinked in the sunlight after the darkened interior of the theater.

"Come on. Now that you've been paid, we're going shopping. The newest star on Broadway needs a wardrobe commensurate with her status. You're a lady's maid no longer, sweet Mary, and will never be again. It's way past time you stopped dressing like one."

At the look on her face, he kissed her cheek remorsefully. "Oh, sweetling, you always look delightful and your clothes are fine. I'm such an ass. What I meant was, let's have fun clothing you in something so stylish everyone will wish to copy the best actress in New York. How about that?"

Mollified, she took his hand and off they went. The shops James took her to were dazzling. Fiona had never seen the like. Even in her forays through the city in the last year, she'd never dared step inside them, but instead had waited in the servants' section while Audrey strolled through the emporiums, even sometimes standing outside while she waited, looking at the display windows. She never thought she'd be inside the Marble Place trying on the lovely clothes she'd only dreamed about. It was their first stop on the "Ladies Mile", as James called it, floors and floors of incredible goods, crystal chandeliers overhead, marble tile floors and Oriental rugs on the floors in the Ladies Dress department, where she bought three dresses, James happily lounging and giving advice, much to the amusement and delight of the salesladies.

After that, they continued on to Macy's, where she bought shoes and stockings, and lovely underwear, blushing when James pointed out the silk and lace that felt best against bare skin, the saleslady giving a discreet but mischievous grin at them. They finished their whirlwind at Lord & Taylor, where she tried on more skirts, dresses and shirtwaists, her newly appointed fashion mentor waiting on a couch, sipping champagne and flirting with the salesladies as she modeled one thing after another.

"No, no, no," James would say. "Peach makes you look sallow. Go bold, darling." He'd nod at the saleslady and quick as a wink, new garments would appear in the dressing room.

At first, Fiona was embarrassed at the women helping her into the garments, but after a while, she became used to it. She stifled a laugh, thinking how shocked they'd be to know she'd never been inside a store buying new clothes in her life before today. At the orphanage, she'd been given her uniform and a dress for Sunday mass, which she'd taken with her when she left with Sean Dooley. He'd never provided a stitch and it wasn't until Cork, when nurse Mary had supplied her with clothing when she left the hospital, that she'd ever had a decent dress, even if it was secondhand.

These were working women, just as she was, just doing their job, and they saw hundreds of women every week in the same dressing rooms. She was no different than anyone else. *But not for long*, she thought to herself. The entire experience was eye-opening. *I am different, and I'll make sure everyone knows it.* The next time she came to any of these stores, they wouldn't simply be helpful, but eager to wait on her. Some of them were even now, and she felt a rush of satisfaction when one of the young salesgirls recognized her.

"Oh my, I saw Romeo and Juliet with my fiancé last week, and I never thought you would be here in person to buy a dress," she confided. "You were wonderful. That color is perfect for you."

After Macy's, they trundled back down to James's apartment, paying a boy a dollar to cart some of the boxes and bags full of the clothes she'd bought. She worried about the money she'd spent, but James scoffed at her doubts.

"My dear, you're getting another paycheck next week. The ticket sales are through the roof." He took her arm, one eye on the lad behind them. "That one will pay the rent and after that, I think we need to look at more spacious quarters. We could entertain, since we're becoming so well known, the both of us. Perhaps something with two bedrooms, not that I don't enjoy my sister warming the bed." He kissed her cheek without missing a step. He winked and Fiona blushed.

She wasn't certain why. The thought of an amorous relationship wasn't something she'd given a moment's thought to, especially after one Sean Dooley, not that her marriage had ever been anything approaching amorous, in fact exactly the opposite. She loved James, but he'd made it clear it wasn't like that for him and she was accepting of that. She needed a friend and James was that and more. Anything closer than that was something altogether different and not a thing she was certain she'd ever be ready for with anyone.

CHAPTER 10

Fiona stared at her image in the mirror as she wiped the greasepaint and makeup from her face. She hated the play, and the character of Laura Cortland. They had just one more week of Augustin's "Under the Gaslight" and she was mightily tired of being tied to the simulated railroad tracks. In Fiona's opinion, this was a revival that should have stayed dead. That Augustin had decided to produce it was not the choice she would've made but his ego always took center stage to anyone else's opinion and novice that she was, she'd not had a better suggestion. Then again, it was his company, thirty strong.

The winter season looked to be tremendous and in just a few months, her star had risen as James had predicted. Her name was now officially Mary Neill. Augustin said there was no point in keeping the Irish, as no one could tell she was Irish when she was on stage anyway and it just led to issues. Truth be told, he was right but even though it wasn't even her real name anyway, Fiona felt some allegiance to her native land and the fact that the Irish were considered lesser and so vilified in New York always made her angry. Still, it was a sacrifice, among others, although she'd seen the sense in Augustin's decision.

"Ready?" James burst in, unannounced as always, cape already over his shoulders. "We're meeting at Lowe's, did you forget?"

She sighed. "No, James, I didn't forget. You're such a nag. Just give me a minute, would you? And, have you ever heard of knocking? I could've been starkers in here."

"Oh please." He plopped himself down on her one armchair. "I've seen that a hundred times. Have you forgot we live together, pet?"

How could she? They'd moved into a bigger flat, one with two bedrooms, so she could have some privacy and he could as well. She loved him like the brother she'd never had, but there were times she wished she'd just gotten her own place. The pace of James's social life had now become hers and it was exhausting. Four nights out of seven, people came for dinner or drinks, and didn't leave until late, eating, drinking, dancing, doing scenes from plays, the walls echoing with laughter and song. The other nights they went out, usually to Delmonico's, James's favorite and once Fiona was introduced to their steak and potatoes, nothing like those she'd ever eaten in Ireland, she became a devotee as well. She loved everything about the restaurant, from the elegant dining room to the kind and knowledgeable waiters, and they had become regular customers, some nights even given their dinners gratis. Like the maitre'd Jean-Pierre said, "when we have stars in our midst, *cherie*, those who wish to bask in their glow come in hordes", and who could disagree with that?

While it was good for their careers to become friends with as many people as possible according to James, from newspaper people to society types to theater investors, it was demanding and she was quickly tiring of it. They were going to have to establish some new rules or she'd grow as mad as Ophelia.

Her world had changed so much in the last year, it was as though it had turned from day to night. Fiona herself had changed just as much, no longer the quiet mousey maid, but a woman of presence who made her own decisions. As much as anyone could in the theater, she supposed. She'd like to change that, too. She'd become well-known and other producers had approached her, as well as James, who had become just as well-known as she had, their likenesses outside the Fifth Avenue theater every night.

Augustin had upped their wages, because he knew full well he had no choice unless he wished to lose them, and both she and James grinned every time that happened. Augustin was making a great deal of money, as were most successful New York theater producers and it was only fair that he compensate the people who made that happen for him.

Quite often people stopped her on the street or in a restaurant or bar. At first, it had been exciting but she was growing tired of the interruptions and their overly friendly approaches, as though they wanted to be her best friend. She had friends and she didn't need others that she didn't know. She'd come to realize theater people were a close-knit group for a reason. They didn't need to explain themselves to anyone nor be judged by them and that suited Fiona quite well.

At least tonight they were going to a restaurant where hopefully someone else could pay the bill. It usually wasn't Augustin, he was such a skinflint. She was making more money than she could've ever imagined but somehow it disappeared, between clothes, rent, food and all the "necessities" James insisted upon, like the best whiskey, food, art, clothing or décor for their flat. He was always broke, just as she was, even though his paychecks rivaled hers. They were going to have a talk, Fiona decided. It was madness, a never-ending spiral.

Lowe's was noisy and crowded as they made their way to a large table in the back, anchored by Augustin, of course. People called their names and hands reached out as they passed, eager to touch their luminaries of the New York theater scene. Fiona smiled in mock regret, patting hands and shoulders as they threaded their way through the tables, pulling the skirts of her emerald chiffon dress away from the floor as she brushed by.

"There you are," Augustin said, clearly miffed they were late. Fiona couldn't care less tonight. She was tired and hoped he wasn't going to be the nasty beast he could be because she wasn't sure she wouldn't snap back at his jibes.

"Well, we're here now," James said, his smile dazzling. "The party can start."

Augustin scowled while everyone else laughed. James ordered them both drinks and they sat down, pulling off their coats and draping them on the chairs. Some of the usual crew were gathered around the table, but there were a couple of new faces Fiona hadn't seen before. A handsome and distinguished older man sat beside Drewry. The older man was accompanied by a very stylish woman, the ostrich feathers in her elaborate coiffure complimenting her face, which would have been pretty if not for the dismissive downturn of her lips. The gentleman smiled at them while the woman stared hungrily. The very look of her made Fiona shiver.

"My, how blessed we are," Augustin said nastily, and waved at the waiter hovering nearby. "Please. My young friends have graced us with their presence and I'm sure are in need of libations for their efforts."

James ignored him and ordered a double whiskey for himself and seltzer for Fiona, their usual. He'd share when she wanted it, pouring a little discreetly into her glass. It was a habit they'd picked up months ago when she'd been uncomfortable ordering spirits in public, or even in drinking them in private. Since then, she'd developed a taste for whiskey but her public image had to remain the chaste ingénue and they'd kept to the role, laughing about it in private. The way Augustin was watching them tonight, she'd be lucky to taste that whiskey at all, as though he didn't know exactly how she and James operated.

Augustin raised his glass. "To a successful performance, once again, and a great run. Next up, I'm thinking 'MacBeth'."

A collective gasp went through the actors at the large table. The Scottish play had a reputation, and so theater myth went, it was a disaster to ever say its name aloud but Drewry just had, defying the gods. No one drank, except for the couple beside him and Drewry himself.

"Don't be ridiculous, it's just a superstition," he said. "How can I produce a play whose name I can't ever say? This little myth has always driven me mad and I can't imagine how this lie ever got started. All right, my little superstitious darlings, after tonight, never again. Does that satisfy you?"

Reluctantly, most drank and sat their glasses down. Fiona was mystified, never having heard of this before, but she followed James's lead, as always, and his face had gone pale.

"What is he talking about?" she whispered in James's ear.

"Everyone knows you never say the name of that play aloud," he whispered back. "Death and misery will follow."

"What?" She mimed it, making a face.

"Believe it, dove," he muttered. "History tells." He looked up at Drewry and smiled. "Good enough, my master. All will be well, I'm sure." He drank as well, and turned back to her. "God knows there's no part for you, Mary, unless you want to age ten years. Can't imagine what he's thinking. He's an actor himself," James sipped his whiskey. "Not a very good one, but he should know better than this."

After that, everyone began chattering about the theater scene, gossip about who was seeing who, and the mood lightened. Augustin looked at James.

"Forgive me for being so remiss," he said. "James Ardrey, this is Samuel Lowell and his lovely wife Victoria," he gestured to the couple sitting beside him. "They're very interested in the theater and meeting all of you. They want to get a feel for the sort of people who will be treading the boards of the productions they finance. And, this delightful young thing is Mary Neill, our Laura of this evening. She's very gifted."

Lowell stood and shook hands with James, his hand lingering, while he nodded perfunctorily at Fiona. *Oh Christ*, Fiona thought. *He's another one.* The wife smiled and it looked to Fiona like a beautiful shark had just opened its mouth. For some reason Fiona hated her on sight. *Get a grip on yourself, my girl,* she thought, *she's just another theater lover with aspirations, not a devil that you should be having mean thoughts about.*

James seemed subdued, but then he always did in the presence of money and, for some reason, refined older gentlemen. Not for the first time, she wondered just who James's family was. She'd seen it before but this time, her senses were on high alert. Lowell wasn't the usual, she had a feeling. There was a reason Augustin had been so displeased with their tardiness and she suspected this was it. She'd learned he'd use anybody for more money to promote his theater and it looked as though the Lowells were the prime candidates being romanced tonight.

The party wore on, and after two more drinks and some trays of nibbles, Fiona was heartily tired of it. She stood up, gathering her wrap. She leaned down and whispered in James's ear.

"I'm going home. I'll see you in the morning unless you want to come."

He grabbed her wrist. "Give me a second. I'm coming with you."

James put on his greatcoat and bowed to the assembled guests, ignoring their cries of dismay. "I'm walking Mary home, darlings. We can't have our lovely star on the streets alone. *Ciao*, it's been delightful."

It was raining. She didn't say a word as they walked the dark gleaming streets to the apartment, only three blocks away, nor did James. He unlocked the door and she went in, throwing her coat on the couch. She lit a lamp and turned to him as he stood on the threshold.

"Get in here, I don't have time for this tonight," she said. He shrugged, locking the door and throwing off his own coat.

"So you're to be a whorin' for him? Which one is it? Him or her? That woman would eat your liver with scones for breakfast."

He had the grace to look confused. "It's not what you think."

"It's exactly what I fuckin' think. You can't be doin' this. What is wrong with you, thinkin' it's fine and all?" In times of stress, her Irish always came to the fore, even as much as they'd practiced, along with the coarse vernacular of the village now coupled with the elegant diction of Shakespeare.

He went into the small kitchen and poured them both a glass of brandy, holding one out to her, and they both sat on the couch, eyeing each other like gladiators. Fiona sipped her brandy and waited.

"Lowell wants to invest in a theater company, and Augustin wants to buy the building. It's going to take a lot of money, more even than Drewry has and Lowell could do it like he's buying groceries, so . . ."

She snorted. "So you have to be the sacrificial lamb?"

He looked at her over the rim of his snifter. "They're very, very rich. And they like actors, so I hear. Besides, it's not so bad."

Mary was tired of this. She loved James dearly but he was so vulnerable while thinking he was so clever and she knew sooner or later his luck would run out. Augustin would use any of them to foster his dreams. She was lucky it hadn't yet been her, but she knew it had been James before. This time she was apprehensive. It was the way Lowell had looked at him, along with that wife, like a leopard spotting its prey, nearly licking her lips.

"This one's different."

"Don't be silly, Mary. He's like any of us, just richer and less likely to be exposed. I'll be fine." He took a long pull on the brandy. "Besides, it's just a night or two. I know I should feel terrible, and maybe I will sometime, but I've done worse." He kissed her cheek. "I'll reform, I promise you."

She felt more than she should allow herself to feel for James. Maybe only because he never laid a finger on her in that way and insisted that wasn't his preference, although irrationally she sometimes thought he might want to. She wanted to slap him but knew that was foolish. Instead, she swallowed the last of her brandy. He was going to do it no matter what she said. She'd deal with the consequences. She didn't know what those might be, but she instinctively knew there'd be some. He didn't know she was very good at dealing with consequences.

CHAPTER 11

They began rehearsals for MacBeth. To her surprise, Fiona was cast as Lady MacBeth which terrified her and required a great deal of makeup, but there it was. Augustin had laughed at her fears which only made her want to do it just to spite him.

James, as expected, was playing MacBeth. Drewry had clearly begun to think of them both as a team. Young as they both were, they outshone the rest of the cast and even Fiona, inexperienced as she was, knew it. James was brilliant, and under his tutelage and Augustin's rather threatening presence, she'd learned quickly and risen fast. The terror she felt each time she stepped onto the stage had dissipated, and as more and more roles came, she'd learned quickly. Unlikely as it seemed, she was born for this—the illusion, the wonder, the joy of being someone else besides Fiona Shanahan, an orphan with no future. Now she had one.

She stood on the stage, waiting for James. He was late. She hadn't seen him before he left for the evening nor this morning before she went to the theater. He walked on, his clothes looking hastily thrown together, very unlike him, even for rehearsals. She tried to catch his eye but he just looked down briefly at his script and quickly lowered his eyes, completely MacBeth to the bone. They began.

"'I have done the deed. Didst thou not hear a noise?'"

She stared at him. "'I heard the owl scream and the crickets cry. Did not you not speak?'"

"'When?'"

"'''Now.'"

"'There's one did laugh in his sleep and one cried Murder!'"

"Stop." Augustin's voice cut through the mostly empty theater like a knife. "You blew some lines, James. Go back."

"They don't matter," James said, his voice low. "I'll get them tomorrow, or the next day."

When he looked up, Fiona could plainly see that he looked haggard, his eyes like burnt cinders, and she took a step towards him. He raised his head and looked at the dark seats in front of him. "Maybe none of this matters." With that, he fell into her arms. She stumbled, lost her balance and they both dropped onto the floorboards.

They were in her dressing room, James sprawled across the one upholstered chair. Augustin had banished them, his disgust evident, and went to rehearsing Act III. Fiona knelt down beside James.

"Get up, James. We're going home to bed. What in hell happened to you last night?"

He looked at her, eyes bleak. This was no place to talk about it, she realized. "I don't want to hear it now, we're leaving and you'll be tellin' me later."

She pulled him up, threw his greatcoat over his shoulders and home they went. He didn't say a word, hadn't voiced a protest on the three-block walk, and had collapsed on his bed while she went to make tea, pouring in a little laudanum she'd gotten from the pharmacy down the street. He was in pain, she'd known that much.

"Drink it."

She sat beside his bed and drink it he did, finishing the whole cup on her urging. He lay back down, eyelids fluttering.

"Oh, no, boyo. It's not to be that easy. Tell me."

He sagged back on the pillows. "Oh Christ, Mary, you don't want to hear this."

"Likely not, but hear it I will," she said. "It was the Lowells, wasn't it?" She knew evil, and it had shone out of that woman's eyes like a lance.

"Yes." The word came out of him, a sigh of remorse.

It came out, piece by piece. He'd seen Lowell once before, an intimate supper after the theater, but last night James had met with them at their townhouse in response to a dinner invitation. He'd been somewhat apprehensive about it and had decided this was the last time he'd try to convince them to invest with Augustin, whether Augustin had finalized his plans or not. Instead, he'd literally been ambushed, drugged and woke to find himself naked and tied to a wheel in some terrible room that resembled nothing so much as a dungeon.

Lowell was there, but in charge had been his wife, wearing leather and wielding a whip, among other things. As he began to tell her of the things they'd done to him, Fiona put her hand gently over James's mouth.

"No, that's enough." She kissed him gently on the cheek. She couldn't bear to listen to any more of the awful words coming from his mouth. "Sleep now."

He didn't need any encouragement, and the laudanum was doing its work well. She pulled a blanket over him and tiptoed out to the kitchen. Her hands shook with anger, and it simmered through her like a fire. She hadn't felt this way since the night she'd burned down the cottage, a rage so great it took her over like a storm rolling across the moor.

She made some tea, adding whiskey and sipped it slowly at the kitchen table, trying not to think about taking up a carving knife and cutting out the black hearts of the Lowells. She knew whatever she imagined they'd done to James, what had actually happened was likely worse. She'd seen it in both of them the first night they'd met, a darkness that seemed hidden to most, but not to a fey Irish girl who'd known evil before. St. Hilda's and Ballyowen had offered all kinds of educational opportunities, especially if you were small, helpless and poor.

She let James sleep and made chicken soup. She wasn't much of a cook, but she knew how to do that. Besides, it kept her busy, that and watching the rain turn to snow outside as the afternoon darkened, the windows clouding over with the steam from the soup.

By late afternoon Fiona couldn't put it off any longer. She heated water for the bathing tub, one of the reasons they'd chosen this particular place, and went to wake him up. He looked up at her, blinking. She put down the cup of tea laced again with laudanum.

"What?"

"We need to get you cleaned up," she said and handed him the tea, which he drank like the elixir it was. She had a very bad feeling he was going to need that, and more.

He sat up groggily and took off his vest, unbuttoning his shirt, spotted with blood. Fiona winced and helped him peel it away. His chest was spotted with burns, about the size of a cigar end, and many small cuts, some of them deep. But it was his back that made her gasp. Slashes crisscrossed his torso, too many to count. She'd expected it, of course, from what he'd started to describe, but it still broke her heart. She helped him into the tub, taking away his bloodied trousers as he shed those too, easing him down into the warm water as he groaned and rested his head on the edge of the porcelain.

The water swirled in pink ribbons as Fiona gently cleansed

his wounds, James leaning forward and sideways as she worked. At last he stepped out and dried himself, wrapping his nightshirt around him. No words passed between them. They ate the soup silently as well, finishing two bowls each, and sat back against the hard wooden chairs, their eyes meeting across the table.

"Thank you."

She nodded. "Of course." She picked up the bowls and put them in the washtub. He sat silent as a statue and then reached out and took her hand, kissing it.

"I was so stupid and so careless."

"Yes," she said. "You were. But you'll heal." She knew that, because she had. There were scars, yes, but the pain would ease even if the memories never did. "What do you want to do about it? Say nothing? Just go on?"

He squeezed her hand, crushing it, and his eyes were lit with anger and, she thought, something extra, a fire for vengeance. There was also a healthy dose of self-loathing that he needed to purge somehow.

"No, I want to expose them for the monsters they are."

She sat down, her hand still in his. "We always want that, James, but it doesn't come easy. Are you sure?"

"Hell, yes."

Fiona smiled, and it was a terrible smile. "Ah, well then. They should pay for what they did to you, and likely many others, in the past and in the future. Although we'll have to be very careful, James."

He sat silently and finally raised his eyes to her.

"Sometimes, Mary," he said, "I don't think I really know you at all, but I'm starting to, aren't I?" He squeezed her hand. "Some very bad things happened to you before you got on that boat. Some day, when you trust me enough, I hope you'll tell me."

"Some day I will," she said, and her smile didn't seem terrible in the least to him, she could see. "Sometimes justice must be served. New York is starting to bore me anyway. I think we're done here."

Now James smiled too. "I think you could be right, my dear."

CHAPTER 12

*M*acBeth, or the play with no name, or the Scottish play, especially to those who acted in it, was a huge success, even ensuring an extended run, right up until Christmas, when the theater would close for a week, giving them all a much needed respite. It was Augustin's idea, and one he'd always followed. Augustin Drewry, not only a brilliant producer and theater owner, was a man who knew how to keep his actors and the whole troupe happy and content.

Fiona and James bided their time, taking no social engagements, seemingly absorbed with rehearsals and the performances themselves. What they'd also done was to find out all they could about Samuel and Victoria Lowell's hidden lives and there was a great deal to find. With little prodding, people had talked to them once the subject was broached, sometimes with a good deal of whiskey, but sometimes not. James was far from the first to be brutalized and quite a few theater people, among others, knew of it, but the Lowells had never been brought up on any charges, much less even questioned.

The worst of it, they'd found, was that people had gone missing, but no investigations had taken place that they could find. It was as though the earth had swallowed them up, and there had conveniently been no families to object or raise an inquiry.

They were beginning to despair of finding anyone with any evidence about the missing actors or at least anyone who was willing to talk about it, when they heard about a young actress named Susan McLeod who had gone missing over a year ago. Susan McLeod had a brother who owned a bar further downtown, a Scotsman who'd been in New York for some time and had a reputation as an honest and respected man. They decided to pay him a visit.

It was late, but still early as bars' hours went. The address was in the Bowery, but the place looked fairly decent, even if the clientele coming and going seemed a bit rugged. The wooden sign over the door was freshly painted in white and green, with "The Red Lion" in bright gilt letters. James shrugged and opened the door for Fiona. It was dimly lit, smelling of whiskey but also of savory meat pies, and many of the tables were filled, mostly with men but a fair amount of women as well, a custom in many Scots or Irish establishments. Their arrival didn't merit any unusual glances as they made their way to the bar. James ordered two whiskies and when the bartender set them down, he pushed a five dollar gold piece towards him.

"We're hoping to talk to Angus McLeod, if he's around," he said. The bartender studied them both for a few seconds. He was a large man, red-haired and bearded and he wiped his hands on his white apron before pocketing the money.

"You're doin' that now."

"Ah. Well, excellent," James said. "We'd like to talk about Susan."

"Would you, now?" The big man jerked his head towards another man behind the bar and wordlessly came around the side, motioning them to a quieter table near the back. They sat down and McLeod stared at them. He didn't look very friendly.

"Well?"

Fiona put her hand on James's arm, pressing firmly and shooting him a glance. He nodded nearly imperceptibly and let her take the lead. They'd done this for a while now and were getting practiced at who was the best choice.

"Thank you, Mr. McLeod. I'm Laura Cortland and this is my husband Alan. We heard Susan's been missing for over a year or so, and we were hoping you could help us find her."

"Who the hell are you people?" He leaned over the table, his face close to Fiona's. "Is this some kind of joke?"

"No. It's just that, well, we're actors, in fact with a company Susan did some work with, and we heard she's disappeared. Maybe you know where she is?"

"If I did, girl, we wouldn't be sitting here blathering about it, would we? She's dead is where she is, and I know who's responsible for it, too, but the police haven't done a goddamn thing about it and likely never will. There's your answer. Now drink up and get the hell out of here. If she'd never gotten involved with the likes of you, she'd still be alive." He got up, his face nearly as red as his beard, but before he could walk away, Fiona stood up and gently put her hand on his arm.

"Please, Mr. McLeod. Does the name Lowell mean anything to you?"

He stared at her, and his face paled visibly, even in the dim light. He sat back down in the chair and stared at them both. "I think we're going to need more whiskey."

Susan McLeod had lived with her brother above the Red Lion, working as a waitress in the bar. She was a pretty thing with red-gold curls, always dancing about as she served and talking about being on the stage. One day she came home breathless with excitement and the news that she was now part of a new troupe that was going to produce musicals. She was quite good, at singing as well as dancing, and while she still lived upstairs, had no time to work in the bar anymore, practicing and rehearsing her skills. No productions had been announced, but she seemed excited about her prospects.

Angus was happy for her, but worried too, especially when she started coming home with expensive clothes, occasionally jewelry, and seemed to have an endless supply of money, more than she could possibly be earning as an actress. He confronted her, worried she was working as a lady of the night and she'd assured him that wasn't so but she had a special friend, just one. He hadn't liked it but he loved his sister even though she also had bruises that he'd seen even though she tried to hide them. One night he followed her to a townhouse near the park and when she still hadn't emerged by dawn, he went home to confront her there when she arrived.

She never did. Angus went to the police, but after desultory inquiries, they shrugged and said young people were always running off and the investigation stalled. When he told them again of the address where he'd last seen her, he was told to drop the matter completely or he would find himself in serious trouble, and likely lose the Red Lion and his livelihood.

Samuel and Victoria Lowell were virtually untouchable, scions of New York society, and Lowell's bank owned a great deal of the real estate in the city. No hint of scandal would be tolerated, especially by the police. They made it clear they viewed Angus as an immigrant troublemaker rather than a brother searching for his wayward sister, and perhaps even worse than that. One of the detectives had suggested that Angus himself might have a motive as to his sister's demise, since she was clearly a wayward young woman and he head of the family.

"And that, my new young friends, is how things still stand," Angus McLeod said, finishing off his whiskey and pouring another. "They killed her. I know it and now you do too, and they will never pay for it."

Fiona and James exchanged glances. *He's right,* Fiona thought, *they did kill her and probably more. James had been very lucky and it was likely because Augustin had known where James was that night.* Her stomach was churning but she downed her own glass.

"Thank you, Angus, for your honesty and telling us about Susan," Fiona said. She put her hand on Angus's arm. "Although I suspected something like this, I'm sorry to say I believe you're right, and we don't think Susan was the first or the last. We're going to make things right, or at least try our best. Susan deserves better."

Tears pooled in the big man's eyes and he blinked rapidly. "Ah, God, wish that you could, but you'll not get any justice in this town, not against them. Best if you just leave it be and let God sort it out. The bastard even owns this building now, according to the police, so it's all I can do."

James put his hand on Angus's shoulder. "They say God works in mysterious ways, Mr. McLeod. Sometimes things do get sorted out."

Neither of them said a word all the way back to the apartment. Fiona made tea and set the cup down in front of James. He put his hands on the cup to warm them and then stared at her.

"Mary, this is a dark road we're on. If we keep going, it could get very bad. This started out as some possible revenge for me, but it's taken on a completely different aspect, especially after everything we've found out and even more so after talking with Angus."

Oh, how well she knew, perhaps better than he did. She put her hands on his around the warm cup. "Have we not decided to mete out our own justice? 'Screw your courage to the sticking place, MacBeth, and we'll not fail.' Susan McLeod and all like her as well as those who might come after deserve our efforts, James."

"Yes, my dear," he said. "I believe they do." He met her eyes. "We will not fail."

* * *

JAMES DIDN'T SEE the Lowells again until MacBeth's opening night, being way too busy with rehearsals and his supposed newly kindled relationship with his girlfriend Mary, to the gossipy delight of the company. He greeted them with lowered eyes, playing the innocent and wounded suitor to perfection, Fiona thought. Wounded, yes, but he managed to give off an air of reluctant longing which seemed to excite both of them, she could tell. She played her part as well, flirting with Lowell and his wife subtly, but she could tell they were becoming intrigued with the idea of a willing couple. Each time they met, she and James always left early, citing exhaustion and lines to rehearse but she didn't miss the glances the Lowells threw their way.

They plotted and planned, sitting up late at night, going over and over the details, saving every penny and finding out all they could about opportunities in Pittsburgh, Chicago and other cities. They befriended actors who'd toured, carefully gleaning information and names, all the while playing up the wonders of New York theater and how happy they were to be a part of it, scoffing gently at the mere thought of ever deigning to tour or venture into the mining towns or the frontier. How droll, they'd laughed, could anyone possibly want to do without Broadway?

The last night of MacBeth, everyone had met at Lowe's as usual, even Augustin's new partners, the esteemed Lowells. Fiona and James had been right on time, dressed to elicit reactions, her bodice low and his waistcoat cut to show off his waist and broad shoulders to perfection. They were noticed as usual by the Lowells, Victoria almost licking her lips. Fiona had glanced at her often, breasts heaving, and Victoria and Samuel both not so subtly looking back. Just as things were winding up, Samuel had met her on the way to the ladies' room, catching her wrist as she brushed by.

"James has led me to believe you might be interested in

coming to our little party tomorrow night," he said, staring intently into her eyes.

"Oh, has he?" She blushed. "Perhaps. He's told me so much about you and your wife. If you promise to be kind and gentle."

Lust flared in his eyes. "Oh, I think I can manage that. Or maybe just a little bit forceful. I think you'd like it."

She fluttered her eyelashes. "I might at that."

He laughed, low in his throat. "I do love actors. I hear you're very imaginative, Mary. As are we."

Fiona pulled away. "So I have heard. Until tomorrow, then." She smiled enticingly and entered the ladies' room, fortunately empty because her stomach was heaving. She washed her hands thoroughly afterwards, especially her wrist.

Back at home lying in bed, she couldn't sleep. They were in a very dangerous game and it wouldn't take more than a slight misstep for it all to go very wrong. It might be the wisest course to simply move on, and leave the Lowells to their fate. Surely someone would soon become aware of their activities and bring them to justice. Vigilantism wasn't the province of a couple of stage actors who needed to get on with their lives. There were other cities and other stages where they would be welcomed, Fiona knew from the inquiries they'd made. Truthfully, she'd like to get away from New York, tainted now and forever for her, and James as well, she suspected.

JAMES DONNED his waistcoat and shot his cuffs. "The servants have the night off when they "entertain". Likely so no gossip will get around. There's no network as efficient as that of servants, trust me."

Fiona laughed. "How well I know. Have you forgotten what I used to do?"

James kissed her cheek. "You've changed so much, I nearly did. Forgive me."

She studied him. "You know, sometime you're going to have to tell me exactly how you'd know such a great deal about the workings of wealthy houses, my darlin'. Once we're out of here."

"Agreed. Now to the business at hand."

They walked to the Lowells', not wanting to risk a carriage driver's memory. At the door, he took her hand.

"Are you certain?"

Fiona nodded. "Absolutely."

Samuel Lowell himself answered the door, a brocaded dressing gown over his shirt and loose trousers, feet encased in velvet slippers. "Good evening, my dear friends. How lovely you came. We've been eagerly waiting you. Please."

They followed him through the darkened entry hall and into the library, softly lit with candles and the flames of a crackling fire. Victoria sat in a wing chair beside the fireplace, a brandy snifter in her hand. She smiled, her teeth showing, as though she was hungry for a tasty morsel. Fiona felt as though they'd stepped into the lions' den, and realized that in fact they had.

"Have a seat, my dears," Lowell said, gesturing to the sofa in front of Victoria. "Let me get you some refreshment."

He busied himself at the bar and handed them both full brandy snifters and retrieved one for himself, sitting between them on the sofa. "It's been some time, James. We've missed you. Here we were thinking you were put off by our last game.

James smiled shyly. "It rather took me by surprise and wasn't quite what I was used to, but it was, well, exciting, in a way." He looked up at Lowell and blushed gracefully, his angelic face highlighted by the firelight. "When I mentioned it to Mary, she seemed quite interested. We like to do things together. Besides, she's a wonderful actress and takes on every role she approaches with enthusiasm. You're very creative, aren't you, love?"

Fiona put down her glass and raised both her arms over her head, stretching sinuously, grinning slyly at Samuel and then resting her gaze on his wife. "I do love learning new things. Teach me?"

Victoria licked her lips, her tongue a bit like a snake's, testing the air. She truly was beautiful, her blonde hair piled high on her head, a few curls playfully dangling here and there on her lovely throat. She was dressed in a filmy green gown that left little to the imagination. "Darlings, we are going to have so much fun. But you're both so overdressed." She laughed. "It is cold outside, but I can assure you it'll be very warm in here for the rest of the evening. Samuel and I never stint on the comfort or entertainment for our special guests."

I can well imagine, thought Fiona, and she wanted to throw her drink in Victoria's face. Instead, she made herself flutter her eyelashes and blush. They made desultory chitchat, difficult for all of them for obviously very different reasons, and finished their brandy.

Samuel Lowell poured them another which they carried with them to the dining room. Apparently there would be no more time wasted in idle talk. Fiona was a bit surprised to see no food on offer nor a table set, but neither of the Lowells ventured a word about it nor so much as an apology. Samuel Lowell paused and apparently pressed a concealed latch hidden in the dining room's walnut paneling. Silently, an opening appeared as a hidden door slid back, revealing a dark passageway into a large room ablaze with candles, lit like a theater ready for a command performance.

She glanced at James, who squeezed her fingers in solidarity even as his steps faltered. Fiona had a sudden urge to grab his hand and run as far away from the house as possible. Surely the police would listen to them and they were foolish to think they could handle this on their own. Instead, Victoria Lowell pushed her ahead, her hand firm on Fiona's back and her breath hot on her neck.

Mother of God, Fiona thought. James hadn't exaggerated. This place could indeed be hell on earth, or at least a haven for devils like these two. She blinked, trying to take it all in, every muscle rigid with shock. The ceilings were high, the walls covered with red brocade, the floors a gleaming black marble. Red velvet couches as large as beds were scattered here and there, among trappings that seemed like something out of a medieval torture chamber, red velvet ropes hanging from some of them. Long filmy draperies, red and black, hung from the ceiling, giving the place a softness it didn't deserve. Around the room stood elaborate iron candelabras, shaped and decorated with vines and the grinning faces of satyrs, glowing with lit black candles as thick as a man's leg. It smelled of some heavy perfume, thick and cloying, probably incense of some sort but to Fiona's mind it might have been sulfur and brimstone.

The art on the walls turned her blood cold: scenes of rape, torture and deviance that no human mind should have been capable of conjuring were depicted in huge canvases set in gold frames. James's hand fell from hers as he stumbled and sprawled onto one of the couches, murmuring the word "run" as his eyes slowly closed. Fiona swayed, the smiling faces of the Lowells the last thing she saw before she slowly collapsed beside him. *The filthy bastards,* she thought, *they drugged the brandy.*

SHE BLINKED, trying to focus but her head felt full of cotton stuffing. She brushed her hand against the bite of something pricking her side. There knelt Victoria Lowell, a silver dagger in her hand and a smile on her face that near froze the blood in Fiona's veins.

"There's my girl. Let's get the rest of these clothes off you.

James will be out for a bit longer, we gave him more than you because it took some effort to get him outfitted without him being troublesome. We thought you'd like to watch, sweetness. We've got all the time in the world now."

Fiona was still wearing her black dress, now with a long rent on one side of it, thanks to Victoria's dagger. The thought that the woman didn't seem to be concerned about her wearing it out of here frightened her badly. They had sorely miscalculated the ruthlessness of the Lowells and their capacity for violence. The plan had been to overpower them and go for the authorities once there was no doubt about their intentions. That, Fiona thought, trying not to panic, had been naïve and foolish.

She stood up, swaying slightly and discarded the dress. Underneath Fiona wore a black corset and stockings, an outfit she'd chosen especially for tonight. She felt like a sad rag doll, her limbs heavy and motionless.

Victoria clucked her tongue, producing a vial of white powder and pouring some into her palm as she watched her. "Here, darling. Take a good sniff of this," she said, pushing Fiona's nose into her palm, holding her hair tightly with the other. "Can't have you dull as paste. You won't be any fun at all and we've gone to such trouble."

With little choice, Fiona followed instructions. She didn't know what the stuff was, but anything would be better than the weak listlessness that had enveloped her, a weakness that would get them killed. Her head exploded. *Sweet Jesus,* she thought, *I've breathed fire.* Tears ran down her cheeks and she bent over, coughing, her nose and brain burning, burning and then numbing, all her nerves crackling like sulfur matches. Victoria giggled, watching her in fascination.

"You're such an innocent little dear. That's better now, isn't it?"

No, it wasn't better, but it was different. Very very different, and Fiona felt a surge of energy like she'd never known, along with another emotion that she hadn't let fully surface for a long time. There were people that simply shouldn't be allowed to continue to draw breath and Fiona knew that with a white pure clarity. She kept her eyes downcast as Victoria took her arm and pulled her away from the sofa.

Victoria ran her hand over the black satin corset. "Lovely, this. Let's keep this on for a time, shall we? Samuel will like it, too." She prodded Fiona with the dagger to the other side of the room and Fiona never felt the prick of the knife, her blood thrumming.

Then she saw James. Just as he'd described from before, he was bound to a wheel, six foot in diameter, naked, his head lolling on his shoulder, his hair in damp curls over his face, and Samuel Lowell stood before him with a gleeful grin, a whip in his hand. He turned.

"Ah, the princess awakes. Lovely outfit. Can't wait to take it off."

Fiona swallowed the bile in her throat and curtsied coquettishly. She was a good actress. That sent both Lowells into gales of laughter.

Victoria stepped up and jabbed James in the thigh with the dagger. Blood trickled down his leg but he didn't stir except for a faint moan. Whatever they'd given him was truly much more than they'd given Fiona. She was on her own but she wasn't concerned about that anymore. She leaned into Samuel, who was clad now only in a pair of silk briefs, his skin hot as she touched him.

"Could I try the whip? I've always wanted to."

He grinned, and looked at Victoria. "This one's a natural. Maybe we should keep her."

Victoria smiled but shook her head almost imperceptibly and Fiona knew she'd been right. They had no intention of letting her or James leave this house alive. They'd probably been on to them from the start but the game was just beginning for the Lowells, although they didn't know it.

Lowell handed her the whip. "Give it a go." He stood behind her, caressing her backside as she brought the whip down on James's leg, the spot she thought would be the least damaging. Maybe it would wake him up, Fiona thought desperately. A thin line of bright red glowed in the candlelight and Lowell sighed, licking his lips like a dog eyeing a particularly juicy piece of meat.

"Nice. But harder. Let me show you." He took the whip from her hand and she positioned herself behind him, taking the opportunity to slide James's straight razor out of the corset boning between her breasts. He hadn't known she'd brought it, but when Fiona spied it in the bathroom before they left, she'd slipped it into the corset and it nestled there like it was meant for such a concealment.

Victoria's eyes were avid, greedily locked onto James's sagging form rather than Fiona as she opened the razor. As Samuel raised his arm for the heavy blow, Fiona felt as though she was in a fast-moving nightmare and the thought of James being ripped into with the whip incensed her. She raised her arm, slicing across Samuel's throat. It was so easy, she thought, almost as though it was meant to be. For a second or two, he didn't move, except to drop his arm, and she worried maybe she'd done it wrong. Then he abruptly dropped to the floor, the whip still in his hand, blood pooling silently beside his white body across the black marble floor.

Victoria stood frozen in shock for a second but then screamed, raising the dagger and lunging at Fiona, her face a rictus of fury.

Fiona ducked and stabbed her in the stomach with the razor. She knew it might not be a killing blow but it was enough that Victoria dropped to her knees in pain. Before she could rise, Fiona thrust her left hand into the elaborate blonde curls, twisting Victoria's neck backwards and cut her throat, too. The woman's body slid bonelessly down to the cold marble floor, her eyes open in shock.

Fiona's blood hummed with the drug and she felt wonderful, as though she could do anything. She gazed at both of them, dead on the floor. This wasn't quite how they'd planned things to go. For a moment verging on hysterical laughter, Fiona thought of Mother Superior who would not have been pleased with the way things turned out at all. Still, penance was penance and Fiona thought this was more effective than fifty Hail Marys could ever be.

Fiona looked up at James, still comatose. What they'd envisioned and planned was incapacitating both of the Lowells, tying them to their various toys, calling the newspapers and the police and getting confessions and long deserved justice, for Susan McLeod and many others. Well. Sometimes you had to work with what you had. God knows, she'd done that before. Fiona wiped the blade clean on the closest red velvet couch and slipped the razor back into her corset.

She went upstairs. In the master bedroom inside the walk-in closet, she found a safe, carelessly left open. She stuffed all the money she found into an empty traveling bag from the shelf. She eyed Victoria's hefty jewel case and dumped its contents in too.

Fiona caught a glimpse of herself in the full length mirror beside the hanging dresses. Blood splattered her neck and breasts, droplets on her legs as well. Tsk, tsk, she thought, this will never do. She yanked a velvet dressing gown off its hanger and wiped herself passably clean. She perused the closet, found a dress that would suffice, and slipped it on, her bare feet making no sound on the thick carpet. There was no one else in the house to hear anyway.

She sat the bag down in the entry hall. From there, she went back to the dining room and discovered a door to the kitchen, where she found a bottle of ammonia and went back to the red room, carefully stepping around the pools of blood, which had gotten considerably larger. She held the bottle under James's nose and he reared back, coughing, his eyes opening but bleary.

"What?"

She made him take another sniff and his eyes opened fully. "What the hell, Mary?"

She sliced through the ropes with her razor and helped him down. He staggered a few steps and stopped cold at the sight of the Lowells.

"What the hell did you do?"

"What I had to do. They were going to kill us, James, like all the rest. Come on."

He found his clothes and pulled them on, stumbling a bit as she led him into the entry hall and sat him down on a bench with his shoes in hand. His eyelids kept trying to close. She put the ammonia bottle down beside him.

"Wait here. I'll be right back," Fiona said.

She went back to the candlelit torture room, staring once more at the bodies, standing over them. That she'd done something terrible, she knew. That she'd had no choice, she knew as well. She'd live with it, as she had everything else. Would she have forgiveness, in the end? She didn't know. Redemption, of a kind? She didn't know that, either. Maybe Susan McLeod would. Perhaps she wouldn't have killed them without the effects of the drug Victoria had given here, but she'd never know that now. It was done.

She tipped over the candelabras and watched as the draperies caught on fire. She left the hidden paneled door open. James still sat on the bench, dazed but at least his shoes were on. Fiona grabbed their coats, picked up the bag and took him by the elbow, shutting the heavy outer door behind them and supporting him as they made their way down the sidewalk into the snowy night. A few blocks down the street, she threw the razor into an alley full of trash cans and rats, a fitting place. The memories she'd have to carry were baggage enough.

***

SHE'D TOLD him all of it, the drugs, the razor, the lack of choices that had sprung from their own overly confident and wrongheaded sense of justice. She'd cried, and so had he, clinging together as the snow fell outside, blanketing the city. She felt remorse now that it was done but as before, fate had taken other choices out of her hands and what she didn't feel was guilt. Nor did he, and they drew strength from each other.

They left a note for Augustin, which he'd find when he returned from his family home in Connecticut, where he'd decamped for the holidays. They expressed their gratitude and regret, and Fiona had a fleeting memory of Audrey Prescott's face as James wrote it out and sealed the envelope. They gave no positive direction of their travels, nor their immediate plans. Simply a young couple dazzled with love who had decided to leave New York for a simpler life, or perhaps one in the widening theatrical opportunities in the vast land that was America. It was no matter.

They had left no traces and had covered their tracks well. Still, there were always whispers or mistakes they might have made in their search for information on the Lowells and who knew what powerful friends they might have had, who knew of their vices and would suspect vengeance rather than accident? Leaving New York was essential for their own peace of mind and perhaps, sooner or later, their freedom. They had no regrets. For both of them, New York had been tainted by the pervading corruption of people like the Lowells, and protected by those who should have been protecting the innocent victims of their perversities.

The train pulled out of the station, heading west. Fiona

opened the newspaper. The headlines were all about a fire that had gutted the home of Samuel and Victoria Lowell, the darlings of New York society, who had tragically perished in the blaze. Investigators had so far not determined the exact cause, but so far it was being ruled a most unfortunate accident, suspected to have been caused by Christmas candles, the culprit of so many holiday tragedies.

James was reading his paper as well. He lowered it and smiled at her over the edge. "Angus will be pleased, don't you think?"

PART II
WHAT'S IN A NAME?

CHAPTER 13

Chicago. It was smelly and cold, was Fiona's first thought as they stepped off the train. Wintry, just as New York had been, but when her hat spiraled away overhead, the porter shrugged apologetically.

"Sorry, miss. That's why we call her the 'Windy City'." He hurried her inside the station, where she stood stamping her feet against the cold as James handled the baggage. They didn't have a lot, and she'd kept one bag in particular with her all the way, rather than in the baggage car. Soon, they were bundled into a carriage and on their way to the Palmer House.

Fiona was pleasantly surprised as they entered the lobby. The place was elegant, palms, music, lovely furnishings, just as nice as New York. Their room was a two bedroom suite high above the city and she could see Lake Michigan, stretching away northwards, blue and beautiful. It looked like the ocean to her. She twirled around and laughed, reaching her hands out to James.

"Isn't it lovely, then?"

He put his arms around her and waltzed her around the room. "Indeed, my lady. I think this will do, for a time. We need some rest and relaxation, I daresay. The toll of the theater, and all."

For a week, they did just that, trying to put memories of New York and especially that night, behind them. They spent most of their time in the hotel, sometimes going down to dinner, other nights calling for room service, Fiona's new favorite. They read, recited lines from Shakespeare and other plays, talked endlessly, much as they had in New York, but now it was just the two of them without the distraction of rehearsals or social activities.

She loved watching James, not just because he was beautiful, she'd gotten used to that, but for the flash of his eyes, his laughter and his nearly encyclopedic knowledge of literature, especially plays and poems. It was almost as though he was a different person, clear-eyed and happier than she'd ever seen him. The bitter sarcasm was gone, replaced by an attitude of acceptance and calm. Leaving New York had been a godsend for him in that way. For her, she was happy to be warm, comfortable, well-fed and with someone she loved who was as kind as he was entertaining. She tried to put the last few weeks completely out of her mind but she didn't always succeed, her dreams a testament to that. She'd done a terrible thing, no matter how justified it might have been. That she was capable of it frightened her quite a bit, and nothing more so than that tiny part that satisfied her as well.

"There's so much to learn," she sighed one evening as the snow fell past the windows, the huge flakes visible in the ambient light of the city. They'd stayed in their rooms, had dinner and read, as had become their usual custom. "You must grow weary of me, my endless questions and ignorance. What an education you have had."

"Indeed. They didn't know what else to do with me, so I grew up in schools." He laughed, but Fiona could see it wasn't amusing for him at all. She got up from the couch and poured them another glass of the velvety Bordeaux.

"You said once you'd tell me about your past," she said. "I've told you mine, after all." She had, too, at least some of it and James hadn't blinked an eye.

He leaned back against the couch. He seemed resigned, but not unhappily so. Maybe it was the wine, their second bottle, but no matter, she'd been wanting this for a long time and maybe he had, too.

"All right, fair's fair. It's not a long story. My mother was Medora Leigh. The name may not mean much to you, but my grandfather's name was George Gordon, and maybe that one will."

Fiona stared at him. She leaned over and picked up a book from the stack on the floor and put it on her lap. "Go on."

"She died right after I was born, in France. I never knew my father, some minor French noble, and they weren't married. When I was two, my nursemaid, who was old and not well, brought me to London to the Leigh family. They weren't thrilled but they had become adept at covering up scandal over the years, so I joined the household, so to speak, another incestuous complication. At least they didn't drown me in the Thames." He gave a bark of what was supposed to be laughter and Fiona winced. She'd never seen him like this, so brittle and defiant.

"I was sent to school at five, and the little time I was home, cared for by the staff. By the time I was eighteen, even people on the street would sometimes stare at my face as though they were trying to remember how they knew me and the Leighs finally decided I had to go. I was at Oxford by then and they gave me a choice: take a modest allowance, change my name and disavow any family ties, or be thrown out of school with nothing. Practicality won out over pride and I opted for number one." He drank some wine and set the glass down carefully, his hand was shaking. "And that is how I became James Ardrey. Sordid little tale, isn't it?" His eyes were on his wine glass.

Fiona leaned over and took his hand in hers. "No, it's tragic. How lonely you must have been as a child, even as an adult. The world is full of awful people, as I well know. I'm so sorry, James."

He kissed her hand. "Don't be, love. It's a long time ago now. I hardly ever think of it."

Fiona knew that was a lie and it explained the fugue states and self-hatred he exhibited now and then. She opened the book on her lap to the picture beside the title page. Lord Byron stared back at her. The likeness was extraordinary, and now that she knew, understandable. James looked exactly like him. She held up the book and he groaned.

"Put that damn thing away. I already know, believe me." He picked up his wineglass. "For some years I did everything I could to emulate him, the men, the women, drugs, whatever it took. 'Mad, bad and dangerous to know' became my mantra, because hell, I was a child of incest. Some people knew, others didn't. I thought somehow if I became him, I could tame the demon. Instead, the demon nearly had me. Getting on that boat to America all I had was my last few pounds and a nasty laudanum habit. Plus a letter to Augustin Drewry from an influential friend in London. I got a job, but fell right back into old habits, habits I didn't know how to break."

He got up and poured more wine, then stood looking out the window as night fell over Chicago, the lights twinkling below and fading into the never-ending blackness of Lake Michigan.

"Then I met you. God, you were so damaged, rather like me. You scared me, though, because the more I came to know you, the more I came to love you, in spite of myself. It was much safer to let you think I only cared for men, otherwise you would've run like a rabbit into a world of wolves and I couldn't let that happen when I'd dragged you out of your safe little nest.

Then my drunken stupidity and ego almost got us both killed. If it hadn't been for your strength and quick wit, we wouldn't even be here. I was useless."

Fiona stared at his back, her mind spinning, trying to process what he'd just said. She opened her mouth, not really sure what she was going to say, when James turned around, holding up his hand.

"Don't say anything, please. I've done my soul-baring for the evening and that's more than enough, and really all I can stand. I'll see you at breakfast. I hear they have a lovely museum here. Perhaps we should go see it in the morning. Good night, Mary."

He sat down his wineglass, kissed her on the temple in passing, and went to his bedroom as usual, closing the door softly.

She sat on the couch for some time, thinking and staring out at the starless night. He was right, she was damaged, and in a dangerous way. She couldn't abide people taking advantage over those who were powerless, and something in her not only rebelled, but sought vengeance. Most of the time, she controlled herself, but the Lowells were what could happen if she didn't.

As to the other, she'd never allowed herself to even imagine being with a man again, not after Sean Dooley and the baby and all the rest of it, and she'd shut that part of herself down completely. Yes, there had been moments here and there, even sometimes when she turned over in bed at night and nestled in James's comforting arms, but she knew he didn't care about that, so she felt safe. She felt betrayed, a bit anyway. She'd trusted him and loved him, never sensing a threat. *That's because,* said a little voice in her mind, *he's never been one and would never be.* Everything he'd said tonight was the plain unvarnished truth, not just about his past but about her. He'd also said the words that scored her heart, 'I came to love you.' No one had ever said that before. Perhaps he was a little manipulative, but she could look past that, especially considering all he'd done for her.

Fiona lay down on her soft bed, pulling the down comforter

over her and before she knew it, fell sound asleep, even though she thought she never would, with the revelations and intense emotions of the evening.

So red, so very red. Everywhere, pouring down the walls, over her hands and face until she thought she'd drown in it. Victoria Lowell came towards her, hands outstretched. "You love it, just like we knew you would, Mary. You're one of us now, just like you were always meant to be."

Samuel appeared before her and swept her up in a waltz, even though she was wearing a nightgown, he didn't seem to notice. He bit her in the neck and laughed, more red trickling down his chin. "Now, let's get to James, he's been waiting so long."

They converged upon him, tied to the wheel and as they neared, his eyes opened in terror. They all seemed to love that, and reached towards him with the knives that appeared in their hands, until Mary screamed and screamed and screamed, trying to thrust them away.

"Stop it. Stop! Wake up, Mary." Warm hands grasped her shoulders and she opened her eyes. "It's all right, love, I promise you."

She gasped and clutched at him, dim in the faint light through the windows, but she knew safety when she touched it, the nightmare dissipating. He lay her back down and climbed in beside her, as they used to sleep, nestling her shaking body into his, pulling the comforter over them.

"Sleep now, love, sleep. All is well."

She closed her eyes and felt safety wash over her. Yes, it was. Now.

Pale winter sunlight streamed into the room and Fiona groaned, turning over to find James's chest in her face. For a moment, she thought they were back in New York in the little flat they'd first shared and then memory surfaced. She sat up abruptly. He slept on, the long lashes cresting his cheekbones, a faint smile on his lips. She brushed his hair from his face and watched him as he breathed softly. She heard a faint knock, the courteous alert from room service delivering their regularly scheduled breakfast. She slipped out on the other side of the bed and rolled the cart into their suite, going back to her bedroom. James stirred, his eyes opening and focused on her as she made her way back to the bed.

"Good morning," she whispered, sitting beside him.

He didn't say anything, just looked into her eyes and gathered her into his arms. She folded into him just as they always had, but this time it wasn't in a sisterly way. When he kissed her, it wasn't on her cheek. Feelings that had buried for so long, maybe forever, overwhelmed her and she surged into him, from lips to the tips of her toes, wanting to drown herself in him. He clasped her to him with a soft sigh, gently pulling her nightgown away as he ran his hands over her body like he was exploring a newfound treasure. For the first time, she had a choice, and it was one she was ready to make. They both had a lot to make up for. Fortunately, they had the time.

"I think the coffee's cold."

"We still have wine."

"Indeed we do."

He kissed her again and they never noticed the sunset.

CHAPTER 14

Chicago became a joy instead of just a refuge. The winter passed into early spring and as the earth renewed itself, so did they, visiting restaurants, theaters, museums, shops, and even parks despite the sometimes icy weather, always returning to their cozy haven at the Palmer House each evening. They'd negotiated a long term occupancy with the hotel because they loved the place and the comfort and safety it provided. Although Chicago could be windy and cold, the year was turning and fairly often blue skies and sunshine greeted them on their endeavors.

This was a city thrumming with life and progress, at the center of the vast country they now lived in, and even in the short time they'd lived there, new buildings, streets and businesses had sprung up seemingly overnight. It was as though the city had thrust out its hands and reached fantastical fingers as far it could into the continent, hauling in agriculture, livestock, raw material and people into a great churning factory that produced the goods and then spewed them back out all over the country. From the stockyards to the factories to the railroads, Chicago was the center, supplying America. It was exciting, fresh and raw, feeding on the energy of those who were building a new country.

Coming from England and Ireland, Fiona and James both couldn't help but marvel at the place. New York was a world of its own, rivaling London and even Paris with its burgeoning sophistication and urbane style, but it couldn't rival Chicago for sheer intensity and growth. In a strange way, Fiona fed off that vitality. She absorbed it with her morning coffee, watching the city come alive, and she knew James felt it too.

They'd studied both the Chicago and New York papers for weeks and months but no mention was ever made of foul play regarding the Lowells and their unfortunate demise at Christmastime so they began to hope perhaps there would be no further investigation and they would be safe from any law enforcement entanglements. Just the same, they decided to keep the names they'd registered under and became used to calling each other by them, until they felt completely secure or moved on.

Fiona hadn't realized it at the time, but James had registered them under George and Juliet Gordon. After his revelation about his family, she'd laughed when she'd discovered the alias he'd used. She thought for a while they were bound to run into someone who knew who George Gordon was, but they never did. Byron had been in the grave for many years and they were a long way from England. Still, it for her there'd been too many names in too short a time, and sometimes it was a bit disorienting.

"You're going to have to get better about calling me 'Juliet'," she chided him one morning over breakfast. "I've gotten fairly practiced, George. I think the maid heard you say 'Mary' the other day and that simply won't do."

"Schooling me. How perceptive of you, dearest Juliet," he said. "I agree. We may be erring on the side of caution, but it never hurts to be careful, does it?"

"No, it does not, dear George." She popped a strawberry into her mouth. "I may not have mentioned it, but Mary was a name I had to get used to. Likely Juliet'll be easier for you."

James smiled and fed her another strawberry. "You'll be my sweet Juliet, always."

"Ha, be careful, George. What would a nice girl like Juliet be doing with Mr. Mad, Bad and Dangerous to Know?"

He grabbed her wrist. "The very thing she's gotten so adept it in such a short time. Let me demonstrate."

She kissed him and they ended their morning back in bed for a time, as they did quite often. She had no complaints. An entire new world had unfolded for her and she loved it. For the first time in perhaps forever, she wasn't worried about what tomorrow would bring, because each day brought happiness and new wonders. She'd been attracted to him from the first minute she'd seen him, or at least since that day on Broadway.

On the other hand, James was nothing if not devious, but she loved him for that, along with everything else —his wit, his charm, so devastatingly handsome, veering dangerously onto pretty, so like his grandfather, and sometimes alarmingly into wild and hedonistic behavior which he could tell concerned her, so he'd curb himself. She sometimes worried that he'd tire of her. She knew she was pretty, too, but the hundreds of hours he'd taken to teach her not just about theater, but life, style, manners, literature were telling. Then again, she was indeed a quick learner. James had said she was fascinating and she chose to believe him, her confidence growing. After all, he'd the experience to know.

Chicago was rich with theaters. They'd been to most all of them, some of the performances wonderful, others not so much, and they'd thoroughly critiqued the actors and the production in the privacy of their suite with great enjoyment. One standout had been the productions from Julius DeMonte's company at the Olympic, and they'd been back a few times as the shows rotated.

"Do you know him?" Fiona said one evening as they shed their evening clothes.

"He's got a reputation," James answered. "He's been here for a time. There was some scandal, can't remember. I don't dwell on those things, given my own history." He smiled ruefully. "I met him once after a show in London, but that was when I was still at Oxford. I'm sure he wouldn't remember me. He left England soon after and came here. Why?"

"He's interesting, that's all," she said. "I heard he does traveling shows, too."

"Oh? Well, that doesn't surprise me, given the number of gypsies in his company, did you notice? You must have, what with the music and dancing I've heard about. It was definitely European, likely Romany."

"I did. I also heard he travels in wagons, like they do."

James laughed. "That's ridiculous, even for an eccentric like him. Can you imagine living like that?" He placed his cufflinks carefully on the dresser.

She smiled. "You know, I don't think it's ridiculous at all. Might even be fun, especially in the summer."

He threw himself onto the bed and put his arms behind his head. "You're just fooling with me, at least I hope so."

"Course I am," said Fiona and turned off the lamp.

The nightmares came that night, but not as bad as before. Victoria Lowell's face was streaked with blood, not like she'd ever seen it at the end, her mouth shrieking as she came at them with a dagger. She woke screaming and James held her close, as he had for all the times before.

"It's all right, love. Just a bad dream. They can't hurt anyone ever again. We did what we had to do."

Fiona turned her tear-streaked face to him. "I know. But it wasn't you that cut their throats. It was me." Sometimes she couldn't help but wonder if it had been James that had to kill them to save them both, if he could have done it.

He kissed her tears away and snuggled her closer. "I know, and I'd give anything for that not to be true. But you saved my life, too, my love. And all of the innocents those monsters would have killed had you not done what you were forced to do."

She sighed, drifting away, secure in his embrace and the knowledge that he was absolutely right.

After that night, the dreams had not come again. Only the memories, and a few niggling doubts but those she had to live with.

* * *

ON A FRIDAY EVENING in late April, they came out of the Burns Theatre on Clark Street after a musical revue, joining the throng of attendees, everyone happy and humming some of the catchy songs they'd just heard.

The theater wasn't far from the hotel, so they decided to walk even though the evening was chilly with the breeze off the lake. A block past the theater, sidewalk traffic was sparse although the street was busy with carriages full of theatergoers. Fiona was wearing a fox fur wrap James had insisted she have, and she was warm as toast even in her silk evening gown. He was magnificent as usual in black, his dark hair streaming over his collar, laughing as she sang one of the tunes from the show.

The man appeared out of nowhere, it seemed, a dark shadow emerging from an alley.

"Fiona."

His face was scarred but she recognized him instantly and fear shot through her, turning her legs to stone, the same reactions she'd always had around the man. She'd thought she was quit of him forever after leaving Ireland. How in god's name could he have found her here?

He looked terrible and the fumes of whiskey and body odor rising from him were just as she remembered. He staggered nearer and grabbed her arm.

"You'll be comin' wi' me, now, Fiona. Took me a lot of trouble trackin' you here, but since I knew you was an actress I figured I'd find you one night comin' from a playhouse, whore that you are. We'll be goin' home now."

"Let her go," James said evenly. "Who the hell do you think you are?"

"Her husband, ye dumb bastard," answered Sean Dooley. "She's got a lot to answer for, boyo. I recognized the little slut the minute ye stepped out of that fancy theater back there."

Sean pulled on her arm and James shoved him aside, breaking his grip. Fiona stepped towards the street to hail a carriage and was brought up short when Sean grabbed the collar of her fox wrap.

"Ye're not goin' anywhere, Fiona." In his hand, a wicked-looking knife glittered in the dim light.

James drove his fist into Sean's stomach and Sean dropped both the knife and his grip on Fiona's wrap, staggering backwards. James kicked the knife into the street and held up his hands.

"That's it, my man. Stop right there. We're calling for the police."

Fiona knew a bad idea when she heard one but James had no idea who the man was. She was going to have to remedy that slight omission from her history, but certainly not in front of the police. Besides, they couldn't afford to draw any close scrutiny.

In the end, it didn't matter. Sean Dooley roared, charging at James like an enraged bull. James sidestepped as elegantly as though he was on the dance floor, and Sean's momentum carried him into the street and under the harness and hooves of a swiftly moving delivery wagon, the wheels carrying his body a few hundred yards down the cobblestones, amid the shouts of the driver and the panicked shrieks of two horses.

Fiona stood frozen with horror until James grabbed her arm and hustled her quickly down the dark street. "Hurry, but don't run," he said softly. "I don't think anyone saw a thing, even the driver, it happened so fast. We were never here."

The Palmer House lobby was dimly lit for the late evening and they strolled nonchalantly through and up to the room. James poured two brandies and put one into her hand where she sat on the couch, trembling.

Fiona's hand shook as she picked up the glass but after two hefty swallows, she felt better. He gazed at her and drank some of his own, waiting.

She told him then, all of it this time: her marriage to Dooley, the baby, the fire and how she'd come to be on the *Adriatic*. James never said a word through the whole recital until she was done.

"Christ, love, that's a story. Makes mine look like a nursery tale in comparison." He shook his head. "So the bastard's been tracking you the whole time. It's quite amazing, really. I've been thinking about how. Did you never notice him back in New York?"

"No," she said. "Well, I thought I saw him once or twice on Broadway, but I thought it was just my imagination. I guess it wasn't. How did he know we were in Chicago, do you think?"

He shrugged. "Not that mysterious, when you think about it. First, your picture was up outside the theater for each production, starting even with Romeo and Juliet. He must've seen one at some point not long before we left. I'm sure you look better than you did gracing the hovel hearth, but with that face, he'd know you."

Fiona groaned. "So, then when we weren't there any longer, he discovered we'd left town, and had the picture . . ."

"Showed it around the train station and got lucky, is what I think," James finished. "Probably had mine, too, and then, *voila!* All the bastard had to do was wait and watch around theaters, thinking you likely worked in one. I do have to give him credit for perseverance. Or perhaps it would be more apt to say, obsession."

Fiona shivered even though she still had the fox fur wrapped around her. James lifted her from the couch and led her to the bedroom, undressing her carefully and tucking her under the sheets. He slid in beside her within minutes.

They lay in bed, replaying the events of the night in their minds until finally she sat up and stared at him. "You think he's dead this time?"

James snorted softly. "Darling. If he's not dead, he's close to it, the poor bastard. Trampled by horses is not a pretty way to go."

"Poor bastard? I'd have pushed him myself but he did the work for me." Her eyes glittered in the moonlight. "You have no idea what it's like to be helpless, beaten, raped, day after day. You're a man, you don't know."

For a long moment, silence stretched between them. Then, soft as velvet. "Juliet. How quickly we can forget. Do you not remember my charming friends the Lowells?"

God, she was an ass, she thought, *of all the men in the world, this one understood like no other.*

"I'm sorry, so sorry," she cried, and put her arms around him, "I'm just upset, and a bit drunk, and, I love you."

"I know, it's all right," he said. "You were a child and you went through hell." He kissed her temple, his arms warm around her. "I know what, my fury. Let's check the newspaper in the morning and if he's not dead, we can visit the hospital and take him out there. I'll be a priest and you a nun. We are actors, you know. And, it's not like we haven't exacted justice before."

Fiona shook her head, but didn't bother to reply. Of course

they'd never do any such thing. Sean Dooley's life had become a hell of his own making. She was done meting out justice and, for all his bravado, James never really had. Her eyes were closing.

"In fact, maybe we need to get back on the stage instead of simply looking at it, now that the subject's come up," James mused drowsily.

She'd been thinking about that for a while, and she knew he had too. It was in his blood, performing, and it had been quite a while. Since they'd left the stage, she'd been missing it too. And, if for no other reason, they could use the money. The cash she'd stolen from the Lowells' house was running out. The Palmer House and their lifestyle had come at a high cost. She still had the jewels but she kept them stashed in a false-bottomed traveling bag and she thought of them as an insurance policy against any unforeseen event that could happen. You never knew, she'd come to learn.

The Chicago Tribune had a small article on the second page the next morning, entitled "Clean Up Our Streets". It seemed another drunken man had run into the traffic on Clark Street the previous evening. The indignant reporter reminded readers this was the third time this year an incident like this had occurred, and it was a safety hazard to drivers as well as horses. Police presence needed to be more thorough and vigilant in their duties to the citizens of the city of Chicago. The man had unfortunately died on the way to the hospital.

There wasn't even a twinge of regret in her mind about Sean Dooley. The only regret she had was for her own lost innocence, but that had been taken from her long ago. Maybe now the scales of justice were balanced.

CHAPTER 15

Another night, another show. At intermission, they stood in the lobby of the elegant Lakeview Theater, sipping champagne, not really that interested in returning for Act III of what was proving to be quite a mediocre play.

"An earlier dinner?" Fiona said, adjusting her chiffon scarf. She looked at James over the rim of her glass.

"Excellent idea," he replied. "Dreadful play. Although there's been some good productions here. Chicago is coming into its own with theater, not that it begins to rival New York or London. Still, give it a few years, and perhaps the help of a few actors like us, and who knows? Perhaps we should approach some of them." He grinned. "You've been hungering for the boards, sweet Juliet. I can tell."

Fiona laughed. "Maybe that's so, but you speak for yourself, my love."

James nodded. "True. You know, the best performances we've seen since we've been in Chicago have been DeMonte's. I wonder if he's in the market for a couple of new actors?"

Fiona smiled. "Getting bored, James?"

He sighed. "Hmm. So, here in Chicago? Take the train to wherever? I don't care, to be honest. I just want to act, and I know you do as well. We've kept our heads down like good little children, but it's time we came to life again, wouldn't you say? I think it's safe enough. Time has passed."

Fiona wasn't so sure. "Maybe, but my instinct tells me if we returned to New York we'd be making a mistake, so I'm not certain we can say it's buried forever."

James grimaced. "So to speak. West, then?"

"The West is a very big place," drawled an aristocratic English voice. "Forgive me for interrupting, I couldn't help but overhear and the word does conjure up memories."

Speak of the devil, thought Fiona. Julius DeMonte stood beside James, dwarfing him a little, twirling a champagne glass in his long fingers. He was impressive, his long white hair falling in waves onto shoulders, framing a face that wasn't just attractive, but compelling, his green eyes staring down into hers.

"Allow me to introduce myself," he smiled. "Julius DeMonte. I've noticed you both before here and there. Such a lovely couple is hard to forget."

James recovered quickly. "George Gordon, and this is my wife Juliet," he smiled. "Thank you for the kind compliment and let me return it. We've been to some of your productions and they are quite wonderful. Delighted to meet you."

DeMonte nodded. "So, are you in the theater profession, Mr. Gordon? You both have that look, and of course, exquisitely informed taste, if you like my modest efforts."

They all laughed politely and Fiona noticed through half-lowered lashes that DeMonte was observing them very closely. "Actually, yes," she said, "we've done a little stage work, but we're currently pursuing other avenues. But your productions are so well done, we've been drawn back to the theater, to watch and perhaps even more, who knows?"

He nodded. "Ah. I'm sure that could be arranged." He stared at James's face.

"You know, I think we've met before, Mr. Gordon, have we not? In London, as I recall." The man was intimidating and she had a feeling he never missed a detail. "But it's been some time."

James, to his credit, smiled. "Indeed, you may be right. But, it's a new country and a new endeavor, isn't it?"

"Oh my yes," DeMonte said and raised his glass. "To America and unknown paths."

"Hear, hear," James said, and they all took a sip.

"I must be getting back in, but it was lovely chatting with you both. Hopefully we'll meet again. Enjoy the play."

"Well, that was interesting," James said, watching DeMonte's back as he walked away. "Quite a memory he's got. Should've known better, what?"

Fiona wasn't feeling so nonchalant. "Let's get out of here. He makes me feel like he knows exactly what we're thinking and quite possibly, what we've done."

James shrugged. "Don't be silly. He's observant, indeed, and I'm very sure he remembers me in my dissolute youth, and of course he knows who George Gordon is, but that's all there is to it. Theater people change their names all the time and he knows that better than anyone, my dear." He took her arm and grinned. "An early evening is exactly what I've been looking forward to, beautiful Juliet."

"Scoundrel," Fiona leaned into him and smiled in anticipation because in truth, there was nothing she would rather do herself.

Two weeks later, an invitation to dinner was delivered to the Palmer House, handwritten on thick cream paper. James read it and raised his eyebrows. "A command invitation from Chicago's theater prince cannot be ignored, my dear. Besides, I'm dreadfully curious."

Fiona shivered. Curious, yes, but apprehensive too.

* * *

THE MOON WAS RISING as the hired carriage pulled into the drive at Julius DeMonte's house on Lakeshore Drive. It was a tasteful Victorian, beautifully designed and landscaped, and Fiona loved it at first sight. Across the street glimmered the sands of the beach, and the currently gentle waves of Lake Michigan. How she'd love to live here.

"Quite lovely," said James and stepped out first to help her down. "Well, well. This should be an interesting evening. '"Childe Rolande to the dark tower came'."

She shot him a look. "You can do this, George."

He grinned. "Of course I can, my darling and so can you."

She was impressed with the house, but even more so with the furnishings. Fiona had never seen anything quite like it, but then even Prescott House hadn't prepared her for the English aristocracy, which, of course, DeMonte was, if James's sketchy memory served. It was all a very far distance from an orphanage and a mean cottage in Ballyowen. While she'd learned a great deal, she'd also learned enough to know there was a world she was just starting to know.

The receiving rooms were magnificent, hung with paintings she'd only seen the like of in museums, the carpets jewels of Oriental silk and the furniture a comfortable mix of upholstered brocade and sumptuous cushions, interspersed with glowingly polished tables full of objects d'art she'd only heard of in books.

DeMonte had greeted them, accompanied by a rather imperious older woman he introduced as Mama Rosa, her hair wrapped in a silk turban. After a glass of sherry and welcoming desultory chitchat, they'd gone into the dining room, similarly hung with art, and even though she was used to the dinners at Prescott House, she was amazed. The glitter of crystal, silver and candles lit the long table, set for twelve, the room itself like something out of a baronial manor house, not that she'd ever seen one from the inside.

Since it had been only the four of them in the parlor, she was surprised to see the chairs filled with members of the troupe she remembered seeing on stage. DeMonte clearly didn't stand on ceremony or society's norms. Fiona was delighted and took her seat next to Mama Rosa, who smiled thinly at her. James was across the table, seated next to a very handsome gentleman of the Romany persuasion, as was Mama Rosa, if she wasn't mistaken, the man's smile divulging very white teeth in his swarthy face as James sat down beside him. The rest of the table was filled with beautiful people of all colors, from ebony to white, dressed in colorful clothing and the meal commenced with the first serving, a soup. A glass in front of each place had already been filled with a pale yellow wine and when she took a sip, the crisp yet buttery flavors of apricot and lime were wonderful. This man knew how to have a dinner party, even in her limited experience.

"Is the the vichyssoise to your liking, Mrs. Gordon?"

"Quite," she managed. "And it's Juliet, please."

DeMonte smiled. "Excellent. Please call me Julius." He was dressed as before in black, in a bespoke suit cut so beautifully it seemed to be a part of him. He was at the head of the table and she was on his right, while James was on his left. A distinction, she was sure, that was significant although she hadn't yet figured out why.

Dishes were cleared and the main course, a large roast of beef, was served, two gentlemen in white coats slicing and delivering meat to their plates, while another server came by with whipped potatoes and gravy. Dishes of asparagus, peas, and other vegetables were set on the table with silver spoons and sauces beside them. Another wine was poured, a red, distinctly different from the first, and she tasted not just earthiness, but hints of cherries. Life was good in the DeMonte realm.

The talk around the table was of the theater of course, with bits of current events thrown in here and there, as well as references to some of the places the diners had traveled, mostly in the south and west, even the frontier. Some had been in Europe, particularly Paris, Venice and Russia and she couldn't help being delighted as they recounted amusing incidents from places she'd never dreamed to go. Glancing at James now and then, she saw he and Julius were engrossed in their conversation, speaking in low tones while she was raptly listening to the other guests, occasionally putting in a "really" or "how exciting" as required since she didn't think they'd be too entranced with tales of Ballyowen's country market days, which were the extent of her travels before boarding ship. She gave most of her attention to the food, which was delicious.

When dinner concluded, DeMonte announced entertainment in the salon, which turned out to be a young man playing a guitar and a woman singing some plaintive songs in a language Fiona had never heard before. It was poignant, and brought tears to her eyes. Sitting beside her, James was affected as well, taking her hand in his and smiling gently.

"Beautiful, isn't it?" he said. "I've never heard the like."

The performance over, everyone drifted away except for her and James, Julius and Mama Rosa.

It was quiet, then, and quite lovely, the fire crackling in the hearth, the brandy in their glasses a molten amber. Fiona relaxed against the soft back of the damask sofa. It had been a truly wonderful evening, in spite of her apprehension. For a moment, her thoughts drifted back to the last time she and James had enjoyed brandy before a fire in someone's home and quickly banished that thought, a sudden shiver running up her spine. That was over and done and they'd made their peace with it.

"So." Julius leaned over and poked the fire. "I hope you've had an enjoyable evening, Mr. and Mrs. Gordon." He gazed at them, his eyes guileless but Fiona suspected he was far from that.

"Indeed." James said. "Thank you for your hospitality this evening, it has been more than enjoyable. The meal was wonderful, and the entertainment exquisite, quite unlike anything I've ever heard. You must be our guest at the Palmer House some evening and allow us to host you."

The woman in the turban said nothing, assessing them with her dark eyes. She made Fiona nervous, her silence and watchfulness unnerving. She had seen Julius and Mama Rosa exchanging glances occasionally, as if affirming something and that wasn't reassuring either.

Julius smiled. "I'd very much like that."

James finished his brandy and stood up. "It's getting late and we mustn't keep you from your rest. Thank you again, Mr. DeMonte."

DeMonte waved his hand. "It's Julius, George, I thought we'd established that at dinner. Please, sit down. I'd like to chat a bit, if you aren't overly tired."

"Of course," James smiled, turning to Fiona, who nodded. Julius refilled their glasses.

"I used to live in New York, back when I first came to America, and I know a lot of people there," he said, gazing at them both. Waiting.

"I'm sure you do," James said, not missing a beat. "The theater world is really quite small. "

"Oh, it certainly is," Julius said. "For instance, an English actor named James Ardrey and a young ingénue called Mary Neill made quite a name for themselves last year in New York. A beautiful couple, rising stars and the toast of the town. Then they just disappeared. Perhaps you've heard of them?"

Fiona's heart froze. She stared at DeMonte as though he

were a snake, poised to strike and maybe he was. She couldn't help herself and clutched James's hand. He didn't seem to notice but had grown very still, eyes fixed on the man.

DeMonte stood up, swirling the brandy in his snifter and pacing leisurely back and forth in front of the crackling flames. He stopped and gazed at them. "Let me tell you a story."

"Once upon a time, there was a beautiful prince and princess who lived in a castle, or near enough, for years revered by everyone who encountered them. But they had a secret life that wasn't beautiful at all. Secrets can be deadly, especially when people get hurt."

He took a sip of brandy and resumed his story. "One snowy night, the castle burned down with the prince and princess trapped inside. Some said the darkness had come full circle for the royal couple and their fate was well deserved." He shrugged and smiled, somewhat mischievously, Fiona thought. "Myself, I love stories, but who can tell what is a story and what may be truth?"

Julius DeMonte sat back down in his chair and crossed his legs leisurely. A log fell in the depths of the fireplace and sparks cascaded over the burning logs. Not another sound was heard in the room, and certainly not one of voices. As the moments passed, Fiona's mind, which had been racing in panic, began to slow. Somehow she didn't feel like a goose led to slaughter, damned for her crimes, if such they were judged. Besides, there wasn't the slightest bit of proof linking them to the Lowells. What sort of game was DeMonte playing here?

James, true to his impulsive nature, broke first. "Lovely tale, if a bit melodramatic. Besides, everyone knows there's no royalty in America." For an actor as good as he was, his chuckle sounded a bit forced.

"Well, that's debatable, who knows who's hiding what, eh *George*? You know, my young friend, for being such good actors, you two are terrible liars."

Fiona felt as though all the air had been sucked from her lungs and glancing at James, he didn't look much better.

The Romany woman stood up, her impatience evident. "I've done my part tonight, Julius, and my bed is calling. Time for this nonsense to stop." She turned to Fiona and James. "Tell him the truth and we can continue on from there, if anyone's a mind to. You're in safe hands. Good evening."

Regally, she made her way out of the room and closed the door behind her.

"Good god, she always takes the wind out of my sails, that woman," DeMonte snorted. "She's not a one for theatrics, just seeing truths. Been doing it for years and always makes me look dumb as Beethoven's bust."

He leaned forward, all traces of levity vanished. "I suspect that at least one if not both of you, since you're clearly a dedicated team, dispatched the Lowells." He held up his hand when James stood up, his face panicked. "Sit down, Byron, I'm talking here. Besides, no one deserved death more than those two."

Fiona pulled James back down beside her. She was done with this. "Sounds to me like whoever did, it was a service to the world. So what is this charade you're puttin' on tonight? If you've a reason, spit it out or we're leavin' your fine house and you in it, fancy man, and be damned to you."

Julius burst out laughing. "God, you're magnificent. My apologies." Fiona glared at him. "Hear me out. Please."

Fiona took a deep breath. James hadn't twitched a finger but he was very good at hiding his emotions, as she'd learned. Whenever she lost her temper, the Irish came out and her fine new accent flew away with the fairies. This better be good or they were on their way west. It wouldn't take long to pack all those fancy new clothes. For now, she waved her hand in agreement and sat back on the cushions.

"One night years ago," DeMonte said, "a lovely actress disappeared after an evening's visit to the Lowells. Only I knew where she was going. The police were not helpful with my inquiry so I made it my business to find out more on my own, and what I found was foul, but also unprovable. The authorities were uncooperative and I was not in a position to convince them to be otherwise. I left New York shortly thereafter, but I've always remembered and berated myself for not taking matters further."

Fiona exchanged glances with James and swallowed the rest of her brandy. "We're terrible sorry about your friend and all, but my patience is worn thin. What do you want?"

"To offer you both my assistance," Julius DeMonte said. "And my gratitude. For her and likely countless others."

"This has gone from deuced uncomfortable to ridiculous," James said. "In the last thirty minutes, we've had our identities questioned, our histories disputed, been termed 'liars' and accused of murder. I've had enough of this and your so-called hospitality, DeMonte."

He stood up and grasped her hand, pulling her to her feet. "Good evening. It's been, well, unusual and if I may say, somewhat surreal. Please have your stable man pull our carriage around. We're leaving."

As if on cue, there was a knock on the door. A tall gentleman, immaculately attired in a well-cut black suit entered and shut it behind him. He looked to be in his thirties, his light hair cut close, revealing his hawklike features and piercing eyes. He gazed at DeMonte and nodded. DeMonte waved him to a chair beside the fire and the man moved like a cat, soundlessly taking a seat.

"Let me introduce you to Mr. Henley," DeMonte said. "This is James Ardrey and Mary Neill, as you know."

Henley gave them a brief nod and brushed back his waistcoat, the gun and holster on his person clearly revealed.

"Please, sit back down for a few more moments and do not be alarmed, my young friends," DeMonte said, "Mr. Henley is my close associate and is to be trusted, not feared. I know this has been a difficult evening for you both, but believe me when I say I have your best interests at heart." He turned to Henley expectantly.

James shot Fiona a look and pulled her back down onto the couch. Her pulse was pounding and she knew his was too, but the smart choice at this point was to listen and decide what to do. The weapon Henley carried made her nervous, but perhaps there was something to be salvaged from this so far disastrous evening, so she said nothing and waited to hear what the man had to say.

"As we thought, the man was a New York police detective," Henley said, glancing over at her and James. "We've been watching them for a few days and they finally sniffed out the Palmer House. He has a couple of associates with him, which doesn't bode well, frankly."

"What?" Fiona stammered but James gripped her hand firmly. She shook him off. "What is he saying?"

"He's saying they suspect you for dispatching the Lowells, Miss Neill, and are here to arrest you," DeMonte said. "I was hoping the New York authorities weren't digging, but the Lowells had some powerful friends." He stared at her, his face inscrutable. "They also had powerful enemies and they keep in touch. If I've figured it out, I should have known some bright young spark in New York might have his suspicions about you, but I didn't think it'd be quite this soon. Once I recognized James, the rest I pieced together for myself. I am hopeful you will accept my assistance, because quite frankly, I think you're going to need it."

Fiona sat frozen on the couch beside James, her stomach turning into a ball of ice. Could they trust these people? She looked at James but he was staring at Henley and DeMonte, his face unreadable.

Julius got up and refreshed their brandies, pouring one for Henley.

"It could be a long evening. I've taken the liberty of having a room made up for you."

CHAPTER 16

She was uncomfortably warm. Fiona threw off the down comforter and opened her eyes to the sky above her. She blinked once, twice and realized she was staring at the blue silk canopy of the four-poster bed in which she'd slept. James snored softly beside her and she propped herself up on her elbows, looking around the room, bits of memory sliding slowly into place. They were at Julius DeMonte's house on Lakeshore Drive. *Holy Christ,* she thought, as the rest of the pieces came together. She sat up, pushing her hair away from her face.

A discreet knock on the door preceded the entrance of a young maid carrying a breakfast tray which she sat down on the table in front of the fireplace, withdrawing with a nod and a smile.

Fiona poured a cup of coffee from the urn on the tray and sat down in one of the blue upholstered chairs beside the fireplace. Sunlight filtered into the room through the gauzy blue curtains and it seemed to be somewhere around nine o'clock. She sighed and sipped the coffee, thinking back on the night before. *Christ on a plate,* she thought, *they really were in a pickle and it was a rum go they'd get out of it without help.*

Julius DeMonte was still a puzzle. As he'd briefly put it to them, he was a rich man, an expatriate English aristocrat who had made a life for himself in America in the theater, as well as another one that was hidden under those layers, one that seemed to be devoted to helping others. People who had made unfortunate mistakes, had been victimized, threatened, tyrannized or wrongly accused, or whose skin was not as white as snow and had suffered for that, or because they were Irish, Jewish or no matter where they hailed from. She had no idea how many there were after his relatively brief personal history last night, but she suspected there were many. What had become clear was she and James were now counted among them.

After Julius's explanation that he was looking out for their best interests as he had for so many others, they'd come to accept that he probably was, especially in light of his revelation about his actress friend. After a long discussion about the Lowells and an even longer one about good and evil, justice and laws and philosophy that had Fiona's woefully uneducated eyes closing, they had agreed to spend the night, see what developed and stay safe from harm's way. Julius had a way about him that inspired trust, in spite of his keeping secrets earlier. Fiona's eyes flicked to the two large trunks that stood to the right of the door. As promised, their clothing and effects from the Palmer House had been delivered discreetly at some point during the night while they slept. She'd never heard a sound.

"Do I smell coffee?" James sat up on an elbow. *Did the man's angelic face ever betray an inner turmoil,* she thought uncharitably, but she nodded, pouring him a cup but setting it on the table instead of bringing it to him. Damn him, he'd have to make the effort to rise as she had. Then, bless him, without a thought he wrapped the sheet around himself and plopped down on the chair beside her, smiling his thanks. He was dear.

"Thoughts, so early in the morn, my love?" He sipped his coffee.

Fiona gestured towards the trunks. "That our host is as good as his word."

James peered blearily at the trunks and nodded. "Not surprised in the least, especially after his little speech last night. Damn me if the man ain't likely right in every word he says."

Fiona nodded. "Now I have to wonder just why he's looking out for us and what he wants for that noble gesture. I thought for a moment about going over to the Palmer House and checking but I really don't have any doubts Julius is right, when you think about it. So there's that."

James gazed at her and picked up a croissant from the tray. "Have to say, as doubtful as I was at the first, my dear, you're absolutely correct." He took a bite of pastry. "Since I'm not the most trusting sort, while you were sleeping, I sent a note over to our friend Smithson the concierge last night via the coachman, handsomely tipped."

He held up a cream-colored note with the Palmer House emblem. "Someone slipped this under the door a while later. DeMonte was right. Smithson confirmed that a man who showed him credentials as a New York policeman was there asking for us. Of course, as a trusted employee of the Palmer House and a well-compensated gentleman," he grinned, "he looks out first for the welfare of his guests and told him we were out, and not certain about our destination nor our return, only that we were expected in no more than two days."

"How clever you are, James."

"Also, there's the Sean Dooley debacle on top of it, which hasn't been brought up, but with Mr. Henley's detective skills, I'd not be surprised if he didn't know that as well."

Fiona winced. "Yes, there's that. I've been a bit fashed,

worrying and all. Maybe we are finished with Chicago, one way or another, and Julius DeMonte, whatever he's got in mind, besides hiding us away from the New York inquiries, could be a way. Or we just get on a train and head west. Since you're so opposed to gypsy caravans."

James rolled his eyes. "Remember, whatever they might suspect, it's all conjecture. There is not a shred of evidence connecting us to the Lowells on that night. Only suspicion, and it all depends on whom they've talked with to get to the point of tracking us to Chicago. However, if Sean Dooley, bless his peasant heart, could do it, I'm not surprised the New York police could do so, frankly, and that's been worrying me."

She nodded. "Oh yes. Still, when powerful people decide they want something, they get it, conjecture or no. I'm Irish, my darlin' dear, and trust me, the English have always done whatever they liked when it came to us, present company excluded, love."

"I'm not offended, and I'm not naïve. But, as Julius said last night, the Lowells had powerful enemies, too. I think he's one of them, and there's likely more."

"Hmm. Perhaps I've lost my mind, but when we meet DeMonte at breakfast this morning, I'm eager to hear what he has to offer. He was fairly mysterious last night, but I have a feeling it's not caravans. I believe we owe it to ourselves, and maybe him, to listen before we make any decision. Are you all right with that?"

Fiona poured another cup of coffee and grudgingly nodded. "I'll hear him out. I warn you, James, if I don't like it, we're leaving just as soon as we can get to the bank."

"Fair play," he said and ate the rest of the croissant. "I can't disagree. The day will bring new developments." His finger slid delicately under the lace of her nightgown bodice, gently outlining her collarbone. "Julius has exquisite taste in borrowed nightclothes. You look as delectable as this croissant. No, I'm quite certain even more so." He grinned. "Before the fun starts, I was thinking we should go back to bed for a few minutes?"

She couldn't disagree with that. You had to take your pleasures when you could. To save herself from complete dissipation, she attempted to look outraged.

"You're a complete scoundrel, James Ardrey."

"You knew that the moment you took my hand on Broadway long ago. Look how far it's taken you, love. So accomplished and talented in so many areas. And you've relished every second of it."

Afterwards, she waited until he was in the bathing room to check. There, inside the larger of their trunks, was her false-bottomed carpetbag and not a single piece was missing, much to her relief.

* * *

THE BREAKFAST ROOM'S yellow silk walls shimmered in the sunlight, the curtains pulled back to give the widest possible view of Lake Michigan, the whitecaps a sugary frosting on the blue water. Fiona and James entered to find Julius already sitting at the table. They filled their plates at the sideboard, crowded with offerings from scrambled eggs, bacon, sausages, kippers, the usual, to mounds of delectable pastries. Pitchers of juice and coffee were on the table. They took their seats but were in no hurry to pick up their forks, too eager and apprehensive about what Julius DeMonte was thinking.

"Good morning," he said, looking immaculate as usual, as though he'd slept for much more than a mere few hours. He wore another perfectly tailored black suit, his linen purest white against his throat. "I trust you found your belongings? I had them removed so you wouldn't have to return to face any unpleasantness. You are of course, free to go where you will."

"Yes," Fiona said, "and thank you. So neatly folded as well."

Julius smiled. "Well, we're not barbarians, my dear. I took the liberty of settling your bill as well. Can't have the Palmer House dunning you."

"How kind," James said. "Please do let me know the total so we can reimburse you."

Julius nodded. "Of course. Now, please, I highly recommend Miss Lally's eggs with herbs and cheese, I swear you've never tasted any more delicious."

They ate in silence for a few minutes. He was right, Fiona thought. The eggs and everything else were outstanding.

James cleared his throat. "At the risk of being rude, last night you hinted that there be some options available to us. We've decisions to make."

Julius leaned back in his chair. "Of course you do. First, as I explained last night, I've nothing nefarious in mind. I've made it a habit to help people when I can. That is all." He sipped from the coffee cup in his hand. "In your case, it was approaching dire straits, according to Henley, so we avoided the worst of it. Which doesn't mean you're both in the clear, as the Pinkertons say. From here, you have some choices."

He stood up and wandered over to the sideboard, picking up a crisp piece of bacon and chewing languidly. Christ almighty, the man was maddening, Fiona thought.

What she said was: "One of them is getting on a train west and there's little time to spare for that."

Julius picked up another piece of bacon. "Well, that's true enough. At least you'd be going in the right direction from the trouble following you." He smiled as though they were discussing the variants of the wind and sat back down in his chair, eyes reflective. "Then again, there's an alternative I'd put to you, if you're interested."

"And that is?" James said, failing to disguise his impatience. "Climbing into those wagons I've heard about and putting on shows for cowboys in some frontier town?"

"No," Julius laughed. "Although you'd be very surprised to find out how truly delightful traveling in those wagons can be. Instead, how about sailing down the greatest river in America in the most amazing showboat ever designed? Rounding out my troupe with two actors who've wowed New York audiences with their performances?"

Well, Fiona thought, when the man dropped a bomb he did so with aplomb, not that she knew what a 'showboat' was, but it sounded intriguing. James looked at her, and his mouth slowly closed as he turned to DeMonte. "What?"

DeMonte pushed his chair back. "Come with me."

So they did, trooping off to his library like ducklings after their mother. Once inside the large room, he directed them to a large table with a model of what looked like an elongated white wedding cake, drawings and designs scattered about around it. He gestured expansively and Fiona and James both stepped up to the thing. It was four stories high with a smaller box perched on top, festooned with lacy filigreed railings and a huge red paddlewheel on the back, and the name gilded on the side was "Queen of Dreams".

"This is a *boat*?" Fiona said, thinking of the *Adriatic*, that vessel from hell. Surely this fanciful thing would sink like a stone in the waves of the Atlantic Ocean.

"Oh my yes, young lady," Julius said. His eyes glowed and the smile that had been on his face since they entered the room seemed permanently set.

"The age of the showboat has returned and this will be the most magnificent showboat to ever set sail down the Mississippi River. I've flown in builders from Germany and England and it's taken eight months to finish her. We will bring shows to the towns on the river with elegance and real theater like they've never seen before. Shakespeare, melodramas, song, dance and, just like our name, leave them with memories and dreams, perhaps to change their lives but at the very least enrich them."

He chuckled, clearly delighted with his showboat and the prospects of sailing on it. It was rather charming, she thought, to see this sophisticated man behave like a boy with a new pony.

"That is the purpose of entertainment, is it not? To make people not only happy, but leave them remnants of enchantment, magic if you will. Who can tell what will become of a person who's never heard a love song or a phrase of Shakespeare once they've done so? That is why I do what I do."

Well, thought Fiona. There was no denying the man was enthusiastic about his project and she couldn't fault him for his view of drama, either. It had certainly changed her life and opened the doors to a world she'd never imagined. Julius DeMonte wasn't quite what she'd imagined either, certainly no Augustin Drewry or greedy theater owner. The man had a vision, and it was an elevated one. She had a feeling Julius had a lot of different visions and this boat was just one of them.

James was entranced, Fiona could tell. He walked around the table, studying the drawings and the model, a smile on his face. After a few minutes, he turned to DeMonte.

"So, a jewel box, then, from the look of the drawings?"

Julius laughed in delight. "You know, then. You've seen the one at Windemere, perhaps?"

"Yes," James said. "Just the once, when I was at Oxford. I roomed with Viscount Edward and the Claibornes invited me home for Christmas. It was beautiful. I think maybe that was the first time I fell in love with theater, watching the Christmas Eve pantomime in that exquisite little venue."

Julius nodded, watching James closely. "I've been to Windemere myself. It was modeled after the Italian style. There aren't many, some scattered around Europe. First one I saw was in a cathedral in Venice. Likely designed back when kings were divine, because even they loved a performance. I don't think one's ever been built here, so we'll be the first, and on a boat. Ha." He laughed again. "I even think it'd be the perfect venue on land, of course, for some of the new frontier towns, but they do come and go with the mining booms. I'll have to think on that some more."

His eyes gleamed and Fiona could practically see the thoughts ready to burst from Julius's brain. "Well, back to the beginning. There's no space for a balcony or boxes, sadly, but I've having them built on a slant so there won't be a bad seat in the house, unless some Southern grande dame wears large ostrich feathers. If that happens I might have to pluck them out. Only 250 seats, I've calculated. Maybe fifty more, I've not decided quite yet."

"Lovely that. For discerning audiences, then."

Julius raised an eyebrow. "One always hopes for that, but we won't be discriminating. If you've never been in the South, you are in for an eye-opener, I assure you. From very wealthy to unbearably poor and everything in between, especially after the devastation of the war. It's not like anywhere else. Never underestimate your audience, I've learned.

"Of course we won't skimp on the amenities, which I want to be nearly as big a draw. A restaurant with fine cuisine, a large saloon with gambling, and cabins for those who wish to cruise with us for a time, for a considerable price of course. It's a new version for an old and frankly, tired model. We're doing it better." Julius pointed to the higher decks. "And of course spacious accommodations for all the players and the troupe, and fair quarters for the boat crew. No one works for me or sails on my boat in less than they deserve. We're going to board at St. Louis and sail down the Mississippi River to New Orleans and back. We may winter there and rest during the rainy season. Then, put ourselves back out in March or April."

He smiled, clearly ecstatic and James smiled back. Well, Fiona thought, these two are certainly peas in a pod with this daft idea. She wasn't so sure and she knew nothing about "showboats" so she thought keeping her mouth shut and ears open, as the nuns used to say, was the best policy. It had served her well enough in the past.

The two of them bent over the model and the drawings, discussing space, accommodations and jewel boxes, apparently some sort of theater, murmuring excitedly about this and that while her attention was diverted to the books that lined the room. This library made Audrey Prescott's look like a simple shelf in comparison.

Thousands of books, with a spiral metal staircase to reach the upper shelves were housed here and Fiona marveled, was drawn towards them. As she rounded one of the wing chairs that faced the shelves, she was surprised to see Angel, the ethereal blonde girl she'd met the evening before, curled up in one of the chairs, a book on her lap. The girl looked up and smiled, then wordlessly returned her attention back to her book. DeMonte had introduced her as his ward but from his fatherly affection towards the girl, Fiona couldn't help but wonder if she was more than that.

Fiona smiled back and continued over to the shelves, her fingertips passing across the leather bindings as she mentally catalogued the various titles: Pliny, Ovid, Caesar, Virgil, Homer, Dante Alighieri, Abelard, Descartes, Locke, Shakespeare of course, and many others she'd never heard of. The enormity of the collection coupled with the scarcity of her knowledge was overwhelming. So much to read, to learn, and places to explore. She turned and watched the two men for a time, bent over the model on the table, animatedly discussing the boat and its design, pointing at this and that on the model and the drawings.

Perhaps what Julius was offering them was a gift, she thought. To base a life decision on someone's library might be foolish, but she coupled that with everything that happened in the last twelve hours, indeed the last two years, and made up her mind. If the man had compiled a library such as this, to her mind he could not only be trusted, but respected.

She stepped back over to the model and took another look. It really did look a lovely thing. The river must be very wide to accommodate such a vessel and to sail down it, living on this beautiful boat experiencing that adventure, was something she decided she wanted with all her heart.

"Gentlemen."

They both looked up at her expectantly, tearing their eyes away from the table.

"I think we need to talk further about this," Fiona said. DeMonte smiled, very much like a cat licking cream. She had a feeling he knew exactly what she was going to say. "Tell me more about the Mississippi River, showboats and a jewel box. I'm a woman that likes new adventures."

CHAPTER 17

Julius DeMonte, Fiona decided, was quite possibly the smartest man she'd ever met. Certainly one of the most compassionate and kind, traits not all that well hidden behind his sarcastic and sophisticated exterior. With all his other accomplishments, the man certainly had a vision. One that she and James were now a part of, along with the entire troupe, all of whom had traveled with him before, and many who were a part of his Chicago theater company. She felt comfortable with them now, having rehearsed with them for weeks. They were an interesting group. Many, like her and James, were from other parts of the world: England, Ireland, France, Spain, Africa and the Romany of course, who brought their own unique talents. All of them to board and live on the Queen of Dreams for a time, as advertised, the most elegant showboat to ever float down the Mississippi River.

The legendary Mississippi, the grand river that divided America. In the last few weeks Fiona had learned a lot about that river, and the showboats that had been entertaining the people and towns up and down its banks for many years, thanks to the library and DeMonte's informative lectures. Those hadn't been just for her and James. The entire troupe, even though they'd traveled with their show across that river many times, had never been on that river, so it would be a joint virgin voyage and anticipation was high. So was their workload. They'd been rehearsing plays, dances and skits for hours each day, Julius dropping scripts off before breakfast.

For the plays, he'd chosen well. Some new American ones, a farce or two, one acts, and from Shakespeare, the lighter ones, or if heavier, highly redacted, Julius's specialty. His experience with audiences outside of the larger Eastern cities, was to give them the main plots and high points, usually with Julius as a narrator, but never expect them to sit through three hours of Hamlet or a Troilus and Cressida. There were some who might appreciate them, he'd said, but many more who would grow bored. Fiona agreed. If there was anything she knew well, it was that small towns and villages were not made up of sophisticated folk but mainly those who appreciated simpler fare.

The basic troupe that lived in the house were those who'd been with Julius the longest. Mama Rosa's son Ramon, a versatile and talented actor, the Acaro family, two brothers and two sisters, were acrobats, jugglers, and actors as well—Josef, Daniel, Maria and Elena, all in their twenties with flashing eyes and curling dark hair, Romany to the core; two sisters, Merry and Ellen St. John, singers, actresses and dancers and clearly Julius's special favorites; George Harper, a burly genial man who acted and did anything that needed doing, according to Julius, and Sean McKean, who called himself a roustabout but Julius said he made a wonderful Falstaff, among other roles; two young French actors, Etienne and Yvette, a couple whose English was impeccable, and the Smithsons, a couple in their thirties, long time actors who Fiona remembered seeing at the theater in Chicago. She and James rounded it out.

Since the evening of the dinner and the frightening discovery that they were being investigated and barely managed to evade the police, she and James had also been guests in Julius DeMonte's gracious house. According to Henley, there had been no further inquiries from the New York detectives, who'd returned there in frustration, according to DeMonte's sources. Fiona knew, as did James, that just because the detectives had reached a dead end in Chicago, didn't mean they were done with them forever. They'd had their quarry in their sights and the fact that they'd gotten as far as Chicago was daunting. She and James, thanks to Julius, had managed to disappear, nearly right under their noses, but if it could happen once, it could happen again if someone was determined enough. Only time, luck and influence from higher-ups could bury the inquiry forever, and she fervently hoped it wouldn't surface again, and certainly not before they were out of Chicago.

She and James had become familiar with Julius and came to trust him, so much so they'd even reverted to their real names, an easy task for her but James had always known her as 'Mary' and for him, 'Fiona' had taken a few days. Julius had suggested they keep it simple, as in James and Fiona Gordon, and they'd agreed. Fiona thought James was happy with the decision, because after all, Gordon really was his family name, and Ardrey had been his own invention long ago, just as hers had been Mary O'Neill.

"I suppose you could pass for another Gypsy if we darkened your complexion so's to match the rest of them. Then again, that would be a trial and I rather like 'Fiona,'" James said, playing with her hair, the long strands entwined in his fingers like dark shining rings. "What does it mean in the Gaelic?"

"The nuns said 'fair' but not to think on it," she said. "That could lead to pride and the saints know that's the gateway to hell."

He chuckled. "And here you are, my fair one, at the very gate itself." He kissed the nape of her neck and she shivered, both from the kiss and the thought of being anywhere near the gateway to hell, even though she knew better. She'd been trying to shake off the worst of the nuns' indoctrination, but nightmare-inducing remnants remained and surfaced now and then. Sometimes Fiona thought maybe that was why she had such a remorseless temper when she'd been wronged, all that repression had kept the fire banked until it had to be used.

"Indeed we are," she said. And it was true, in a way. Of all the roads they could've taken after New York, this one hadn't ever entered either of their minds, and a river nonetheless. It seemed a dream, but one that was shortly to become reality.

She was excited but apprehensive at the same time, nearly the like of the boarding the *Adriatic*. When she thought back on that voyage, the sickness and the luck of disembarking with Joel Prescott, avoiding the poverty and derision most of the Irish faced upon arriving in America, her heart fluttered. So very fortunate, she'd been, and meeting up again with James, despite the Lowell debacle, had been another gift.

As Julius was fond of saying, "life takes many turns" and Fiona had taken those words for her own, so prophetic and so true. She was leading a charmed life, she sometimes thought, but it had come at a cost of others, not that she'd had much of a choice. She couldn't dwell on that, she knew. There was a future to be had and days of discovery ahead.

She looked at James where he sprawled beside her on the bed overlooking the moonlit lake. She curled her arm around his neck and kissed him soundly. "I love you, James Gordon. How lucky I am to be here with you."

"Ah Fiona," he murmured, his lips on her neck. "I am the blest one. You, my little Irish wench, have turned me upside down, inspired me and saved me, especially from myself. We are just beginning, my love." He reached over her and turned off the lamp. "Tomorrow we leave for St. Louis, but tonight is ours."

***

JULIUS HAD RESERVED two train cars for them all, luxuriously appointed, with sleeping berths and in the two days it took to reach St. Louis, Missouri the train passed by a blur of countryside, spring green and flowering with life. This was just the beginning of the American plains Fiona had heard so much about, and she was disappointed not to see a storied buffalo or an Indian, much as she glued herself to the window hoping to do just that. Sometimes Julius and James, smiling at her efforts, brought her tea during her vigils, remaining discreetly silent most of the time.

"They're mostly gone, love," James said, planting a soft kiss on her temple. "Progress, so they say. It comes with a price. They say that, too."

When she looked up at him, his eyes were sad as he gazed at the landscape passing before them. She decided at that moment that perhaps progress wasn't a good thing, not when other things had to die to make it happen. Growth was inevitable, but 'progress' from then on, had a new meaning for Fiona. She'd spent a great deal of time in Julius's library. Perhaps too much.

And then they arrived. St. Louis. The famous American city in the very middle of this vast country where everyone departed, a gateway to the west, the north, or down the river. Explorers, trappers, settlers heading west and north, people traveling up and down the river, and boats carrying the wealth and produce of the plains and the farms of the west into the cities east.

While nowhere near the size of Chicago, the place buzzed with life, especially at the train station, porters and baggage men shouting and people crowded onto the platform, passengers both coming and going. They didn't have a chance to explore the city and find out any more, because from the minute they'd pulled into the station, a dozen wagons were loaded with their baggage, from trunks full of costumes to artfully painted sets. More wagons were piled with excited chattering entertainers, technicians and helpers, including Fiona and James, clambering onto the wagons with the rest of the troupe.

Through the city they went, and even though it was early May, a warm and humid breeze caressed their faces. She could smell the river as they approached, a mossy damp and slightly fishy odor that wasn't altogether unpleasant, very unlike the salt tang of the ocean. They hadn't seen Julius at all since the evening before at dinner, but when they arrived at the riverbank there he stood, directing all the chaos like a magician waving his wand and things were miraculously moving and disappearing into the places they belonged.

Anchored on the wharf in front of him, on a river so wide it nearly looked like an ocean, floated the most beautiful boat Fiona had ever seen. The Queen of Dreams, just like the model she'd seen so often in Julius's study.

The Queen was magnificent. Three, no four stories high with a square little pilothouse painted with red trim on the top. She dwarfed the other craft anchored nearby, both in size and sheer elegance, her glossy white filigreed railings and red paddlewheel glowing in the afternoon sun, her name spelled out in gilded letters along the second tier. This was a vessel truly worthy to be called the Queen of Dreams.

A sigh was all Fiona could manage and James put his arm around her shoulders.

"I know, love. Damn me, but Julius was not exaggerating. My god, this is quite the incredible boat."

They weren't alone in their wonderment. Nearly everyone on the wharf, from cargo loaders to captains to people strolling along the docks, were enthralled with the Queen, eyes riveted to the great boat. Women with parasols had stopped, their escorts beside them, staring at the steamboat that transformed the rude wharf into a launching pad for the fantastic.

The entire troupe was staring at the Queen in awe as well, climbing down from the wagons and milling around the dock, murmuring to themselves. Fiona was sure she saw Ramon and Maria cross themselves and Mama Rosa made the sign against the evil eye. Sometimes the incredible invoked that response. Fiona was close to crossing herself and invoking Mary and Jesus as well but she resisted. It had been a long time since that had happened, in fact the day she left St. Hilda's and it hadn't done her any good then or since.

Stevedores were already unloading luggage and sets and trunks of costumes and moving them onto one of the gangplanks while Julius stood on another and waved his hat. Very theatrical, Fiona thought, especially for Julius, who never seemed to exhibit raw enthusiasm. Now he did. She thought she could even discern a rosy blush on his normally pale cheeks, but she may have been mistaken in the sunlight. That would be so un-Julius-like, she thought and rather than elbowing James, she kept still, quite delighting in her observation. She was as fascinated by Julius as she was by the showboat. One was a finished accomplishment while the other was a never-ending enigma. Julius's voice rose above the din of the docks.

"My friends, this is the Queen of Dreams, your new home and theater, awaiting your presence, your love and your talents. Come aboard and become acquainted with your new home. I have selected accommodations for you on one of the upper decks. For now, there are refreshments and lunch awaiting us on the main deck while we finish loading cargo and supplies."

The rest of the troupe surged forward en masse, although politely, onto the boat, but Fiona and James held back. He helped her down from the wagon and they waited, walking to where Julius stood on the wharf, and Fiona's earlier suspicion was right. Julius wasn't just the cat who'd had some cream, he was sated with it, thrilled at the physical embodiment of his creation, and his eyes twinkled above rosy cheeks. She wasn't likely to doubt him again.

He grinned. "What do you think, Romeo and Juliet? It's not Verona, but then again, you're not dead. Quite a fine alternative, wouldn't you say?"

CHAPTER 18

On the wharf side of the Queen of Dreams, huge double doors on the low-ceilinged main deck were open, and temporary tables piled with food and drink were set out of the way of the cargo loading area. The troupe surged into the space, chattering and exclaiming over the boat and the river, filling their plates from a mouth-watering array of dishes, and glasses of champagne punch were filled over and over. A smiling rotund man in a white chef's hat was presiding over it all, directing servers as they came and went, usually with just a look or a hand gesture, clearly in charge of his culinary world. In spite of the chaos, he seemed unperturbed and his pleasant face was kind, not impatient.

They followed Julius to the main buffet. "Andre, you've outdone yourself with such a rudimentary dining space," he said, shaking the man's hand. "This is Fiona and James Gordon. Darlings, this is Andre Frontenac. I stole him from the Hotel St. Louis. He's in charge of everything we eat and drink, as well as *Enchante*, our restaurant."

Andre grinned. "*C'est vrai.* But I was easy to entice, no?

Because I am a man of the river and who can resist this opportunity?"

"Who indeed?" James said. His gaze slid to the platters on the table. "Oh god, shrimp *diablo*, and do I see lobster bisque in that pot?"

Andre smiled. "*Vraiment.*"

Julius patted James on the shoulder and smiled at Fiona, moving away. "Enjoy. We'll go up to the higher decks after lunch."

They filled their plates and took two glasses of punch, wandering out to the rail to watch the river as they ate. James rolled his eyes in ecstasy at the first spoonful of bisque and Fiona laughed.

"This is going to be a wonderful trip on the river, if for nothing else than the food, you glutton."

James nodded, his mouth full. Fiona took a bite of the shrimp and was amazed at the tangy flavor of the chile. It didn't take either of them long to finish off every bite. Whatever else, they were going to be extremely well-fed, she thought.

Back inside, they dropped their plates onto a serving cart as half a dozen men entered the room, all dressed in dark blue uniforms with gold braiding and brass buttons, replete with stylish brimmed hats in the same colors. Julius chatted with them for a moment and turned to the company.

"Allow me to introduce you to your captain and crew. These outstanding gentlemen are in complete charge of this floating wonder and we are all not only obligated but indebted to them for their skill. We are under their care." He turned to the man beside him and if he could have bowed, Fiona thought, he would've, but even for Julius, that would have been a bit much.

"This is Captain Abel Hamilton, who will be guiding us on our journey," Julius said with a flourish of his arm. He rattled off the rest of the crew's names, although they were quickly forgotten because all eyes were riveted on the captain and rightly so.

He stood close to six foot six, even dwarfing Julius, who wasn't a short man. His ebony skin gleamed, and the brilliant smile that lit up his somber face was infectious. A collective sigh rose from the company and Fiona's wasn't the only one. James seemed quite surprised, but he shrugged his shoulders and focused his attention on the Captain.

"Good afternoon." His voice sounded like God's, Fiona thought, sonorous, deep and reassuring, more so than any actor she'd ever seen on the New York or Chicago stage.

"I am pleased and honored that Mr. DeMonte has chosen me to guide you all and captain this magnificent boat." He looked over the people assembled and it seemed that his kind brown eyes saw every one of them. "I grew up near this river and as a boy, watched the boats go by. From the simple rafts to the keelboats to the steamboats, in war and peace, I knew I wanted to be one of the people that were on board. Not just on board, but in command."

He looked over at Julius. "Thanks to him, I am." He nodded at DeMonte who returned the tribute. "You are in my hands and those of my capable crew and I promise you this will be a peaceful voyage you will always remember with great satisfaction." He bowed slightly, calm and in command and everyone felt it. The applause echoed around the room and off the water. He stepped into the crowd, followed by the entire crew, shaking hands and chatting before they left the deck, climbing the stairs.

Fiona turned to James. "He was impressive, don't you think?"

James smiled. "Very much so. I wouldn't have expected less from Julius. To have a black man as our captain is a stroke of genius and I'm sure one that came with careful thought." He lowered his voice. "Likely the last time any of his relatives were on a showboat they were either loading it or performing in one of what they called 'minstrel shows'".

"What do you mean?"

"America is the land of the free, but for his people it's been a very long road, and one that still comes with prejudice, Fiona." He looked over at Julius, who was talking with Ramon and some others. "You know how the Irish are viewed in New York? It was much worse here. His people were slaves. Surely you've heard of the civil war and what happened here?"

She stared at him blankly. What was he talking about? She felt stupid and somewhat ashamed. Her world had been narrow, she knew that, but she'd worked diligently to educate herself, reading into the night, many nights, but somehow she'd missed what was right before her eyes. The history, not far distant apparently, of this country and its people was something she'd missed in her pursuit of the literature and philosophy of those long dead.

"No, I have not, James. I don't know anything about it. I'm from Ballyowen, you remember? People there don't think about much of anything except their potato crop or making poteen. Since I got on that cursed boat to come here I've only been concerned about myself, and then you. I guess I have some reading and research to do. Captain Hamilton looked to me like a magnificent man and no different than any other except for the color of his skin."

James shrugged, whether apologetically or because he was bored, she couldn't tell.

She moved away, and her mood lightened. The rest of the afternoon was taken up with a tour of the Queen of Dreams. From the main cargo deck, through the low boiler deck, with its seven steam boilers, up to the cabin deck, where the theater, salon and restaurant were and onto the next where the troupe would be housed and even up to the Texas deck and the pilot house, where Captain Hamilton and his crew would guide them safely down the river.

Fiona was dazzled, there really was no other word for it. The restaurant and salon were replete with glass windows so big that the river and the city of St. Louis were depicted beyond them as though they were almost part of the boat itself. Chandeliers glittered from the ceiling, while the tables were already set with white linen and silverware, rivaling the most elegant New York restaurants. The bar in the salon was stocked with the finest wines, rums, whiskies and bottles whose contents gleamed back reflected again in the mirrors behind the polished oaken bar, from crystal clear to pale green, hundreds of sparkling glasses stocked in the cabinets, awaiting the desire of the patrons.

She couldn't imagine anyone not being enchanted to be in these places, grasping James's arm and exclaiming as each area was revealed. He was similarly impressed, she knew, and to think all this was on a boat, for heaven's sake. She'd never expected this and sophisticated as he was, she knew James hadn't either.

And then, the jewel box. So now she knew. She'd been speechless before, but those times had been due to fear, shock or terror. This time was from sheer awe, stepping through the padded double doors amidst the troupe, twenty-six of them, following Julius, with Angel at his side, into an enchanted realm. It was quiet except for the hiss of indrawn breath in every throat as they all turned and craned their necks around the theater. The walls were painted a sky blue, with gilded and ivory panels along each side, each with a painting of a castle or chateau in a pastoral scene. Overhead the ceiling itself depicted what Fiona could only term 'heaven', somehow a perfect imagining of such a place, far beyond what any sour-faced nun in a cold Irish church could have thought of, it was a blue sky with fluffy clouds and angels floating among them, the colors swirling as though being blown by a rapturous breeze.

For ten rows on each side of the center aisle, carpeted in dark blue, fifteen theater seats fanned out in a gentle curve, covered in the same hue of blue velvet, their backs and armrests carved gilt wood, the entire seating area and aisle sloping gently down to a small orchestra pit below the stage. Above them, framed in the same dark blue velvet curtains, held back by golden ropes, the stage glowed like a jewel, the backdrop a painted Arden welcoming forest, the polished warm oak boards inviting them to walk on and work their magic.

Julius stood in the center of the stage. "Your workplace, my friends, for the next six months at least, and maybe much longer. Thoughts?"

From hush to hubbub, everyone began to exclaim and chatter, gesturing at the walls, the ceiling, the stage, trying out the chairs, some rushing up to the stage to hug Julius, wandering backstage, hands caressing the velvet curtains. Fiona stood motionless beside James.

"It's like a fairy tale, isn't it?" James said. "Absolutely exquisite. Julius has really outdone himself. Good god, I had no idea."

Fiona nodded. "Yes. It's beautiful, so . . . I can think of no other word." She leaned over and whispered in his ear. "What's a 'fairy tale'?"

He stared at her for a moment. "My darling girl. You have had a childhood straight out of one, I think." He put his arms around her and kissed her hair. His voice was husky. "I shall attempt to remedy that. If I could go back to Ireland, I'd do more than that to those cursed people who raised you."

He kissed her again and took her hand. "Let's get on that stage and congratulate our creative leader. He deserves all the praise we can muster."

Fiona couldn't agree more. They made their way up to the stage to Julius. While James moved to shake his hand, she threw her arms around him, and he hugged her back.

"Thank you, thank you," she murmured. "It's so magnificent,

the boat, this, all of it. And especially for what you've done for James and me. I don't know what else to say."

Julius gently pulled back, gazing at her. "I'm glad you like the Queen and very happy you like what I've done with her. Your efforts are going to make this stage come to life, my dears, which is all I ask."

He took Fiona's hand and still held on to James's, raising them both, turning back and forth to address everyone. "On to the next deck, my friends, where you'll all be settled into your quarters. We have exciting days ahead, and a lot of hard work." He grinned. "I'm just the director, it is all of you who will create the magic, joy and yes, dreams as we progress down the river on the Queen. We'll meet up afterwards in the restaurant for dinner at seven and go over our plans for tomorrow. Go, enjoy."

CHAPTER 19

Tonight would be their first show. Fiona lay on her back, watching the play of light on the ceiling from the morning sun reflected off the waters of the Mississippi. A soft snort from beside her and James rolled over, burying his head beneath the pillow and slept on. All to the good, she thought. He was a beast when he was tired, and they had only had two days of rehearsals and getting to know the lovely jewel box theater as well as the showboat itself, still anchored at the wharf in St. Louis.

It had been inspiring but hectic, and even with Julius's warm manipulation, stressful for all of them. Some of the troupe were hesitant about the river, and Fiona had heard tales of shipwrecks, ghosts and river monsters off and on now for weeks, but they'd magnified in the two days they'd actually been on the boat. She didn't believe a word of the tales. She knew the real monsters lived among them, and looked just like everybody else. As far as she knew, there weren't any on this boat, though.

They would stay in St. Louis for a week, according to Julius, put on performances and then launch downriver. He wanted to work out any issues with the theater and restaurant before they set off and also to give St. Louis a taste of just what the Queen of Dreams could offer, which was considerable. The city and its inhabitants had watched for months as the boat came to life and it was only fair, he said, to allow them to be the first to see what all the fuss had been about. Besides, the calliope had only been installed late yesterday afternoon, so Julius said. Fiona didn't know what a calliope was, and from the looks on the faces of the troupe when he'd mentioned it, neither did they, but she was sure they'd all find out very shortly.

She sat up and looked around the room. It was luxurious and well-designed for the small space. The bed took up a third of the area, but left room for a wardrobe, two chairs and a table, and a mirrored dressing table with a washstand, all new and glossy with paint, just like the Queen herself. Fiona threw off her nightgown and dressed in a simple yellow muslin gown. She ran a brush through her dark curls waving here and there around her head and onto her shoulders and splashed cold water on her face, looking at her reflection as she dried her cheeks. Dark green eyes, creamy skin and cheeks that would always have that Irish tell of soft rose. She knew she was pretty, some said beautiful, but it was a face that had sometimes led her to sorrow as well as good fortune. Still, she wouldn't trade it. She was here and she'd survived. Not bad for an old hag of eighteen, she thought, smiling at herself. *Your wicked ways haven't taken that much of a toll. Yet.*

She thrust her feet into velvet slippers and glanced back at James, still sound asleep as she softly shut the door and walked out onto the deck. It was early and though she could hear sounds from the kitchen below as well as the boiler deck, no one was about on this one. She stood at the railing and watched the river flowing by, mesmerized by the swift current. Out in the middle a flatboat floated past and she watched as a man stood on the tiller, steering the boat on its journey.

"Safe passage," she murmured and waved as he passed by. She wondered where he was going down that long river.

"Good wishes are always needed," Henley said, appearing at her side. "You are kind to give them to a stranger on his way."

She spun around. The man had cat feet, Fiona thought, but she wasn't displeased to see him. He was reassuring, in all ways. Capable, strong, clever, and handsome, but she drove that thought away. Henley was strength, and that was all she wished him to provide and he did that admirably. She liked him very much, but James found him intimidating, she knew. That Julius DeMonte trusted Henley with his life, and the lives of those he cared about, was all Fiona needed to know to trust Henley implicitly.

"I'm not that much of a humanitarian," she said and saw Henley's quickly hidden smile. "Just wishing the man a happy voyage, is all. We should all have the grace to do that, I'm thinking."

"Absolutely." He put his hands on the rail, staring out into the river. "It's early, could I interest you in some coffee?"

Inside the restaurant, Andre's minions had set out coffee, croissants and bowls of fruit, but there was no one else at the tables as of yet. Theater people were not renowned for keeping early hours, Fiona knew well. She and Henley poured themselves coffee and Fiona took a croissant from the tray, the pastry still warm in her fingers. She'd already learned Andre's croissants were the best thing she'd ever eaten.

They sat down at a table beside the window where they could still watch the river traffic flowing by. It was never too early for that, apparently. The Mississippi was a busy conduit, she'd learned. Henley stared out at the passing boats, his face serene.

Fiona took a bite of croissant and moaned softly. Henley chuckled.

"Andre really outdoes himself with those, doesn't he?"

"Holy mother of God," Fiona said, swallowing. "The nuns at St. Hilda's might come to life if they tasted these, because they come as close to divine food as anything I've ever tasted."

Henley laughed outright and Fiona popped more of the croissant in her mouth and smiled back at him. He sipped his coffee while she finished the pastry, which didn't take long. She eyed the buffet and sat back, deciding to wait.

"You grew up in Ireland, then?"

Fiona shrugged. "Yes, I suppose so, if you could call it that. Survived is more like it."

Henley waited but Fiona had no more to say on that and certainly not to this man she hardly knew. He seemed trustworthy but no one but James had breached that wall.

"How about you, Mr. Henley? Where are you from?"

"New York. My father had a farm upstate but I wanted to see the big city. I was a policeman there for a time until I went to work for Julius."

"Oh?"

"Meeting Julius was a turning point for me, maybe just like it's been for you. The man's like that, as you've likely noticed."

Fiona knew that was true, but she leaned over the table. "What happened?"

Henley finished his coffee and sat the cup down. "Long story, not needing to be told now or maybe ever. I will tell you this, Fiona." He stared at her. "Julius changed my life. He's a man who values truth, honor and justice, and those are things that don't always fit into the 'laws of the land' or the strictures of cities, police departments or churches. He cares about people and making things right and I agree with him with all my heart. That is all I needed to know then, and why I am here with you this morning."

He smiled to soften the seriousness of his words, and briefly touched her hand where it rested on the table beside her empty plate.

"Thank you for sharing your breakfast with me. I have some work to do in a bit, but I wish you all the best for your performance this evening. I'm eagerly looking forward to it."

The restaurant was coming to life, people wandering in, smiling hello to Fiona and Henley and taking their seats. Waiters appeared and began taking orders. Fiona and Henley pushed back their chairs and stood up when the most amazing sound Fiona had ever heard split the air.

Everyone looked up and ran outside to the deck to see where the sound was coming from, including Fiona and Henley. It was like bells and brass and a strange kind of piano had come together, to make a strange sort of music, in fact a song she recognized as "Them Golden Slippers", a dancehall favorite. It was compelling, and it resonated across the river and all over the waterfront. It went on for a few minutes and then stopped. Only then did they hear the cheers and clapping from the wharf.

"What in seven hells was that?" Fiona said to Henley, who laughed like a six-year-old.

"It's the calliope, Irish," he said. "All showboats used to have one, calling the people to the river and letting them know the showboat had come. They've been out of use for a while, but Julius wanted to bring it back. Just like he brought back this boat, to create a little magic in a hard world. Like it?"

Fiona stared at him. Would she never get used to this country? Then she laughed along with him. "I don't like it, I love it."

He smiled. "Thanks for sharing your breakfast."

He walked away down the deck. Fiona watched him go and thought about calliopes and Henley and Ireland and James and Julius and all that had led her to the Queen of Dreams and this moment. Life took many turns, she thought and just when you least expected it.

* * *

St. Louis loved them. They'd loved them for the last five nights, as they'd performed a redacted Romeo and Juliet, Romany folk songs like the ones Fiona had first heard in Julius's drawing room, risqué dances and acrobatics that sometimes defied belief. Julius certainly knew how to put on a show. So did everyone in his troupe, including Fiona and James, the newest members, who'd been given starring roles.

"You were incredible," James whispered in her ear. "As was I, of course." He laughed softly. "This was a grand idea, my love."

She couldn't fault that, or deny his words. They'd done a great show, over and over. But then, since their debut together in New York with this same play, it'd been a success the like of which she couldn't have imagined then. She'd heard the indrawn breath of the audience, especially the ladies, when James stepped onto the stage. They'd adored him, and their reluctance to leave after the show, hoping to catch a glimpse of him, had halted their husbands as they strove to go to their homes. Fiona also knew that when she had entered the stage, a hush had fallen, and her innocent Juliet was the stuff of dreams. When she'd joined James after the performance still wearing that white gown Juliet had lived and died in, those same husbands had slowed their impatience as well as their steps, devouring her with their eyes as had their wives. They sought what they'd never have, from her and James, and rightly so, because that was the magic of theater.

Fiona laughed as she clasped James's hand and the entire troupe took a final bow, on this their last night in St. Louis. Applause and cries of "Bravo!" echoed from the angelic ceiling on their final night in the city. Julius, clad in a black velvet robe, his magnificent hair flowing onto his shoulders, stepped onto the stage and the applause intensified for a few moments and died down as he held up his hands.

"My friends, thank you for your gratitude. St. Louis has been very kind to us and we are pleased to have been so welcomed in your lovely city where so many begin their journeys. It is our fondest wish to make you happy, entertain you and leave you with endless memories of our time together. We will return to you with new productions, music and more to give you delight and fuel your dreams."

He paused dramatically, because of course, this was Julius. "Because that is what we strive to bring to you, with love from all of us here on the Queen of Dreams." He bowed with a flourish. "Good night, and we will see you next spring."

PART III
DOWN THE RIVER

CHAPTER 20

Most mornings it was Fiona's habit to stand at the railing with her coffee or a croissant in hand, a silent sentinel who took in the dawn, the wind, the currents and the vibration of the deck beneath her feet, driven by the engines and the river itself. She'd started the first day they'd left St. Louis and now if she missed a morning, she felt as though her day hadn't properly begun. James made no secret of his disdain, pulling a pillow over his head each morning and usually muttering something unpleasant about cottagers and porridge but Fiona didn't care. She loved the river and the wonder of it and the boat had become her world. She never felt confined, as some did, like James, because she felt as though she was part of something special.

They steamed along in grand style, stopping at small towns and even villages, according to Julius's itinerary. Wickliffe, Carruthersville, Osceola, Tiptonville, so many small towns, villages and landings that they began to blur together, the houses and buildings perched beside the river, the green hills rolling away to the farms in the outer areas. Usually they only spent one night in each of them, the joyful calliope alerting the inhabitants to their arrival each afternoon, while children white and black ran alongside the boat as it slowed its pace and docked at each place. The excitement was contagious and before dark, a large crowd had assembled. Even if the town was just a tiny village, people came from the surrounding farms and inland villages and the restaurant and the theater were always full.

She'd noticed that Julius's prices were extremely variable depending upon where they were and the resources of the people in the area, sometimes in poorer areas hardly charging anything. Some had come just for the spectacle of the boat and had never thought to be able to afford to attend the show, but Julius always made it happen, if they were of a mind. The ticket-takers always bowed politely as they admitted the patrons, no matter if they were dressed in patched homespun or silk, or if they were white or black or Indian, ignoring any snide comments or sneers. He especially liked the children, and set up a couple of rows right down in front so they could see well and not have to peer over the heads of the adults.

Fiona had done her homework as well, and read the history of America's civil war and its mission to free the slaves. Then she went on to the native people and was horrified at what had happened to most of them, asking questions of people about the Cherokee especially who had lived right in the path of the showboat but were mostly relocated. Ireland was far from alone in making life difficult for the poor or disenfranchised and while America prided itself on its freedoms, it hadn't always extended to people who looked different. It was harrowing and every time she crossed paths with people who were not of her color, she felt a deep empathy with them. There were many on the boat, from maids to sailors to the captain himself and she knew Julius had engineered that, as did he did so much else.

She ran into him one morning as they left a town called New River, the first time she'd seen him alone in a while. Since they'd left New York, she'd once again felt herself changing into someone more, just as she had on leaving Ireland. Another incarnation, she smiled to herself. But this one was different. The river was different. Its soothing rhythm, the endlessly flowing current and the green banks that slid by were nearly hypnotic. Even the flow of people's speech, the further south they went, became smoother and less hurried, accompanied by their actions in many cases, and Fiona could feel the tension slipping away from her shoulders day by day.

"Good morning, Fiona," Julius said. "I notice you out here almost every morning and you look much happier than I've ever seen you. The river agrees with you, doesn't it?"

She nodded, blushing, and took a sip of her coffee.

"I like what you do," she said.

"And what is that, exactly?" Julius smiled, his café au lait in his hand where he stood beside her at the railing as the boat got underway.

"A lot of things," Fiona said. "But especially the lower ticket prices and the area for the children. It's something special and not something most people would think to do. But you do."

Julius shrugged. "It's how it should be, Fiona. I just believe in allowing people access to things that could better their lives," he laughed a little, "even if it's just a theater production. You never know what the catalyst for change might be, but I try to never ignore the smallest thing. I learn from experience, you might say."

He peered at her over the rim of his coffee cup. "As do you, I think."

Fiona felt a shiver run down her spine. Sometimes Julius saw too much. For a fleeting instant she wondered how much he'd like her if he'd seen her cut Samuel Lowell's throat. Sometimes she was tempted to confess but the temptation always passed. "True, but I hope to learn more. You've given me and James an opportunity that's worth much more than money, or an escape route, Julius. You've given me a chance to learn and gain perspective. My simple gratitude really doesn't begin to cover it, but you have that and more."

Julius nodded, remaining silent as they stared out at the water. Then he kissed her lightly on the forehead.

"All shall be well, Fiona."

He pivoted on his heel and strode off down the deck. Even a few months ago, she would've flinched at this gesture but she knew much better now. This was Julius and this was the dawning of a new Fiona. She watched him go and once again knew how fortunate she was.

As word spread downriver from St. Louis, the number of people the little towns brought to the showboat always amazed Fiona. The theater was always full to the last seat, with people standing outside on the deck, listening and happy to just be on the boat.

Their shows varied, the main play sometimes Shakespeare, or Drewry or another playwright, most of whom Fiona hadn't heard of before, but whose lines she had learned, both back in Chicago, and on the fly as they steamed down the river, Julius handing out new scripts many a morning, which they rehearsed all day, and for the more intricate ones, a few days while they fell back on old standbys which everyone knew very well, especially the troupe. Fiona marveled at their expertise and adaptability, but then she knew they'd been with Julius for years and had learned not just their lines, but how the man produced and staged every moment.

She spent most of her free time, what there was of it, reading. Shakespeare, plays, and scripts had to come first but she squeezed in everything else, too. She needed to get to the level of the other actors, James included, who'd done most of these plays many times, while she had only done a few. Fiona came to realize that she had a memory for lines and it served her well, but even at that, she breathed a sigh of relief when occasionally the evening's performance didn't include her, or at least didn't include a play she wasn't familiar with.

While not as driven as before, sometimes she felt like a fraud in comparison, but that was a feeling she'd learned to deal with in New York. James knew, like no one else, her anxieties and he always soothed her worries.

"Fiona love, you must trust yourself," he said, smoothing back her hair. He turned her shoulders gently to uncover her face where she'd buried it in the pillow. "You're inexperienced, that's true, and not had a long career in this business, but you're also something quite different. You're a brilliant actress and there's not a person, professional or not, who's not been only impressed with your performances, but loved them."

"Truly?"

"Truly." He kissed her gently and lay back down on the pillow beside her. "Irredeemable rogue that I am, when I saw you that day in New York, I think I fell in love right there, so I wanted you to be a part of my life. There was something about you that made me think you might be a good actress, apart from just how you looked. As though you were used to playing parts, perhaps, and melding into whoever you needed to be to survive." He smiled ruefully. "Indeed, how right I was about that, eh?"

Fiona sat up and glared at him but he held her gaze. Ah, hell. He was right. She'd been acting, sometimes to survive, since she was old enough to know what the word meant. Standing on a stage doing it for money wasn't that much different. She just had many more roles to learn to think of herself as a professional but that didn't mean she wasn't good at it.

She sighed and flopped back down. "Thanks, James. I'm not searching for praise but you know how I am."

"I do, Fiona. Now go to sleep."

After a while, lines running through her head, she did. He

was good at reassurance, she knew, especially when it was linked to his own success. But, that was the theater, after all.

* * *

THEY SPENT two nights performing in Cairo, Illinois, she and James giving them Romeo and Juliet again, and then steamed back down the river. It was growing warmer every day the further south they went and even after New York summers, Fiona had never felt heat and humidity like this. No one else had either, apparently and in Cairo, an ugly but fairly industrialized town, Julius contracted for the installation of large fans in the theater and the restaurant both, operated on the steam power of the boat itself. It helped, but by the end of each performance, they were all drenched in sweat from the costumes and the lights, and Fiona suspected the audience wasn't any more comfortable, especially those who'd gotten dressed up in their finery to attend.

Still, everyone seemed to be in good humor. She figured they were most likely used to it. Although she hadn't really missed Ireland's misty green hills before, she did now and James wasn't having an easy time of it either. Whiskey seemed to help him, and he'd been drinking much more than he ever had in New York. If she mentioned it, he quelled her with a look and she dropped the subject. His ill temper never reached that of Sean Dooley after downing a jug of poteen, so Fiona decided the best course was to ignore it.

At lunch the next day, usually when everyone in the troupe gathered in the restaurant, Julius had an announcement.

"Let me start by thanking you all for your hard work and learning the ways of the showboat and the river. I'm proud of you all. We'll be arriving in Memphis tomorrow. It's the largest of the cities since St. Louis, and one known for its rowdiness, but also one hungry for entertainment, which we are coming to provide." He grinned, gazing out at the people he'd gathered together. Fiona took a last bite of her chicken salad and focused her attention on Julius. She knew him well enough now to know there was more coming.

"As planned, we'll be doing the Scottish play. Memphis has always had a penchant for violence and it's just the play for them."

Everyone laughed on cue, but since not a one of them except for Julius and Henley, perhaps, had ever been to Memphis in their lives, they didn't know just how true his words were.

"We will be joined in Memphis by some old acquaintances who'll be stepping in and accompany us to New Orleans. It's lucky they happened to available, as that will allow us to rotate some of the roles and give you all an occasional respite."

James wasn't happy about new actors coming on. "This isn't good. Bringing in new actors mid-stream, so to speak," James said, looking out at the river, "isn't terribly conducive to the harmony of a troupe of players. I should know, believe me."

"I'm sure you do," Fiona said. "Can't see where we've got anything to do about it except go along. Julius seems to have things well in hand."

James shrugged and reached for the bottle of wine on the table. "Maybe. I suppose we'll find out soon enough. Christ knows he could put on a minstrel show with all the darkies he's got working on this boat." He poured the remainder of the Bordeaux into his glass and sat back. "It ain't my show, we're just going along for the cruise, as it were, m'dear. I daresay, this river is a foul-smelling piece of water and I'd give my soul for a northern clime. Feels like we've been trapped on this scow for years."

Fiona knew whenever he lapsed into his old London fop speech he was unhappy and turning quite nasty towards one thing and another. Some new aspects of James's personality were emerging on this voyage and Fiona found most of them distasteful. From the amount of wine he'd had, he'd be napping all afternoon, another trait that she found unsettling. What she didn't know, watching the river flow by, was what to do about it. She remembered the French phrase she'd learned well, *plus ca change, plus c'est la meme chose.* The more things change, the more they stay the same. Oh, how well she'd learned that.

They'd docked in Memphis the next day, but no performance was planned until the next evening, giving everyone a much-needed break. They'd slept in, and Fiona rose before James, who was as usual sated from drink and wandered out onto the deck after picking up a croissant and coffee from Andre's picked-over buffet. As she watched from above, Julius stood at the gangplank, welcoming a woman and two men as they stepped aboard.

"Darling!" exclaimed the woman, giving Julius a hug and kissing him on the cheek. He responded but not with quite such enthusiasm. She was beautiful, her blonde hair pulled back in a tight chignon, her lovely face clearly revealed as she turned to the two men who accompanied her.

"This is Jonathan Hargreaves," she said, pulling forward the first man behind her. He was handsome, with a dark beard and moustache, slim and dressed well in his gray waistcoat. He doffed his fashionable hat and took Julius's hand. An actor, no question to Fiona's mind.

"Thank you so much, Mr. DeMonte," he said. "What an opportunity you've given us. Haven't seen you since that one night in Philadelphia. Mavis here has been telling me all sorts of stories about you." He laughed. "I can assure you I don't believe half of it."

"Oh, that's unfortunate, they're likely true," Julius said with a sanguine smile. He turned to the second man, standing behind Hargreaves. "And this is?"

"Charlie Sitwell," said the second man, a stocky individual clad in a plaid suit with an interesting vest embroidered with red birds of some sort, his black hair shorn close to his scalp. His eyes were like those of a raven, beady and sharp. He held out his hand and Julius shook it briefly.

"So happy to make your acquaintance, Mr. DeMonte. I've heard such good things. Please forgive my intrusion, but when Mavis and Jonathan told me about this fabulous showboat you've been steering down the river, I was anxious to come and take a look for myself." He turned around and waved his hand as though to encompass the entire boat. "It's incredible."

"Thank you," Julius said, but his tone wasn't as warm as the one Fiona had become accustomed to. "I'm only hiring two new actors, Mr. Sitwell. Were you planning on cruising with us?"

"As a matter of fact, I hope to, now that you mention it, Mr. DeMonte." His voice couldn't have been more toadying, Fiona thought, and it didn't inspire trust.

"Charlie's a man of adventure, Julius," the woman called Mavis said, squeezing Julius's arm. "He's also a gambler and we hear you have quite a saloon on board."

Julius stared at Sitwell. "I run a clean house, Mr. Sitwell. Many do not. Any shenanigans and you're sitting on the riverbank. Do I make myself clear?"

Mavis and Sitwell exchanged glances during the awkward silence that ensued. Fiona was beginning to wish she'd been closer when someone whispered in her ear.

"Guy looks like a rounder to me, Irish."

Henley grinned at her, holding his finger to his lips. Mama Rosa stood beside him, a scowl on her face as she looked down at the figures below.

"I was thinking the same thing myself," Mama Rosa said. "A weasel."

"I can assure you," Sitwell spluttered, "I would never deal a rigged game."

"Since I don't know *you*," Julius said, "I can't know *that*, can I, Mr. Sitwell?"

"Julius," Mavis began and Julius held up a hand.

"We shall see. Since you're not a part of my company, you will be paying the standard rate for a stateroom, as we would charge any guest. I assume you're prepared for that?"

"Of course," Sitwell replied, looking injured that such a question would be asked.

"In advance, of course," Julius said silkily, ignoring Sitwell's deepening embarrassment. He turned to Mavis. "Now that's out of the way for now, please come on board. Our boat manager, Nigel Bidwell, will show you your quarters and arrange Mr. Sitwell's fees."

A dockside porter struggled up with their luggage and the ever-efficient Nigel had been standing behind Julius out of Fiona's sight. He exchanged a meaningful glance with Julius and escorted them inside. Fiona liked Nigel immensely, as did everyone. He ran the showboat and the company's business affairs with kind but precise efficiency and had little patience or time for silliness.

Julius watched them leave. The three watchers on the upper deck hadn't moved a muscle but Fiona was not in the least surprised when Julius turned and stared up at them, a smile playing at the corners of his mouth.

"Well," he said. "It's always an excellent idea to have witnesses to these conversations. I'm sure you'll all agree. I look forward to seeing you at lunch."

Henley and Mama Rosa silently walked away in different directions while Fiona stood at the rail for a few minutes longer. Julius wasn't one for mistakes, but he may have just made one. She wasn't sure, but somehow she had the dread sense that a serpent or two had just entered their Eden.

CHAPTER 21

"For God's sake, Julius," Mavis said from the front row where she'd come in to watch rehearsal, "she's a fucking ingénue. Nobody in their right mind is going to believe her as Lady MacBeth."

She tromped up onto the stage where they were rehearsing. "I know this part inside out. Let me bring some reality into this."

Utter silence fell over the theater and Fiona froze, standing as still as one of the backdrop columns, staring at James whose mouth was open in shock like the rest of the company and then at Julius, whose face was a marble mask as Mavis made her way up the stairs and stood before him.

"As much as I appreciate your helpful comments, Mavis," Julius said smoothly, "apparently the New York audiences and critics disagree with you, as do I. Fiona is brilliant in this role."

Mavis's face turned a blotchy shade of crimson but before she could say a word Julius took her arm and turned her towards the stairs. "If you insist upon participating in this particular performance, perhaps I could write you in as Banquo's ghost? It's really the only possible role left."

A choking sound that certainly didn't come from Julius was

heard. James frowned but a few members of the cast had turned away to hide their smiles. Fiona nearly burst out laughing. James had been flirting outrageously with the woman and she wasn't feeling over sympathetic.

"It might be prudent," Julius continued in a mild tone, "if in the future you have casting suggestions, to check with me first. We'll discuss your upcoming parts soon. Now, if you'll excuse us, we have to get on with rehearsal and I'm sure you'll be more comfortable elsewhere."

The door closed behind her on her way out and Julius turned back to the assembled players. "Now where were we?"

Mavis Thornton and Jonathan Hargreaves had been introduced to the company at dinner the night before. Julius had been voluble about their talent and how grateful he was they'd just happened to be in Memphis at the time he needed more actors. It was a fortunate occurrence and everyone had been very welcoming to the newcomers, shaking their hands and chatting during the meal and afterwards.

Fiona had mentioned her eavesdropping at their arrival to James and he hadn't seemed too concerned. He trusted Julius, as did she, but still, there was a vein of corrosive worry that thrummed every time she looked at the newcomers. Today had only made it throb and she looked at Mavis Thornton with even more suspicious eyes.

They went on with rehearsal, and after the play portion was done, the musicians and dancers came on for their time. Neither Julius nor anyone else mentioned a word about Mavis's interruption. Fiona and James went into the saloon and sat at the bar, ordering drinks from the bartender and watching Charlie Sitwell deal poker from his table across the room. His table was unusually busy. Mavis and Jonathan were seated near him and after a quick glance at Fiona and James, turned back to their conversation.

"She's lovely, but quite a bitch," James said casually, taking a sip of whiskey. "I can't imagine why she thinks she had a right to question Julius, or you."

Fiona shrugged. "Nor can I. I think they have a history of some sort but whatever it is, he's not too accommodating. She's definitely not partial to me."

James raised an eyebrow. "Not just this afternoon, then?"

Fiona blew out a breath. "Oh, no. Last night she looked at me like she wanted to stick her knife into my liver and have it fried with some tatties, God love her putrid soul."

James laughed. "Christ, Fiona. How did I miss all that?"

"I think it was the raspberry cake, James. You seemed devoted. You couldn't take your eyes off her cleavage." It was also the quantity of wine he'd swallowed but she didn't mention that. She poked him softly in his midsection and he rolled his eyes. He had put on some weight, thanks to Andre and likely, the drink. "After the Lowells, I guess I've become ever more suspicious about people and their motives than I was before, which after Sean Dooley is saying a lot, love."

"Surely she's not that bad?"

"Hmmph. Never discount nasty even if it's wrapped in a pretty package. If there's anyone that should know that, it's you."

To his credit, James grimaced and finished his whiskey, calling for another. Fiona didn't think he needed another but she'd learned to never get between a man and his drink the hard way.

"I know I'm a little too careful sometimes," she said, sipping her own whiskey, "but after all we've been through, I can't help myself and it's no bad thing, is it?"

He shrugged. "Not really."

"Besides," she said. "That woman is odd, and so are her friends. Jonathan Hargreaves is just as slippery as he is charming, and whether he's a good actor or no, remains to be seen. As for that gambler," she nodded towards Charlie Sitwell, "he's a weasel if I ever saw one. Julius spotted that right away and warned him before he ever set foot on this boat. I trust Julius's instincts and I am not sure why he let him on board to this very minute, James."

He slid elegantly off the bar stool and offered his hand. "Nor am I, my dear, but truthfully at this moment, I don't really give a bloody damn."

Fiona finished her whiskey and took his hand. "Truthfully, neither do I, at this very moment." She imitated his English accent to perfection. "Time for a nap, what?"

"Why don't you repair to the boudoir or what passes for it on this floating scow. I will join you shortly, after I enjoy a couple of hands of poker or whatever game Sitwell is dealing. I'm feeling lucky."

She didn't see him at dinner. In fact, she didn't see him until she woke up the next morning, his snores and the smell of whiskey both overwhelming.

* * *

THEIR FIRST NIGHT in Memphis drew rave reviews and an audience that was beyond enthusiastic, waving hats and cheers. Julius was right, this was a rowdy town and its inhabitants were that as well as welcoming beyond all expectations. They played there for another week, drawing crowds and fans from the surrounding counties. Fiona was pretty sure that some of the theater-goers were starstruck second and third comers, but that was all for the good. She knew she'd been good, maybe beyond that. They all had.

She'd learned this part, one of her first on the New York stage, unsure and fumbling the first night but finding her feet after that and it had been a resounding success. Reprising it for the people of Memphis, many of whom had never seen Shakespeare or a theater as elegant as the one on the Queen of

Dreams, was head-spinning. James as MacBeth was magnificent and Fiona, her hair pulled into a tight bun and pale lined makeup, shone as Lady MacBeth. Julius beamed at both of them after each performance as though they'd been headlining in London or New York. Fiona felt vindicated beyond anything she'd hoped for, especially after Mavis's snide comments. That the woman had made her doubt herself, even for a second, made her angry and even more determined to prove herself.

Perhaps Mavis had only made her better and in a perverse way, she was grateful to the woman. Sometimes, as the philosophers she'd been reading for a few weeks had said, adversity only made you stronger. It seemed to be true. She blessed Julius, not for the first time, for his library and for just, well, being who he was. Half the women in the company were in love with him, as were the women in the audiences they played to, but not Fiona.

She'd never known a father, although she supposed Julius was of an age to be that, but for her Julius was a mentor and a man she'd come to look to for wisdom and assurance. That was a role he filled to perfection. That he seemed to genuinely care for her and even James's welfare wasn't usual in this world, but then he wasn't your usual man by any means.

At breakfast that morning, people had clapped when she and James came into the restaurant, somewhat later than Fiona's usual. They were grateful and a bit embarrassed, but it was nice to be recognized by your peers.

"Thank you," James said, taking her hand. They bowed slightly and sat down at the nearest table. "If it hadn't been for all the work done by everyone else on that stage and behind it, no one would have noticed us, I assure you." The standard star actor's remarks, Fiona knew, but it still held true.

"Not so," a few voices called while others repeated "Bravo". Fiona smiled, knowing she was blushing but she couldn't help it. James poured them both some coffee from the silver pot on the table and she buried her face in the cup. When she looked up, Mavis Thornton was staring at her and knowing she'd been caught at it, the woman stood up and came over to the table.

"Fiona," she said, pulling out a chair. "Good morning, and good morning to you, James." Her smile lingered on James's face as most women's did, as though she'd forgotten why she came to table in the first place. *You are a slatternly slut under that fancy exterior,* Fiona thought and fought the impulse to fling the contents of her coffee cup at Mavis's face. Instead she smiled sweetly and waited for Mavis to say whatever it was that had brought her to their table.

"My dear," Mavis said, settling herself and her satin skirts onto the chair, "I must abjectly apologize to you for my outburst the other day. You were truly magnificent as Lady MacBeth and I am mortified that I doubted you and Julius for one second."

She's quite an actress, indeed, Fiona thought. "Think no more about it, Mavis," she said. "We all make mistakes, don't we?"

James choked on his coffee and coughed into his napkin while Fiona kicked his ankle under the table.

True to her training, Mavis smiled benignly. "Yes, my dear, we do. Now that I am aware of your considerable talents, that's not one I'll make again." She placed her hand on Fiona's. "It is my fondest wish we can be colleagues and friends, since we'll be working together for some time. I only want the best for the company and for the Queen of Dreams."

Fiona slid her hand out from under Mavis's, thinking of the skin of a snake. "I'm sure we'll work together well. I always find it beneficial to learn from those so much older than me who have so much more theatrical experience. It's a rare gift, I've found."

James made another choking sound and slid his chair back, mumbling something about bacon and made for the buffet table.

Mavis watched him go and returned her gaze to Fiona. Her blue eyes were like ice chips. "I think we understand each other perfectly, darling."

"We surely do, my new 'friend'." Fiona's smile was equally cold. "After all, there's so many roles in Shakespeare, both young and, well, mature. We'll be ideally suited for them, I'm sure Julius would agree. It'll be such a pleasure to work with you, Mavis."

The woman nodded, trying to disguise the rage that was making her nearly incapable of speech and took herself off to her table with Hargreaves and Sitwell. Fiona felt a fissure of uneasiness down her spine. If Mavis had been an ambivalent enemy before, she was an implacable one now. While the conversation had been gratifying, it had been foolish on her part. She and James had enough enemies and they certainly didn't need any more. Especially ones confined with them on a showboat with no place to go. She wasn't sure the woman wasn't capable of throwing her overboard some dark night, from the look in her eye. Even Julius might not be able to get her out of this mess she'd made all on her own.

CHAPTER 22

*D*ays and weeks passed as they went down the magnificent river, through so many towns Fiona couldn't remember all their names. So many performances. Some went outstandingly well while with others, the audience seemed a bit mystified, but still appreciative. Julius never seemed perturbed in the least. His goal was to bring theater to many who'd never seen it before and they were assuredly doing that, along with receiving accolades from those who had. Who could tell what the future implications could be to a person who'd just seen and heard things that might inspire them to a bigger ambition? If she'd been able to see a rendition of any Shakespeare play when she was an orphan at St. Hilda's, it may have changed her in many ways. Or not. That was the conundrum, she thought. Life took many turns, as Julius said. At least he provided a pathway for those who were willing to venture down it.

Even things had smoothed over with Mavis, although Fiona made it a point to socialize with other members of the troupe, which limited her time with James these days. He spent most of his free time and late evenings in the saloon, drinking and gambling, much of it in the company of Sitwell and Mavis. At first Fiona had been jealous, then worried but as the days passed, she'd come to realize she didn't miss his company very much. She could scarcely remember the last time they'd made love, and that especially should have alerted her that a sea change had crept into the relationship she'd once cherished.

"Morning, Irish."

Fiona smiled and waited a bit for Henley to join her. She'd found Henley was a morning person, too. Most everyone else was still asleep this early but she enjoyed his company. Half the time they just strolled in companionable silence, but over the weeks, they'd come to know quite a bit about each other and she liked him a great deal. She'd been very intimidated by him the first night they met but she'd found he was an easy man to trust, just like their employer. It was nice to have someone to spend time with and just talk about anything, the way she and James used to be able to do.

They both loved the river, especially in the cool of the morning. A gentle breeze, mostly from the movement of the boat itself, wafted through her dark curls and felt good on her face. It smelled of green growing life, earth and the wild slightly pungent smell that was the Mississippi.

They would arrive in Greenville, one of the larger towns on the river, this afternoon. Tomorrow night they were putting on Sheridan's "A School for Scandal" and it was a new one for Fiona. She played Maria, the young ward of the village squire Sir Peter Teazle and Julius had cast Jonathan Hargreaves in that role, while James played the young Charles, Maria's love interest. Mavis had been cast as the villainous Lady Sneerwell, and Fiona could hardly stop herself from giggling every time she looked at Mavis's face in rehearsals. That Mavis wasn't thrilled about her role was putting it mildly but it suited her very well indeed. Sometimes Fiona thought Julius was tormenting the actress on purpose.

For her part, Mavis had taken to openly flirting with James, which Fiona thought was a way to get back at her and James seemed to be enjoying it, his ego inflated. The entire farce was beginning to irk Fiona. This morning, more annoyed than usual, she mentioned it to Henley, who laughed outright.

"Christ, Irish, can you imagine any man with eyes in his head taking up with her when he could have you? Don't be ridiculous."

Fiona glanced up at him, startled for a second and then snorted. "Ha. Mavis is glamorous even if she's a bit raddled and sometimes I think James misses his former dissolute life. I think he liked being a bad boy. Men are fickle creatures, Henley, I've discovered that much. It's sad watching the old cow mooning over him." She glanced over at his face and the giveaway of a quirk on the side of his mouth made her stamp her foot in exasperation.

"Stop that."

Henley looked down at her, brown eyes perfectly innocent. "Stop what?"

"I saw that smirk."

"I wasn't smirking, I just found your description of Mavis as 'raddled' amusing, and accurate, of course. I'm sure she'd prefer 'woman of the world' but I think your description is more apt for the old . . .woman. I've found it's not really the age, it's the experience that tells." He tried very hard to keep a straight face but once Fiona grinned at him, he chuckled.

"Mother of God, you're a tough one, Henley," Fiona said, nudging him in the ribs with her elbow, which made him miss a step. "Let's get a cinnamon roll, what do you say?"

He rolled his eyes but took her elbow and steered her towards the restaurant. "Maybe it'll sweeten your disposition but I rather doubt it."

Fiona shrugged. He was right, as Henley usually was. There was no point in worrying about Mavis, James or any of that. She was actually quite happy floating down this wonderful river, acting and receiving applause each time she did, and maybe for the first time in her life, feeling truly secure, thanks to Julius and the man beside her. It was a long way from Ballyowen or New York.

* * *

THEY PLAYED two nights in Greenville, but the "School for Scandal" wasn't as well received as Julius had hoped. The morning after the second performance they were still docked there, and Julius, at lunch where everyone was in attendance, made an announcement.

"People, we're going to be here for a couple of days but no more performances. We're at a halfway point before we dock in New Orleans and there's a great deal to come when we leave here. Take this time to relax, rejuvenate and," he smiled, "rehearse of course, there's always that. We'll be stopping in Vicksburg next and "As You Like It" will be our main play, as well as the usual accompaniments. So far, this has been a magnificent voyage and I'm terribly proud of all of you. This has been a transition that all of you have weathered famously and you've performed at the peak of your quite formidable skills for me and all our audiences." He bowed to the assembled company. "You deserve a well-earned respite."

Everyone applauded, grateful for the break. Fiona glanced at James, who was still hung-over as usual these days but he didn't seem very surprised or even interested in what Julius had to say.

"Fine with me," James said, finishing off his brandy. "I could use some time to myself." He smiled brightly at her. "From the stage, I mean, darling." He glanced around the room. "I think I'll go play some cards. I'm sure you can amuse yourself for the rest of the afternoon?"

Fiona's heart sank. He'd been gambling a lot the last few weeks and she didn't think he was winning. She needed to check on how low their funds were, something she'd been remiss at, not really wanting to think he'd go behind her back. Still, she was beginning to wonder. Cash they had equal access to, but she'd still kept the Lowell's jewels hidden. After all, she thought, she'd earned it, while James had been the one that needed rescuing. She tried to not let those thoughts surface often, but right now, they were surfacing as much as she tried to tamp them down. What bothered her more at this moment and had for some time now, was that she didn't trust him anymore. Loved him, yes, but trusting him was becoming difficult, given his behavior lately. He was subtly turning into a person she hardly knew. The drinking, the gambling, the nonsense with Mavis and who knew who else was becoming tedious.

She wondered why they were stopping in Greenville, of all places. She wanted to talk to Julius, or at least Henley, who probably knew the answer. Greenville wasn't exactly a metropolis or a place they'd load on supplies, but then, what did she know? She pushed back her chair and gathered her skirts.

"Have a lovely afternoon, James," she said, kissing him on his cheek. "I'm going to take a nap."

"Excellent plan, my love," he said, smiling at her. "You need to take some time for yourself too. This damnable river can be tedious. I'll see you at dinner, or thereabouts."

Not likely, considering your behavior lately, she thought, but walked out onto the deck. It was warm and there was little breeze. She looked over at the town and thought about what Henley had told her about Greenville.

Greenville had been razed to the ground during the American civil war. Every building, down to the foundations, had burned. The inhabitants of the town had taken refuge on surrounding farms and plantations all of which had found themselves under the threat of the same fate, but as the army had marched on to Vicksburg, they'd been spared. Greenville had been rebuilt after the war, the entire town a monument to courage and tenacity.

Fiona couldn't help but think of the Irish towns and villages destroyed by the famine and the brutal hand of the English landlords, most of whom had not had the determination or even the scant resources and warmer weather of the southerners who had faced the same disaster. She was curious about the people who lived in this place. America seemed to instill a heart in people that spoke to her, that called somehow to who she was, a woman seeking a better life, or at least a land that gave inspiration and hope to anyone that did. For her, that had been true, along with a great deal of luck and, yes, the willingness to do the hard tasks that most would not. She was under no illusions about that.

There were three wagons being loaded at the wharf below from the storerooms on the bottom deck. Curious, she went down the stairs and found Julius and Captain Abel Hamilton, dressed not in his uniform, but a linen shirt and pants, overseeing the process.

"Good morning," she said softly, coming up behind them. "Looks like a busy one."

Julius turned swiftly. "Ah, Fiona. Good morning to you, my dear. Yes, we are unloading supplies for Captain Hamilton." He didn't elaborate but he didn't ask her to leave, either, so Fiona continued to stand nearby and watch.

There were a great deal of supplies, and she couldn't help but wonder why a riverboat captain would need them. Henley came down the stairs a few minutes later and his eyes flicked to Fiona but he passed her by, and spoke with Julius. She couldn't hear most of the conversation but a couple of words, "plantation" and "trouble" filtered through and she couldn't contain herself, sidling closer.

"Gentlemen." She smiled. "I know this is none of my business, but I'm curious and if I may be of assistance, I'd be delighted. If you'd rather I went back to my own pursuits, I can surely understand. And, I saw nothing." She tried to look naive and even batted her eyes a little.

Julius laughed and Henley rolled his eyes, while Hamilton just stared at her.

"Irish, curiosity killed the cat," Henley said. "Your call, Julius. She's not quite the innocent she makes out."

"Oh, I know that quite well," Julius smiled but his gaze was appraising and Fiona knew right then and there that Julius knew exactly what she'd done in New York, as much as she'd tried to gloss over any details or let James bear the brunt of their actions. He couldn't know, but somehow he did. Her heart beat a little faster. Ah well, she thought, what's done is done.

"Up for an excursion, Fiona?"

"What?" She saw Hamilton turn away, a small smile on his usually stoic face.

"We're taking a little trip to Mr. Hamilton's plantation. You might enjoy it, and I think it might be a welcome diversion for the more curious." He whispered something to one of the deckhands and the man scampered off. "We'll get you a proper hat. Can't have the sun ruining that lovely Irish complexion, can we?"

Mr. Hamilton had a plantation? Fiona's mind was whirling but she stood mutely and within a minute, the deckhand came back and handed her a large brimmed straw hat, replete with white satin ribbons. She put it on and it fit perfectly. Julius smiled and offered her a hand up into the nearest wagon, loaded to the brim. Henley joined her on the seat and flicked the reins as Julius waved. They were off and she had no idea where they were going. All she knew was that at this moment, wherever it was, she very much wanted to go. Curiosity wouldn't kill this cat and with Henley beside her, she was secure enough for any "excursion" whatsoever and there was no one to gainsay her. She was quite sure James would be otherwise occupied and once again, as was happening often lately, she didn't really care.

CHAPTER 23

Rather than pepper Henley with questions she didn't think he'd answer, Fiona sat back on the wagon seat and enjoyed the ride. Well, as much as she could. The seat was hard and the road was bumpy and before they'd gone out of sight of the Queen of Dreams she wished she had a pillow. She glanced over at Henley who smiled serenely back at her and didn't seem to have the same problem. Ah well, then. Two could play this game.

It really was a lovely day, cloudless blue sky, which made her grateful for the hat, and she studied the town they were passing through. Greenville was a pretty little town, all the buildings new, the businesses prosperous, the streets clean and orderly with people going about their business on this fine morning. As they passed into the countryside, the trees soared over the narrow road, birdsong rampant in the green dappled sunshine, the air fragrant with the smell of growing things. It was warm, but the slight breeze of their travel made her comfortable enough.

"How far are we going?"

"About another eight miles," Henley answered. "We're going to Abel's plantation, Heart's Ease."

Fiona looked at him. "Nice name, that. So Abel has a plantation. He's certainly a man of many talents, isn't he?"

Henley grinned. "Oh, yes. You shouldn't be surprised. Julius has a way of finding people that are, as I'm sure you've noticed by now, Fiona."

She didn't bother to respond to that and the miles passed in silence until they came to a set of iron gates set into two granite pillars. They were open and Henley drove through, down a long drive lined with live oaks, pulling up beside a large white-columned house. A slim woman dressed in white, her hair caught up in a red turban atop her head, stood on the portico and Henley put on the brake, jumping down and striding up to her. She embraced him, her dark face lit with pleasure, and he gestured to Fiona to join them.

She jumped down from the wagon and up the steps, where Henley caught her arm, helping her up the last one. Better late than never, Fiona thought, and turned her attention to the woman.

"Fiona, this is Amaro Hamilton, Abel's wife," Henley said. "Amaro, this is a friend of ours from the boat who's come along today."

Amaro's lovely face lit with a smile and her voice was soft and welcoming. "Pleased to meet you, Fiona," she said, and held out her hand, which Fiona took in hers. "Any friend of Julius's is always welcome here."

It wasn't just her soft warm hand, but the woman herself that enchanted Fiona. She was regal and comforting at the same time, her dark eyes reflecting kindness and compassion. Fiona dropped her hand with reluctance.

"Come in, come in," Amaro said. "I've sweet tea and lemonade waitin'. How far behind are the others?"

"Not far," Henley said. "We had no trouble, especially with

Missy here." He glanced at Fiona and smiled. "How are things here?"

Amaro led the way into the house, through a long hallway and into a high-ceilinged parlor where pitchers of drinks were set out with glasses and plates of cookies. "It's been real quiet for some time now." She smiled ruefully. "Maybe it's calmin' down now, but we always remain cautious."

Fiona was horribly curious, but she said nothing, instead taking in her surroundings. The house, both inside and out, was beautiful, the epitome of southern charm and grace she'd heard so much about. How had it come to belong to the Hamiltons, she wondered, knowing the little she did about the terrible civil war that had rent the United States. She had a feeling those questions were about to be answered without her even asking.

They sat on the comfortable sofas, drinks in their hands.

"Fiona's from Ireland, Amaro," Henley said, settling back on the cushions. "She's new to these shores, but learning about America and she's a very fast study, I've found. Tell her about Heart's Ease, would you? I think she'd like to hear it."

Fiona drank off half her lemonade and rested the frosty glass in her hand. "I would, please, if you'd like to tell me," she said, locking eyes with the woman across from her. She sensed this was going to be story that had more than few rough spots, perhaps similar to her own. Perhaps Amaro did too, the woman's eyes assessing Fiona a moment longer before she nodded. Then she told her tale.

When the Civil War broke out, Amaro was a child, a slave on this very plantation, then called Stanford Hall, her mother a cook for the Stanfords, the white planter and his family who owned them. Stanford enlisted in the Confederate Army, a colonel, along with his three sons. His wife Amy, a cruel woman, was left to run the estate and she did so with relentless enthusiasm for a time, especially with a whip, sometimes in her own hand. Abel was the son of one of the maids, and put to work in the fields along with Amaro and a host of other children, as was the custom. By 1863, the male Stanfords had all died in battle and Amy was an embittered woman, made even more cruel by what she saw as injustice to her family, taking out her hate and anger upon anyone she could, frequently children and the women in her household. One night she beat Amaro's mother to death with a skillet and Amaro hid in the slave quarters, with Abel and his mother, who had fled the big house too.

The Union Army burned Greenville to the ground and the town's inhabitants fled to the plantations, except for Stanford's. Amy's reputation had spread and no one wanted to take refuge with a madwoman. When Amy came for Amaro, Abel's father killed her with a machete, but not before she'd shot him. They buried both of them in the fields and not one person ever testified to Amy Stanford's fate, either to the Army, who spared the plantation and its buildings, or to any other citizen of the town. She wasn't a person who would be mourned. The former slaves drifted off here and there and the place was abandoned to the kudzu vines and the forlorn cotton plants which never again were harvested by anyone.

Abel and Amaro made their way to New Orleans and worked in a restaurant there, the famous L'Occitane, where one night they met Julius DeMonte, a frequent visitor. They had saved all the money they could, and their admittedly unrealistic dream was to return to Greenville and rebuild Stanford Hall, a house of horror, into a place in defiance of its past, where former slaves could make a life, a cooperative effort where everyone had a voice, a job, and a share of the profits.

Julius liked them, and he liked their idea. He acted as their agent, and between them, they bought the abandoned plantation for little more than the back taxes. The dream flourished and became reality, through enormous hard work. Many of the former slaves returned to build a life of independence and hope at Heart's Ease. It wasn't easy and there were many days when Amaro and Abel wondered if it would ever work. Once the plantation was on a firm footing, Abel had apprenticed himself to a riverboat captain, his desire for navigating the river a lifelong dream as much as the need for an income for Heart's Ease.

Amaro laughed softly at this part. "That man, I swear, he was born with wet feet and I just don't know where he got it from. He loves that ole river like nobody I ever saw. Just like I love this land beneath my feet right here. He's a mix of the two of us and our loves, that Abel. I'm hopin' one day he'll just land right here and sit on that porch with a whiskey but it ain't happened yet. If nothin' else," she patted her belly under the starched white apron, "this one finally might keep him around a l'l more." She sat back and sipped her tea. "We're some of the lucky ones, and God knows I thank him for that."

Fiona stood up and put her lemonade on the table. She went to Amaro and kneeling down, embraced her where she sat. Amaro patted her head and rose up, holding Fiona in her arms. "You got a story too, girl, I know that. Pretty and sweet as you are now, that ain't always been the case, I can tell."

Fiona found it difficult to speak. This woman had been through hell and come out the other side and she knew that her own journey was yet to be finished. She stepped back and dried the tears on her cheeks. She knew Henley was watching her closely and she composed herself and sat back down on the sofa beside him.

"Thank you, Amaro," she said. "I appreciate you trusting me. You're quite remarkable, as is your husband."

Henley coughed just as they heard the unmistakable sound of wagons pulling up outside. Amaro jumped up and ran to the hallway and Fiona turned to Henley before he could follow her out, her hand on his arm.

"It's not over for them, is it?" she said. "The people around here aren't as accepting as they could be, are they? That's why you let me come with you. Proper white Southern lady, or something of the sort."

He nodded. "True, as usual, Irish. Be assured you were in little danger, however."

"I never thought I was," Fiona said, staring into his eyes. "Else I wouldn't have ever gotten into that wagon, hat or no damn hat. Then again, Henley, it's not like that pistol on your hip is a secret, although the one in my bag might be."

He grinned. "Not to me." He took her hand and they went to the porch to greet Julius, Abel and the others.

The wagons were unloaded and Fiona was given a tour of the property, which was impressive, while Julius and Abel rode out into the fields, talking crops, rotations, harvests and money matters before they even left the house. She still couldn't quite put together Julius's involvement here, but it wasn't really any of her business. The man seemed to have many interests, many more than the theater.

She helped Amaro in the kitchens in spite of her protests and they sat down to a magnificent meal: baked ham, sweet potatoes, greens and the most heavenly biscuits, drowned in butter and honey. Andre couldn't have done better. Dinner was a merry affair, the wine and whiskey flowed freely and Fiona never turned down a refill, comfortable in her surroundings and with the company she kept.

After dinner, they sat out on the porch as darkness fell, sipping brandy and watching the fireflies swoop around the lawn. They would be spending the night here and going back in the morning, she'd learned. She wondered what James was getting up to. Likely nothing she'd want to know about, she thought, but he was his own man and had made his own decisions long before he'd met her.

"So it's been quiet?" Julius said.

"As Amaro says," Abel returned and Amaro nodded.

"Yes, for now. I think the worst is over. They's always goin' be some who don't care for what we've done here, but the law's on our side and they know it."

Julius shook his head. "My dear, that's not always the guide to go by. People can be rotten, as we all know, law or no law. You'll just have to keep your guard up, as you always have."

"I know that," Amaro said. "The men here know that, and everyone else. We ain't some babes in the woods, you know."

Julius sighed. "I do. But that doesn't stop me from being concerned. Once we dock in New Orleans, Abel will be back on his way upriver to you, and we'll be back to business as usual. We both wanted him to be the captain for the initial voyage of the Queen of Dreams, but I don't want to worry about you all in the meantime."

Abel's baritone voice was deep and reassuring. "We'll be fine, Julius. I can't think of anything else. This woman," he put his arm around Amaro, "and all the people here are invested and will keep things safe. I have no doubts." He strolled down the portico a ways. "After all the supplies we delivered today especially, I think we're set. We take care of what's ours, and that's the way it is."

At that point, Fiona knew for sure they hadn't been just delivering flour and feed. She'd been invited along as cover, she suspected. The wooden boxes on the wagon she and Henley drove were full of guns, as she'd surmised from the outset. She hoped fervently they wouldn't be needed, but she was glad they'd arrived safely.

It was quiet on the porch for a time. Fiona tossed back her brandy. She hadn't been going to say anything, since she was about as out of her element as she could be, but she cared about these people, and she was grateful Julius and Henley had trusted her enough to come to this wonderful place built on hope and raw courage. It struck a chord in her, one she didn't know she'd had until hearing Amaro's story this afternoon. The Irish and these particular Americans had a lot in common. Repression was always the same, no matter the land where it surfaced.

"Thank you all for bringing me along today," she said. "I admire what you've done here, so very much, and I only wish my more of own people had displayed the courage you have. Don't be afraid to use any method you have to defend your rights and property. Julius is right, the law doesn't always defend the righteous, I learned that in Ireland. You have to do that for yourselves and you did."

Embarrassed by her outburst, Fiona sat down hurriedly, wishing she hadn't opened her mouth among these people who clearly knew much more about this situation than she did.

"Thank you, Fiona," Abel said and reached over and touched her hand. "I was not certain about you but Julius assured me you were to be trusted. I have no doubts anymore that he was right, as he usually is."

Julius laughed and the mood lightened. "It's a curse, the gypsies always said it." He finished his brandy and Amaro left to bring more, smiling at him. "I know people. And, Fiona?" She could see the gleam in his eyes even in the dim light. "I know you."

"I believe you do, Julius," she said. "I'm thinking the gypsies are always right." He nodded, not breaking his gaze. Fiona found she didn't mind.

Amaro re-appeared with the bottle, and everyone's glass was refilled.

"To Heart's Ease, and good friends," Abel said and everyone echoed him, raising their glasses in the sultry fragrant air, the gently cooing of mourning doves echoing in the still night.

CHAPTER 24

They left after an early breakfast the next morning, the air still cool but Fiona knew that wouldn't be true for long. This time, she rode with Julius, while Henley and Abel took the first wagon, and two deckhands from the boat the second, and leaving a good distance between them to lessen the dust from the road. They kept a companionable silence as they traveled under the canopy of trees but after a mile or so, she turned to Julius.

"Why?"

He'd tied his hair back and wore a large straw hat, his white linen shirt spotless, looking the epitome of the Southern gentleman planter. Julius was good at roles. Now he smiled, keeping his eyes on the road. "Why what, Fiona?"

She snorted. "It's your mission in life to help people like a bloomin' saint, then?"

"Well, yes, I suppose it is. Of course, I'm very good at helping myself as well, my dear. If I wasn't, I'd not be able to do much for anyone else, would I?" He chuckled. "And you know perfectly well I'm no saint, or have you forgotten the St. John sisters?"

Fiona's cheeks reddened in spite of herself. "No I've not forgotten, but that's not what I meant and you know it."

"I put a couple of those marvelous peach muffins in that sack at your feet, Fiona," he said. "Would you hand me one, please? I do love Amaro's cooking."

She fished out a muffin and handed it to him, which he took, deftly putting both reins in his left hand and taking a large bite.

"Ah, delightful." He glanced over at her. "Now where were we? Oh, yes, the saint part. Hmm. Are you up for a tale, Fiona? We've miles to go, after all."

"Yes," she said, biting back the rest of her words. She'd been waiting for this since Chicago.

"Well, then, you shall have it. My family name is Cargill, and my father is the Duke of Sandhurst, a rather cruel and uncaring man, out of Essex. I believe he even owns a couple of estates in Ireland, and I'm sure your people aren't making out any better than the English ones that he holds sway over.

"I'm the fourth son, and that's not an auspicious thing to be. The first son inherits the estate, the second goes for a soldier, the third becomes a vicar, and number four, namely me, is generally up to no good. I filled that role perfectly. By the time I was seventeen, my reputation was notorious, my habits worse and I'd whored and gambled my way to heights unknown to men of thirty." He chewed reflectively on another piece of muffin.

"Not to say it wasn't a learning experience, since I even went on the stage and found I had a flair for the dramatic. It may have even saved me at the time. Finally, I had complications with the royal family and my father made me an offer. Take a large sum of money and disappear. I took him up on the offer and came to America, first New York, then New Orleans, and Chicago." He laughed. "Land of opportunity and indeed, it was."

Fiona took a muffin herself. They were delicious. "For a poor lass from Ireland, that's quite a tale, Julius. I think there's a great deal more. You were a dissolute rake, from the sound of it. So how did you become a person who took care of others, or even cared about them?"

Julius glanced at her. "Right to the point, eh Fiona? Truly, it wasn't much of a leap. One of the reasons I absconded to London at fifteen was the way my father treated not only me, but anyone who was less powerful than him, which included damn near anyone but the king himself. It made me heartsick and for a time I only wanted to escape and drown my feelings. A few years later, it became something else. Making up for him, making up for all the people damaged by those who hurt others or only cared for themselves. If I have to break a few laws here and there, I don't live by the laws created to keep men like that in power, in America or England. I live only by the law of fairness and justice and I've fashioned my life to make sure I can keep doing that." He laughed and it wasn't mirthful, but harsh. "Every day I think of how much my father would hate what I do, and I know I'm doing exactly the right thing."

Fiona finished her muffin in silence, and fed the last crumbs to the birds as they passed. She knew there was a history but she hadn't quite expected this. She felt like a bit of an ass. Perhaps a mile passed before she worked up the courage to respond to him.

"Thank you," she said, and put her hand on his arm. "And thank you for taking us in. I understand a lot of things better now. And then there's the South, Heart's Ease and all of it, the way things are. The war's over and people are free, but I don't think the hatred ends, does it?"

Julius sighed. "No, it does not. As Amaro said, they are constantly vigilant and it's little different all over the South. Every day new repressive laws are being passed that eat away their rights and every day somewhere black people are being murdered while the law turns a blind eye. I do what I can, as do others, but it's a finger in the crumbling dyke against a flood of ignorance and hate. You're just beginning to understand and I think you might relate more than others would."

He patted her hand. "Now, perhaps you'll favor me with the truth about yourself, if you are of a mind. We've lots of time and truly, I am curious."

And so she did, from St. Hilda's, Sean Dooley, the baby, Cork, the Prescotts, Augustin Daly, the truth about what she'd done to the Lowells and even the encounter with Sean in Chicago. She'd never told anyone all of it before.

Julius never said a word as the words tumbled out of her mouth as though she had no control over them. The miles passed and she felt as though she'd been talking to a mythical kindly priest who understood her sins and forgave them, not that she'd ever known one. He handed her a linen handkerchief at one point and she realized her cheeks were wet with tears, but he never said a word until he pulled the wagon over on the side of the road and put his arm around her.

"It's all right, Fiona."

"No, it's not. I'm a murderess although I never meant to be one. You'll likely leave me here by the side of the road with no regrets."

Julius laughed softly. "Girl, I'm not leaving you anywhere. I saw it all in you from the first. You're a survivor and you've done what you had to do because you choose to live. Some people just need killing, so don't ever think badly of yourself for doing what you had to do. You were a child that hardened into steel and now a woman who's used that strength. You're a wonder is what you are."

Fiona sat back on the seat and looked into Julius's eyes. He stared back at her. "The thing is, I don't feel guilty. I'd do it again, all of it. That worries me."

He sighed. "It shouldn't. You're young, Fiona. Your life is a long road. Bad people and bad things may happen again. Take what you've learned and refine it. Never regret doing what you must or what's right."

He put his hands on her shoulders and turned her to him. "You're eighteen years old and you've lived and learned in those scant years more than most people will ever experience. Because you're clever, bright and determined, you've weathered those experiences. I saw it in you the first night I spoke to you.

"James, now, is a charming rogue and yes, I knew he was Byron's grandson but it was you I was interested in. I knew it was you that had dispatched my old enemies, not him. It's not in him, even to defend his life, or yours. I appreciate your honesty today and I owe you. I had laid plans for the Lowells but you saved me the trouble. Getting you away from Chicago was my pleasure." He picked up the reins. "We will say no more about that, ever, as I'm sure you'll agree."

He pulled the horses back onto the road and Fiona felt as though an anvil had been lifted from her shoulders, and her mind. Julius DeMonte, whether he liked or not, was a saint to her.

A few miles away from Greenville, Julius turned to her. "I think I may have made a mistake or two, Fiona."

"Oh?" Fear surged through her. Surely he didn't mean her.

"Mavis."

"Ah, yes. She is a wrong one, that harridan." She should've had more faith.

He laughed. "We've suspected Mavis may have some, shall we say sinister motives for joining us and so we sort of arranged for her to do so. Charlie Sitwell is a wrong one as well. Hargreaves, well, he's just a poor soul she dragged along. Now, she's gotten James involved, I fear."

Fiona sighed. "James makes poor decisions sometimes. Well, you know that now."

Julius nodded. "I know you love him, Fiona, but since we've shared so much today, I must caution you." He glanced over at her. "I'm not certain he's the same man who left Chicago. He's been gambling and drinking a great deal, maybe worse, with Sitwell and Mavis. Those two are the worst sort of opportunists. We're watching them closely."

She knew all too well that James was falling back into habits he'd only mentioned as being in his history and she wasn't sure what to do about it. The very worst part of it was she wasn't sure she had the same feelings about James she'd had before and she didn't know if she wanted to do anything about it at all, except walk away.

After two days of revelation, returning to their shared stateroom was the last thing she wanted to do. Instead, she put her arm around Julius's shoulders and kissed his cheek.

"Thank you for everything," she said. "I'll keep my eye on James. The showboat must go on, even with Mavis. We'll work it out, if you let me be a part of that."

"Of course I will, Fiona."

Henley and Abel were waiting on the dock in front of the Queen of Dreams to greet them. Fiona smiled at Julius, hopped down and went up the gangway. For now, the boat looked like the home she'd never really had and she was yearning to feel the river flowing under her feet. It felt like a vein of life pulsing through her and she'd come to love it.

* * *

"Where the hell have you been, Fiona?" James's face was angry, red blotches marring his handsome cheeks the second she walked into their stateroom. "I've been frantic with worry and none of these people have provided me with any answers. For all I knew, you fell into the river and drowned."

With his hands on his hips, he looked like a lord demanding answers from a servant, even though his clothes were rumpled and whiskers sprouted on his usually clean-shaven face. His eyes were glassy and though he reeked of bourbon she thought there could be something more. She'd suspected laudanum for some time.

"I'm fine, although you haven't asked that," Fiona said. "I went with Julius on a delivery." She didn't want to volunteer any more information, no matter his concern, which didn't strike her as compassionate, but accusatory. "There wasn't time to inform you, James. I'm sorry, but I did ask Dahlia, one of the maids, to let you know I went with Julius. Did you not see her?"

James sneered. "One of the maids? They're all bloody wogs, Fiona. I don't talk to those pickaninnies." He rolled his eyes. "Now that I think of it, one of them kept pestering me while I was playing cards with Charlie but I shooed her off. No matter. What were you thinking?"

Fiona couldn't believe her ears. All this time she'd known James she'd never heard this sort of nonsense come out of his mouth, but then she supposed they'd never really interacted continually with any people of color until they'd come to St. Louis. She was appalled, especially after the last two days. She wondered if she'd ever really known him at all.

"Sorry," she said again, but it wasn't really meant for James right now as much as it was her own inability to see past his charming façade. All she really wanted was to not listen to him anymore. She was weary from the long ride in the sun and flung herself down on the bed. Her eye landed on her trunks beside the wall, her clothes flung here and there. She was quite sure that wasn't how she'd left them yesterday.

"Were you looking for something, James?"

He stood beside the bed, glowering in his self-righteous anger and her question seemed to catch him off guard. "What?"

"Why are my clothes scattered everywhere?"

He coughed, buying time, and sat down beside her on the bed. "You have no idea how happy I am to see you, darling." He kissed her on the cheek and then seemed to remember her question. "As to that," he gestured at her heaps of clothing, "the thing is, Fiona, I needed some money."

"Why?" She already knew the answer.

"It's only temporary, of course, but I seem to have found myself a bit short lately. A spot of bad luck, as it were. Charlie's been quite accommodating but there it is."

"How much did you take?"

He looked away. "We get paid at the end of the week, as always, so it's all right. Besides I'm sure you stole Victoria Lowell's jewelry, Fiona, and it's past time you shared that with me. You've dragged that carpetbag around whenever we relocate and it then it mysteriously disappears. I'm not an idiot, you know and I highly doubt that's your makeup and toiletries in there the way you treasure it. If you love me, you'll support my needs and now I'll need some of your precious stash because I do owe a bit more."

She sat up. "You lost all the money?"

"Well, yes." He wouldn't look her in the eye.

Fiona sat up. The nasty little weasel. She couldn't believe what she was hearing. "I do not have anybody's jewels stashed away anywhere, James, so likely you are an idiot. More to the point, there was three thousand dollars, our entire fortune, in that trunk the last time I checked. Have you lost your bloody stupid mind?"

He hit her then, backhanded, just the way Sean Dooley used to do it and it felt just the same, as though she'd never left that cold broken-down cottage in Ballyowen years ago. It hurt, but the real pain came from inside her, surging up like a black wave. She didn't have a poker to hand, so she threw herself at him like a banshee, fists flying recklessly but landing at least one good punch right on his nose, gleeful when she heard the bone break and his scream.

"You bitch!" He came roaring back at her, shoving her hard

against the wardrobe, the blood from his broken nose splattering over the quilt and her dress.

Fiona couldn't seem to draw a breath and he loomed over her, his fist ready to descend.

"Oh no, you don't, boyo," Henley said, dragging James away from her by his hair. "We don't beat ladies where I come from."

He threw James against the wall like a soiled napkin and came over to Fiona. "Are you hurt?"

She shook her head. "No permanent damage, I'm thinking. Not the first time, but sure the first time in a while. Nothing a little stage makeup won't fix."

Henley looked dubious at that but turned his attention back to James, who was staggering to his feet.

"Get your things, man. You won't be staying here."

James glared at him, mopping the blood from his nose with a lace handkerchief. "Of course I will, she's my wife."

"No," Fiona said quietly. "I'm not. Get out, you feckless bastard. Get your clothes and move into Mavis's room. I doubt you'll be a stranger to the place."

Henley stood motionlesss, looking between the two of them and Fiona could've sworn there was a tiny quirk at the side of his mouth.

James glanced cautiously over at Henley and bent to his trunk, shoving in clothes and toiletries, all the while glaring at Fiona. "You'll be sorry for this, Fiona. After all, I know quite a lot about you, in case you've forgotten. You're far from the innocent you pretend to be, you little whore. You'll be begging for me to take you back after a day. I've made you who you are and don't ever forget that."

At those words, Fiona wished again she had that poker in her hand. "You sniveling coward, get out of here before I lose my temper completely."

Henley laughed and looking at his face, James finally came to realize he was on very shaky ground. He dragged his trunk out the door and Henley kicked it shut behind him.

Henley poured some water into the basin and wet a cloth. He handed it to Fiona, who sat back down on the bed and gratefully patted the cool wet cloth on her face. It was going to bruise, and she was no stranger to just how long it would take to disappear.

"Quite a day or so, eh, Irish?"

"As James would say, 'I daresay, what?'" Fiona looked up at him and couldn't help but laugh. "Actually, I'm relieved it happened because at least he's gone and that's been brewing for a while. Clean break, more or less. Thanks for the help, Henley."

"Ah, no need, girl. I heard the commotion and thought I'd step in to be sure you were all right." He laughed. "If you'd had a weapon, I think we'd be burying the bastard."

Fiona grimaced. "Well, not my weapon of choice, but actually I did, as you know quite well. But theft, cheating and being a racist ass don't deserve the death penalty so there you have it. 'Course had he come at me again, and if you hadn't come in when you did, I can't swear I'd have stuck with that opinion."

Henley gently pulled her to her feet. "Let's go see Andre and get some ice for that face. I also think you could use a brandy, maybe two. Join me?"

"Thank you, kind sir," Fiona said. "Let's to it before my face gets any more swollen. They could even blame you. They're a gossipy lot on this boat. Like being back in the village square on market day, truly." She grinned at him and found that it hurt.

"Cheeky wench." Henley pulled the door shut behind them.

CHAPTER 25

She woke to the gentle movement of the boat, heading downriver once again. Slats of sunlight streamed through the blinds. She'd slept very late, something she usually never did. She closed her eyes and turned over on the pillow, wincing as her bruised cheek pressed on the soft down and the memories of the night before came flooding back. She glanced over at the door and was relieved to see the bolt was firmly drawn.

She cried a little, then. For James and the life she'd imagined they'd have together. It was never going to be now and she felt nothing for him, the betrayal had been so hurtful and so damning. The regret stemmed from her blind belief in him. *Girl,* she thought, *have you learned nothing in this life about trusting men and their promises?* Perhaps this time, a little voice said, you have.

Fiona turned over and stared at the ceiling. She had troubles, yes, but she thought for a time about Heart's Ease, and Greenville. Those people, both white and black, had known trouble. There was a difference between the two. Greenville had rebuilt what they had, with the same culture that had existed, but hopefully a little wiser than before. Heart's Ease had rebuilt what should have been, not what was, its reconstructors embuing their work with hope, justice and yes, dreams. It was impressive, far beyond what she'd expected when she'd set off on that wagon beside Henley three days ago.

As Julius was fond of saying, life takes many turns but what he meant, Fiona thought, was that people should learn from those turns and use that knowledge to further their own journeys. What was her dream, anyway? She felt like she'd been running from something for a long time, instead of stepping onto a road that would take her to what she wanted from her life. A serenity, perhaps, or at least a feeling of security long enough to decide how to achieve it.

She flung off the sheet and put her feet on the floor, scrunching her toes into the thick rug. What she wanted right now, aside from going down this river to New Orleans, was her money. Whatever else happened, she'd need it. That would go a long way to restoring her faith, certainly not in James, but in herself.

Maybe it was time she had a dream of her own. What she knew for sure was that a woman had to look out for herself in this world, and right now that was dream enough.

* * *

"OUR LITTLE IRISH colleen is going to wake up with a sore face and a bad temper this morning," Henley said, sipping his coffee. They were having breakfast in Julius's private stateroom, going over accounts and the events of the last few days. Fiona had become part of those events.

Julius smiled and took a bite of his omelet. "To be sure, the poor darling. But I can also guarantee you she's going to wake up with a head of steam for vengeance, not that I can blame her. Fiona is no cringing flower. She's going after Sitwell and her money, I assure you."

Henley sighed. "Julius, I may not be the best man for the job on this one."

Julius peered at him over the rim of his teacup. "Why is that?"

Henley looked out the window and Julius chuckled.

"You devil, you've fallen for her, haven't you?" He didn't wait for an answer. "You know, if I was a bit younger, I'd be vying for her myself. But, I think of her more as a daughter, damn me. She's a lovely thing and that spirit . . ."

"All right, yes, but I'm certainly not going to do anything about it except support her. This girl has been cruelly used but her wits never desert her," Henley said, his cheeks flushed. "I know she can be dangerous, but the strange thing is I rather like that, too."

"As do I," Julius said, popping a strawberry in his mouth. "The plan was to draw out Mavis and Sitwell, as well as using anyone that might fall into their net. It's rather sad it was James, but not that unexpected."

I think Mavis and Sitwell's goal is two-pronged. To steal from us, of course, was always their main goal. But from what you overheard before you intervened last night, I think our foolish James has divulged, in his drunken ramblings and worry over his gambling debts, that he thinks Fiona has a stash of jewels which she's not been willing to share with him. With James's loose tongue, they've kept him drunk and given him laudanum, taking all his money and expecting he would cajole her out of anything more."

"They are going to find they bit off more than expected there," Henley said. He'd not much appetite, but he picked up a piece of bacon and chewed reflectively. "If Fiona has the Lowells' jewels. What do you think?"

Julius smiled. "I think she may have. She's told me a lot but left that out. She stole some money, she admitted, and I can't imagine her passing up the contents of the witch's jewelry box if it was nearby. Christ knows, she'd earned it." Julius leaned back in his chair. "I've had a long run at this, Henley, as you know, and I may have been too complacent. Too many people, too many cargoes, sometimes the odds just get higher and higher that somebody figures a least a part of things out.

"I wasn't sure what to do with Mavis and Sitwell until they made a move, and frankly, I didn't think that would happen until we were closer to New Orleans. I never expected they were just looking for the money in the Queen of Dreams safe, but figured they had bigger things in mind, like our suppliers. Which, frankly, was why I let them on board in the first place. I want to know what they know and how they discovered anything at all about my activities on the river and elsewhere. Now, on top of that, they're after more, if said items even exist." He refilled his coffee cup. "And there's Fiona, who's a wild card in more ways than one."

For over twenty years now, Julius DeMonte had been smuggling emeralds, spices and French brandy up the river from New Orleans, and guns and ammunition down it. He'd never meant to become a smuggler but the nature of the thing had appealed to him. Taxes and tariffs had always irked him, free soul that he was, and he thought of them as illegal burdens imposed by a government that used them as legal theft, benevolent as the American one generally was.

Besides, it was an excellent way to replenish the funds from his father that he'd started with but had delved into deeply. He loved the theater but in order to do it properly and assure that those talented souls who depended upon you were compensated well, ticket sales couldn't always be relied upon. But smuggling could, and it had proved to be fairly safe and very lucrative.

Before he knew it, Julius had built an empire, founded on compassion and a hatred of injustice. His love of theater and a way to move cargo had coalesced in the Queen of Dreams. Of course it was extravagant, but how wonderful this turn down the river had been and, under his direct supervision for a change.

Before they'd even left Chicago, he'd gotten word that Mavis and some confederates were nosing around, asking questions they shouldn't have even known to ask, and decided the best way to deal with her was to invite her into his world, the better to know what she was up to. He'd been waiting for her to show up at each port and she'd not disappointed. Keep your enemies close, was Julius's motto, until it was time to dispatch them, one way or another.

He looked up at his younger companion. Michael Henley had been working for him for ten years now, and Julius trusted him like a son. He was clever, trustworthy and ambitious, never a bad thing in Julius's mind. Henley had been invaluable. He'd kept his romantic liaisons discreet and never binding, from what Julius could discern. An interest in Fiona was an unexpected twist, but he was curious as to how this might develop. Fiona was a lot like Henley, to Julius's mind: clever and he suspected, with bigger aspirations than even she knew.

Henley put down his napkin, and Julius could tell he wasn't at peace with the turn of events. He wasn't worried. But he could tell Henley was.

"If they knew Fiona a bit better, they'd be wise to be a bit wary, is what I think. This could be an interesting day."

Julius put his hand on Henley's shoulder as he stood up and turned for the door. "It's going to be fine, Henley. It'll all be sorted. I'm thinking we should put James Gordon ashore at Natchez. What do you think?"

Henley shrugged. "That way he'd be able to go up the Trace or catch another boat going south, his choice. On the other hand, he could be useful in determining what Mavis is up to. If our lovely Fiona doesn't accost any of them."

"I'll think on it," Julius said. "Try and keep Fiona out of

trouble for a few days, if you can. I was planning to stop at Vicksburg, but I think we'll pass it by and spend more time in Natchez, a better audience anyway. Such a genteel town, Natchez. I've always liked it there."

Henley snorted. "And the Widow McClain, as I recall."

Julius had the grace to look pained. "Oh dear, my sins have come full circle. Don't mention this to the St. John sisters, please. Cicely McClain is a treasure."

Henley shook his head. "It's a good thing you have just as good a head for business as you do for pleasure, Julius. Keeps you balanced and me gainfully employed."

"Dear boy, it's an art, and one you should be grateful for."

"Oh, believe me, I am, as you know damn well," Henley said, and shut the door behind him, and he heard Julius chuckle as walked out onto the deck.

FIONA DRESSED CAREFULLY, even in the heat, because clothes gave her courage. She was a woman outfitted for battle, one she fully intended to win. She wore a suit of dark green twill, and she added a high-necked lace blouse under the tight-fitting jacket with flared sleeves. Her face was a colorful mess of blue and purple on the left side and she spent quite some time with stage makeup trying to cover it. From a seat in the audience, it might suffice, but up close it wasn't quite enough. She fluffed waves of hair over the worst of it. Not perfect but still, it would have to do.

It wasn't like the people she was looking for were unaware of what had happened the night before. Charlie Sitwell was a cheat, and she was quite certain Mavis was his helpmeet in his endeavors, fleecing the unwary when they sat down at his table. Gamblers were one thing, cheating people out of their money was another. Especially when it was hers. She put her feelings about James, good and bad, aside. If he hadn't been aware enough or so enticed with drink, lust or god knows what else, that he'd lost their stake, it was Mavis and Sitwell's fault, not only his. It had been planned, and she was going to get the money back, no matter what it took. The naive girl from Ballyowen was no more. She'd learned a great deal more than she could have ever anticipated on this voyage.

CHAPTER 26

Fiona stepped out onto the deck and locked her door. James undoubtedly still had a key and she'd have to get that back. She'd hidden the carpetbag with the jewelry under a board she'd pried up from the bottom of the wardrobe but with a prolonged search he'd likely find it. She'd wanted to put it in the safe but she found she didn't want to have it that far out of her control. Besides, she didn't trust anyone that much, even Julius.

It was silly, she knew that, but somehow she thought of that bag as her future, even though it was a hard-earned and unpleasant remnant of her past. Although every time she touched the bracelets, earrings and necklaces in their gold and silver settings, they fell through her fingers like cold hard nuggets of remorse. The rubies were the worst. She couldn't look at them and not think of the blood necklace she'd drawn on Victoria Lowell's throat. She shuddered involuntarily. What she'd done was over and she knew she'd do it again under the same circumstances. Besides, this was no time to think about the past. The present was more than enough to deal with today.

It took a moment for her eyes to adjust to the dimmer light

in the saloon after the bright sun on deck. The crystal chandeliers multiplied in the mirrors behind the bar lending the place an air of enchantment. Wafting cigar smoke and whiskey perfumed the air but it wasn't all that unpleasant. People stood here and there at the roulette wheel or leisurely playing blackjack or faro. She paused near the door for a moment and caught sight of Charlie Sitwell sitting at a table, shuffling cards. He was dressed flamboyantly as usual, his waistcoat embroidered with purple flowers. He was alone and she sighted in on him like a hawk, ignoring the other distractions in the room.

"Mr. Sitwell. May I have a moment of your time?"

Startled, he dropped a couple of cards and looked up at her. His eyes slid quickly from side to side as though looking for reinforcements but none came. He coughed.

"Good afternoon, Mrs. Gordon. What a surprise."

"It shouldn't be." She stared at him coldly. He seemed struck dumb, not even offering her a chair. She sighed and pulled out the one beside him and sat down, settling her skirts.

"What can I do for you?" He said, swallowing nervously. You should be unsettled, Fiona thought, you cheating rat.

"I understand that James has been doing some gambling with you, Mr. Sitwell," she said, "and it seems to have not gone terribly well for him."

Well, yes, Mrs. Gordon," Sitwell smirked, relaxing at last. "Lady Luck can be an elusive mistress, so they say."

"Unlike Mavis. She seems quite available indeed."

Sitwell blinked and coughed again. "I wouldn't know about that, Mrs. Gordon."

Fiona sat back in her chair and gazed at him. "I think you know a great deal, Mr. Sitwell. Don't hide your talents. Perhaps you should go on the stage yourself."

Sitwell barked out a little laugh but he didn't seem amused. "Perhaps, but I'm fairly content doing what I do."

"Which is what I wish to discuss," Fiona said. "Let me be

blunt. You have stolen three thousand dollars from me under the guise of honest gambling and I want it returned immediately."

Now Sitwell did laugh wholeheartedly, while Fiona stared at him. He patted her arm. "My dear, I think you're under some delusion. I've never sat at a table with you. I think this discussion is over."

Fiona brushed her sleeve where his hand had touched her as though she were dusting off gravedust. She surprised him and put her finger under his chin, pushing it up a bit and moved much closer, her face inches from his.

"Sitwell, this discussion is just getting started, I assure you. It will go well for you if you are civil. Now where were we? Oh yes, you owe me three thousand dollars. The money James lost to you is mine."

His face red, he shoved her hand away from his face and shoved his chair back a few inches. "You're out of your mind, girl. James is a bad gambler and that's not my fault. How do you think I make a living if not for people like him?"

Fiona smiled, her eyes and demeanor icily calm. Sitwell's face lost its ruddiness and instead began to pale. That particular smile of hers sometimes had that effect on people, Fiona knew and for the first time, he seemed to take her seriously.

"Let's quit playing around here," she said quietly. "James had help in losing that money, from Mavis and from you. I'm aware that gambling is a risky business but I think sometimes when a player is impaired by drink or drugs, say, it's ethical to stop him from playing. You know, in a just world with ethical people."

Sitwell opened his mouth and Fiona held up her hand. "I tell you what. Let's make a deal. James's foolishness is his own mistake, encouraged or not. I'll say nothing to Julius. Let's say I just want my half back. Fifteen hundred dollars. That sounds more than fair, doesn't it?"

For a few minutes, the only sound in the saloon was the

murmur of conversation from the few patrons and clink of glasses behind the bar.

"My dear," Sitwell said with a smarmy smile, his earlier unease dissipating. "I can see you're distressed but what you're suggesting is ridiculous. People play cards, people lose money. I'm not responsible, nor is Mavis. I suggest you counsel your husband and take out your displeasure on him."

Fiona gazed at him silently for a few seconds and Sitwell grew restless. He shuffled the deck of cards in his hands, the pasteboard images falling with a slight susurrus. "If you don't mind, madam, I've a living to make and you sitting here haranguing me is not contributing to that endeavor." He sat down the deck of cards. "And, James owes me quite a bit more, in case you'd like to pay up now."

Fiona stood up, ignoring his last remark and slid her chair back in. "Thank you for your time. As the nuns always told me, there's an easy way and there's a hard way and God bless the sinner who can't see the difference." She stared into his eyes and Sitwell squirmed a little in his chair, a bit unnerved. He broke her gaze and began to shuffle again.

Fiona walked slowly away, just as Mavis entered the saloon. Ostrich feathers bobbed from her hair, blue to match the bright satin dress she sported. She stopped and put a hand on Fiona's arm, her eyes warm and friendly.

"My dear, how fortunate it is I ran into you. We must talk. Poor James is completely distraught, and I must ask you to reconsider." Her face was nothing but sympathetic but it only made Fiona want to break her nose too. Instead she composed her face into a mask of innocence. They were actresses, after all.

"Is that so?" Her eyes wide.

"Oh, I cannot tell you," Mavis sighed. "He spent the night on the floor in my room, as a friend, completely respectable of course. He was devastated by your behavior and longs to make things right between you again. Please say you'll speak with him."

"How's his nose?"

"What?"

"Does it look horrible? I hope so," Fiona said. She leaned into Mavis's ear and whispered. "If you're not careful, Mavis, I'm going to give you a matching one. Tell another lie and my patience could snap. Voila! My fist to your face."

Mavis jerked away as though she'd been scalded. "You little bitch. You have no idea who you're dealing with. You're going to be sorry."

Fiona smiled. "I don't think so." She had the satisfaction of seeing Mavis's composure slip a bit before she turned on her heel and walked out the door into the sunshine.

There was no doubt anymore about what had occurred and what she had to do. Fiona took a deep breath and walked swiftly back to her stateroom.

Henley stood at the end of the deck and watched her unlock the door. He'd been standing by the bar and seen it all. He threw his cheroot into the river, sighed and strode towards Fiona's stateroom.

* * *

FIONA UNBUTTONED the suit jacket and flung it carelessly on the bed. She took a deep breath, glad to shed the confines of the stylish mode. The lace blouse with its high collar quickly followed and she stood in her silk shift, feeling immensely better. She really didn't mind the heat in the South, but today it was combined with the stifling feeling that she'd failed miserably in her goals and she had been eager to divest herself of anything that contributed to her frustration.

She splashed water on her face despite the makeup she applied so carefully in covering the bruises and stared at herself in the mirror. Black curls framed her face, and dark green eyes gazed back at her, nearly matching the color of the bruise blossoming underneath the heavy foundation. That the rest of her face was still creamy with rosy cheeks seemed an aberration. One was either evil or good, but she looked an unsettling combination of both.

"Nice." She said out loud and then laughed at her reflection. She'd had worse and she'd go on, as she always had. The knock at the door startled her and she turned towards it like it held an enemy, although it could be a friend. Still.

"Who is it?" She stood by the door and her voice was loud.

"It's Henley, Fiona. Let me in, please."

She sighed with relief and unbolted the door. Henley came in, promptly bolting the door again. Today, instead of usual black suit, he was in perfectly tailored gray. Fiona raised her eyebrows.

"Are you as worried as I am about someone unfriendly stopping by? Lovely suit, by the way."

"Funny." Henley looked around and pulled up the one chair while Fiona perched on the bed. "You've certainly had an interesting day so far, Irish. Stirring up the natives, is that how you plan to get your money back?"

"Were you in the saloon, or just eavesdropping outside? Almighty Christ, is there no privacy on this boat?"

He shrugged. "Very little, and you might keep that in mind. I was at the bar, actually, when you came in. You were very intent on your quarry and never noticed me. You'll have to be more careful from now on."

Fiona's eyes flashed angrily. "Don't be tellin' me how to do things, man. I don't need a keeper."

Henley stretched his arms over his head and locked his fingers together behind his head. "I'm not your 'keeper', Fiona, but I am someone who'd like to see you live a long life. If you plunge heedlessly into situations like you did today, that may not be likely. You seem to have a knack for trouble."

Fiona snorted. "I'm still breathin, aren't I?'

Henley sighed. "True." He gazed at her silently.

For a few minutes neither of them said a word, looking at each other across the small space. Fiona finally gave up.

"All right," she said, and held her hands out to him. "I know my temper gets the best of me and march in like some Irish legendary hero. Right will win because it's right, is my rather stupid motto sometimes. I got a lot of bruises for that as a child but it seems I didn't learn much from them."

Henley reached over and took her hands in his. "Maybe you learned to keep on fighting." His hands were surprisingly soft but strong and she liked the way they felt.

"Maybe I did, at that."

Henley stood up, still holding her hands and stepped closer. He bent and kissed her gently on the temple. Fiona sat as though paralyzed, not moving a muscle. But Henley did, dropping her hands and taking two steps back.

"I'm sorry, that was completely inappropriate. I only came to ask you to be cautious. We have no idea what Sitwell and Mavis are likely to do now and I don't want you caught in the middle of it."

Fiona held up her hand. "Henley, stop." She smiled, shaking her head. "First of all, there's no need to apologize. Second, I am in the middle of it, especially if I want my money back, and believe me, I do."

She stepped close to him and put her hand on his cheek. Oh god, it would be so easy and so wrong, to allow herself to have any feelings for this man except friendship. "Thank you."

He nodded. "I understand, Fiona. I do. But sometimes money isn't the most important thing in life, you know? Just be careful. I know you don't want a white knight but don't make me worry, and Julius, too. All right?"

"I swear. Really."

Henley looked skeptical but he let himself out and she bolted the door behind him. She caught her reflection in the mirror and only then did she realize she'd been wearing only her white silk camisole with her suit skirt. Ah well, she was pretty certain he'd seen distressed women in much less. She grinned at herself. Maybe sometime she wouldn't be so preoccupied.

CHAPTER 27

The Queen docked in Natchez that evening around dinnertime. Fiona was in the dining room with the St. John sisters, enjoying herself immensely. They were quite lovely, Merry with her flaming red hair, and Ellen a sultry dark-haired beauty. Fiona could certainly see why Julius favored them and she loved their carefree attitude and sophisticated outlook on life. She could learn a lot from them, and they had been kind and welcoming with her, taking her under their generous wings each time they were together. Fiona regretted she'd not spent more precious hours with them instead of James and she meant to remedy that from now on.

"Open your mouth, Fiona," Merry ordered, holding a toast point loaded with little round things on it. Fiona obeyed and moaned in appreciation as the flavors exploded in her mouth.

"Good, eh? Caviar." Merry popped another into her own mouth and rolled her eyes. "Food of the gods, right Ellen?"

Ellen shrugged. "Not my favorite, but it's tasty. Now, this she-crab soup with sherry, please feed this to me on my deathbed, will you, Merry?" She took a sip and quickly lowered her spoon for more.

Fiona agreed. The food from Andre's kitchen had been a revelation, as had so much of everything she'd discovered as she'd traveled into the heart of the South and she loved it all.

"Where's that handsome rascal James?" Merry mumbled, her mouth full of caviar.

Fiona managed to look sad and in a way, she was. "We've had a falling-out. I think it could be permanent."

Merry looked at Ellen and they contrived a sympathetic look but it didn't last long. They obviously knew more than they'd let on.

"Fiona, my dear, that man is a rogue and you're better off without him. Even though we met you as "Mrs. Gordon", I think perhaps that was not so?"

"You are right," Fiona said. "On both points. Could everyone see this but me?"

Ellen patted her hand. "Of course not, darling." She glanced at her sister who nodded. "Merry and I are rather astute observers of the human condition. Comes from being with Julius for so long, I think." Her delightful laugh tinkled. "Don't be silly, now, Fiona. You can trust us to be discreet, and please," she reached across the table and touched Fiona's shoulder, "come to us if we can be of help. Even at midnight to share brandy and sympathy. In fact, especially then."

The waiter came and whisked away the empty servers and dishes. Fiona looked regretfully at the empty caviar platter and Merry laughed. "Such a devotee, and so soon."

Fiona grinned. "I'm a quick learner even though I'm Irish. I know excellence when I see it."

The sisters exchanged glances once again. "And not just in food, my dear, if I may be so bold? I mean, James is adorable but one can grow weary of just that. Maybe someone a bit more capable? Men are like food, there's so much to sample."

"You two are a delight and there's not much hidden from you, I can see that."

"And bright, too." Merry raised her wineglass. "Fiona, our new sister."

They clinked glasses and the waiter brought more dishes: baked oysters on the half shell, and steak with bearnaise sauce. He also brought another bottle of wine and refilled their glasses as they bent to the delectable food. He even brought small dishes of potatoes with cheese sauce and Fiona could've blessed him. If she lived to be one hundred, she'd never stop loving potatoes, because if it wasn't for potatoes as her entire diet she wouldn't have lived to be an adult.

"I'd better pace myself," Merry said with a laugh after a while. "We've got lots of time before Julius's meeting tonight. It sounds like there may be some changes ahead. Do you know what play he's got planned for Natchez, Fiona?"

"No," Fiona mused. "I really don't. We were going to do a couple more "School for Scandals" and maybe we still are, but I can't say what he's got in mind." Privately she thought how horribly awkward that would be, with James and Mavis, but as the saying went, "the show must go on" and she knew it would, bruised face and bruised feelings taking second place.

Ellen shrugged. "We'll know soon enough. Won't change much for us, of course, but I hope you don't have to do 'Romeo and Juliet' with you know who. That would really require some acting, Fiona."

Merry snorted. "I'll say, but then, you're a crack actress, darling. You can do anything."

Julius had called the meeting in the theater for the entire troupe at nine that evening and when Fiona, Merry and Ellen walked in, most of them were already there. She saw Mavis and the back of James's head where they were sitting in the front row. They took their seats and after a few minutes, Julius walked up onto the stage, dressed casually in a linen shirt and trousers. He clapped his hands and the murmuring quieted.

"Good evening, people. Thank you for coming." He smiled.

"Been a nice little hiatus for a couple of days, hasn't it? I know you all needed a rest and I thank you again for all the incredible hard work you've been doing since we set out on this adventure. It's not over yet. Since we bypassed Vicksburg, we'll be here in Natchez for a few nights before going on downriver to Louisiana, first Baton Rouge and the Crescent City, New Orleans, where we'll be moored for some time. I've gotten word they are eagerly anticipating our arrival, and I know you all are anticipating New Orleans.

"It may be my favorite city in all the United States, sort of a little bit of Paris right here in the American South, and I hope you love it as much as I do. Coming in on the Queen will be grand way to experience it for the first time for most of you."

Julius pulled a stool from the wings, settling himself. He gazed out at the assembled group, sensing some in his audience were restless. Fiona noticed George Harper and Sean McKean standing in the wings as well. If Henley was Julius's right hand, those two gentlemen were Julius's left. They were genial burly men who handled just about everything to do with the performances, from scenery to unruly playgoers, and occasionally performed themselves. Fiona liked them both but on seeing them, her suspicion that this wasn't just an ordinary meeting was confirmed. She grasped Merry's hand, and Merry squeezed it, acknowledging her own unease. She'd noticed Sean and George, too and she raised her eyebrows and shrugged.

Julius cleared his throat. "We'll be doing 'School for Scandal' for two nights here in Natchez, and then 'Romeo and Juliet' for the next three, along with our usual variety acts, so really nothing much will be different, except for a minor casting change here and there. When we arrive in Baton Rouge, we'll take a day or two to rehearse something new, and then in New Orleans, our entire repertoire will be decided, since we'll be there for some time."

People began whispering among themselves and Julius held

up a hand. "So, nothing really different. I apologize for the delay but I wanted to reassure you all that we're on schedule and all is well. If you have any questions, please?"

It seemed no one did, or not that they cared to voice in public rather than private, but the "minor casting change" remark did raise a few eyebrows, but that happened often in the theater. People began to file out of the theater and onto other pursuits for the evening. Fiona, Merry and Ellen, among a few others, including James and Mavis, were curious and still sat in their seats.

After a few minutes, Julius came down the stairs and sat beside James, talking softly but after a few words, Mavis stood up, her voice shrill.

"You can't do this, Julius! Who in hell do you think you are?"

Fiona and the St. John sisters exchanged looks as Sean and George came down from the stage and stood beside Julius and James, now on his feet as well. Fiona gasped when she saw his face. His eyes peered out, surrounded by skin that resembled two large bruised plums, and his nose matched them perfectly, swollen far beyond recognition from the perfect Roman nose he'd had not a day before. His mouth turned down in a snarl as he caught sight of her.

"Fiona, this is all your doing," he shouted, "as if I didn't know. You've likely been sleeping with Julius and half the troupe for months, you lying slut."

Julius moved so quickly he was a blur, holding James's chin in his hand, snapping it back to face him.

"That's quite enough, James. I was hoping some semblance of good breeding and manners would quell some of your deluded nonsense, but I sorely underestimated your capacity for either one." He stared into the younger man's eyes. "And that, my young friend, is why you're leaving the boat this evening, rather than in the morning. But leaving it you surely are."

Mavis opened her mouth to protest again but a look from

Julius quelled her and she sat back down. Clearly she didn't want to share James's fate.

Julius released his hold and James turned away, rubbing his chin. He still stared defiantly at Julius. Fiona and the St. John sisters sat quiet as mice, exchanging glances but not even whispering between themselves. This wasn't a performance Fiona had ever expected to see in this theater.

Julius held out a packet and James took it sullenly. "What's this?"

"Three hundred dollars and a letter to a friend who runs a theater company in Savannah, Georgia. I've told him you're an astoundingly good actor, which you are, and nothing else untoward. Sean here will accompany you to pick your things and take you into Natchez, where you can find transport."

James turned to his companion. "Come on, Mavis. We can do better than this filthy barge."

"Well, actually, darling, it's been quite delightful, but I think not. You'll do fine on your own." She turned to Julius with an ingratiating smile. "He's really a lovely actor. Savannah's got quite a theater scene, I hear. Delightful town."

James paled visibly under his bruises. "Julius, for God's sake, you know me. What in hell am I going to do in the wilds of the American south? My family will never forgive you for this travesty."

Julius shrugged. "You forfeited any claim on aristocratic privilege, dear boy, with your actions. Your family couldn't care less, but I think your grandfather would have thought of this as a grand adventure, so rise to the occasion. It very likely could be the making of you. By the time you get to Savannah, your face should look much better. You're clever, so use that to your advantage."

Fiona actually felt sorry for him, so much so she started to rise but Merry's hand was like a death grip on her left arm and Ellen's clutched her right.

"No you don't, my friend. We're not letting you make the mistake countless women have made before," Ellen hissed in Fiona's ear. "Once they hit, they don't stop. You know it as well as we do, but in case you weakened, we thought to remind you."

Fiona sat back down. They were right and she knew it, but it was very hard to watch the man she thought she loved be turned out to fend for himself. It wasn't as though James was a hardened frontiersman. He knew nothing but city streets and lighted stages.

"There is one little thing, though," Mavis said.

"Oh really, and what might that be?" Julius's voice was soft and sweet as honey and Fiona knew a warning when she heard it. Mavis was oblivious, however.

"Dear James does owe Mr. Sitwell a bit of money. Perhaps Fiona or you would be willing to settle that for him?"

Julius seemed unperturbed, glancing down at his fingers where they lay curled on his lap. "Mavis, my dear. I was undecided, but now I think you would make a stalwart companion for James on his journey, much as you've been one for Charlie Sitwell since you boarded this boat."

He gazed at her and Mavis's face went as pale as James's, even under her makeup, which was liberally applied as always. "Sean will help you with your trunks as well. I'll take care of your pay and have it ready for you on the pier. As you say, Savannah is quite the up and coming theater town. I'll give you a reference as well."

Julius smiled benevolently and watched with interest as Mavis erupted. Fiona had to admit it was quite a performance.

"You bastard, Julius," she screamed. "I should have known better than to think you'd be a gentleman, or trust you for a second. You'll get what's coming to you some day, you lying scum."

Julius rose and gave her a weary smile. "Goodbye, my dears. It's not as though I haven't given both of you every opportunity.

People will always be who they are and sometimes they just can't change. It's most regretful." He motioned to Sean and George, who came to stand by James and Mavis like sentinels, or guards, which Fiona supposed they were at this point. Julius passed Fiona and the St. John sisters without a glance but she knew full well he'd known they were there from the beginning.

She watched as the two men followed closely behind James and Mavis, who both threw venomous glances at her as they passed. They left the theater and Fiona slumped back in her chair. She felt as though she'd been in a battle, but in fact it was Julius who had fought it for her, a stalwart knight if ever there was one.

She said goodnight to Merry and Ellen, hugging them. "Thank you for being here with me. You're both very kind."

Ellen sniffed. "No, we're not, at least not usually." She took Fiona's face in her hands, delicately and kissed her cheek softly. "You're special, Fiona, and you deserve better than you've been getting. Sleep well, sweetheart."

Fiona walked down the deck to her stateroom but hesitated outside the door. Instead of going inside, she settled herself at the railing, watching the lights of the boat play across the ripples of the river, like phantom lights that glowed and disappeared with the current. It soothed her for a time. She felt strange, justified but regretful at the same time. James had been a large part of her life, in fact giving her a new one that she couldn't have imagined when she'd stepped off the *Adriatic* so long ago now. She'd always be grateful to him for that. All that had happened since then was a mixture of wonderful and terrible, but he'd still always been there for her, until now. Tutoring her had been to his advantage as much as hers, she saw that now, but still, he'd been the mentor and force she'd needed. His betrayal had been so sudden she'd had trouble adjusting to it but when she thought back, the traces had been there all along but she too blind to see.

Movement and raised voices on the main deck disrupted her thoughts and she peered down. Sean and George Harper were escorting Mavis and James from the boat while a porter loaded their trunks onto a wagon.

"Don't touch me, you cur," James snarled at Sean, shaking his hand off his arm. "I don't need assistance from the likes of you."

James helped Mavis onto the wagon seat beside the driver. She was crying but Fiona couldn't tell whether it was real or faked. That was the way with Mavis. James didn't seem too interested in her travail, one way or another. Perhaps he'd discerned that he'd been taken in by her and Sitwell, but then James liked to blame others for his misfortunes and the prime targets this time were Julius and of course, Fiona herself.

As they pulled away from the dock and into the night, Fiona watched them go and then concentrated her gaze once again on the river. She didn't seem to have much luck with the men she'd been with, either by circumstance or choice. It was time she concentrated on herself alone. She took a deep breath of the sweetly scented night air. For an almost giddy moment, she was happy, despite the guilt over the past. Truthfully she thought, she didn't feel all that guilty anymore, but she did feel something else. For the first time, she felt free.

CHAPTER 28

Natchez was a lovely town, beautifully laid out with wide streets, parks and gracious mansions lived in by equally gracious people, all very welcoming and full of that Southern charm and an ease of manner that Fiona found captivating. It had been a productive and good few days and they only had two more nights here. "School for Scandal" had gone very well, with Josef and Maria Acaro stepping seamlessly into the roles previously played by James and Mavis.

Tomorrow night they'd perform "Romeo and Juliet" as their main attraction, and Fiona's new Romeo was Ramon, who'd played the part many times in the past. Their rehearsals had gone very well and she was looking forward to the shows, the new actors having blended easily into the vacancies left by those gone.

She'd finally begun to feel relaxed, and with the exception of occasionally crossing paths with Charlie Sitwell, on her way to being secure. Why Julius hadn't tossed him out along with Mavis and James was a mystery to her, but not one she wanted to delve into. He must have his reasons and she didn't really want to know those either. Serenity was hard come by and Fiona was enjoying hers. Tonight the theater was dark and, somewhat surprisingly, Julius had invited her to accompany him to a dinner at his friend's house, an invitation Fiona had eagerly accepted.

The languid evening air was heady with the scents of night-blooming jasmine and magnolias as they walked the few blocks to the McClain house. Captain Hamilton walked on one side of her and Julius the other and Fiona had never felt as safe as she did on this night, even strolling through an unknown town. She was also intrigued and could hardly wait to meet the Widow McClain, as Henley as called her. Another of Julius's special friends, perhaps? She'd been surprised by Julius's request, but Henley said he likely thought she needed a respite from the boat after all the trouble and she took him at his word. She'd chosen a white dress with lace and ruffles and when she'd joined Julius and Abel at the deck, Julius had laughed with pleasure.

"You are a true Southern belle tonight, Fiona," he'd said, twirling her around so her skirts flared and even the normally stoic Abel had smiled.

Torches were lit at the gatepost of the house and along the crushed oyster shell drive where an imposing three-story columned mansion glowed ghostly white against the flickering flames, its windows aglow with welcoming light. The front door opened as though their approach had been awaited and they were ushered inside the hallway and shown into a beautifully appointed parlor where their hostess greeted them.

"My dear," said the lovely woman dressed in yellow brocade, her dark hair streaked artfully with silver. "So wonderful to have you here again." She clasped Julius's hands in hers and kissed his cheek, turning to Captain Hamilton with the same enthusiasm, and another welcoming kiss. Clearly they'd met before. Then she turned her attention to Fiona.

"And this beautiful creature?"

"This is Fiona Gordon, Cicely, one of my players and a young woman who reminds me a great deal of you, actually," Julius said. "Fiona, Cicely McClain, the doyenne of Natchez."

Cicely took Fiona's hand and smiled warmly. "So happy Julius brought you here tonight, Miss Gordon. I think we're going to be good friends." She tapped Julius smartly on the shoulder with her floral-painted fan. "Although he is mighty fond of hyperbole."

"So kind of you to welcome me, Mrs. McClain," Fiona said, glancing at Julius. "And though he is fond of hyperbole, in your case, it is justified."

Cicely McClain nodded her head in appreciation. "You see, Julius, we all understand you perfectly. You have no secrets here."

Abel Hamilton laughed. "It's always a pleasure to see you, Cicely. It's a rare woman who truly understands our Julius, but you certainly do."

Cicely shrugged elegantly and both men chuckled. Fiona knew she was an observer to a reunion of old friends, but she didn't feel awkward, especially when Cicely took her hand and led her into a small supper room, leaving Julius and Abel to follow. Fiona glimpsed a much larger dining room through an archway and was grateful they'd have a cozier setting.

Here a small round table was set for four, covered in snowy linen, and Cicely showed Fiona to a seat between her and Abel, with Julius on Cicely's other side. Two dozen white candles lit the room, the walls papered in turquoise silk. Crystal glasses glittered and the elaborate silverware shone under the small but exquisite chandelier, the pure white china glistening. A waiter poured a delicate white wine and served the crab stew, glistening with the sherry that he deftly sprinkled on its creamy surface.

"Please," Cicely said, picking up her spoon. "I thought we'd get started early and have time to attend to any business after dinner. Besides, Julius, I know how much you love my crab stew and yes, I did make it myself."

They needed no urging and Fiona thought she'd never tasted anything more delicious, even Andre's version, of which she'd grown very fond. They made inconsequential small talk while they enjoyed the food, Julius regaling them as well with tales of the showboat and the trip. The roast chicken, sweet potatoes with pecans and honey and the fluffy biscuits that followed were as good as the crab stew, and Fiona gave a small moan when the peach cobbler with whipped cream came from the kitchen.

Abel chuckled. "Fiona, it seems you've become fond of our cooking down here, if I'm not mistaken."

She blushed. "I have, it's true. I will have to take a lot more turns around deck from now on if I'm not to look like a puffball, I'm afraid." She turned to Cicely. "Thank you for a fabulous dinner, Mrs. McClain."

"It's Cicely, Fiona," the widow said. "I'm happy you like it. So tell me more about how you came to be in Julius's troupe. Such an adventurous life you've led compared to me, born and raised here in Natchez." She sighed. "One little trip to Paris when I was nineteen, otherwise I've never left these shores. But Ireland?"

Mother of God, Fiona thought, how do you explain St. Hilda's and Ballyowen to a woman who'd never known hunger, poverty or mistreatment? You don't, she concluded in a heartbeat, but there was something in the woman's eyes that made Fiona think perhaps there was something in her past that might have caused profound pain. Even so, she had to lie and knew Julius's eyes were intent on her.

"Ah, well, it's not all that exotic, Ireland," she said. "Not the sort of place fine young ladies would find to their liking, I fear. I myself come from a small village and most all my family came to America long ago though I was just a simple country girl, I was glad to finally get the opportunity myself. When I became an actress, which my dear departed mother would probably not be happy about," here she crossed herself, "bless her soul, it was lucky chance that I came to Chicago to live with my Uncle Patrick. There I attended the theater often and met Julius who offered me a part. One thing led to another and he offered me the chance to come on the showboat. Now, here I am, fortunate enough to have met you as well."

Fiona thought she heard a small choking sound from across the table but when she shot a glance at Julius, he was sipping wine, his face bland. Cicely didn't seem to have noticed and Abel was studying his own wineglass in excruciating detail.

Cicely put her hand on Fiona's. "I am the fortunate one, Fiona. Come, everyone, let's go into the library, shall we? The windows are open and the evening has cooled."

They ensconced themselves in the soft sofas amid the shelves of books, a room that was always Fiona's favorite in any house. Someday, when she was lucky enough to have a home of her own, a library was the only room she'd need in it, she thought. Well, and a bedroom, she supposed.

Brandy snifters were set out on the table beside them, and everyone took one in their hands, warming the glass with the heat of their palms. They talked of theater, of the planting season, the river and the weather, safe topics each of them knew something about. Fiona leaned back against the soft cushions. Tonight, it felt good to be off the boat and in a house that wasn't moving.

When they heard horses outside on the lawn, both Abel and Julius reacted swiftly, heading to the open windows, which reflected not simply the small pathway torches, but large ones, carried by several white-hooded men on horseback, the flames towering above their heads.

"Christ, they've gotten bold," Abel swore. "Amaro said last

month they were at Heart's Ease again, too. We didn't bring those guns any too soon."

"I won't have it," Cicely said, stamping her foot in emphasis, hands on her hips. "These hooligans are too cowardly to even show their faces. My guns are in the study, Julius."

Julius held up a hand. "Let's see what they've got to say before we up the ante on this, Cicely."

"I don't care if they say the Lord's Prayer," Cicely snapped. "They're on my property and I can tell you right now it's not going to be anythin' I want to hear."

Julius put his arms around her and after a few seconds she put her head on his shoulder. He looked at Fiona and she moved silently to Abel's side. The men outside hadn't said a word but they didn't need to. Their presence was menace enough.

"Who are they?" she whispered to Abel.

"They've gone by many names, but the latest is the White League," he said softly. "Used to be pretty quiet but lately things have started up again, my guess is underground now, sort of unnamed, against any farm or plantation owned by black people, and white people who help them. Cicely falls into that category. She's got two plantations where she's given co-ownership to the former slaves her husband owned. She's a brave woman but some people just can't accept that the South has moved on. So they intimidate, frighten and sometimes worse. This sort of thing never dies, it just takes different forms. They're racist cowards."

"Widow McClain," yelled the lead rider outside, pulling his horse a few steps in front of the others. "Send out the riverboat gorilla and we'll be movin' on tonight. That's the price you pay for puttin' good white men out of work and settin' down to table with an ape. Have to teach you a lesson and bring down God's judgment on you."

Fiona gasped. "Surely he can't be meanin' you, Abel?" But she knew he did the minute the words came out of her mouth.

"Oh, I do believe he does, Fiona," Abel said dryly.

Cicely headed to the door as Julius tried to stop her, assuming she was heading to her gun cabinet. Fiona was momentarily aghast at how quickly a gentle evening had turned into chaos. This wasn't how things were supposed to go in the South she'd come to fall in love with. Afterwards, she would swear something just snapped inside her, maybe a long-buried memory, maybe a loathing for injustice, or she'd just had enough of cruelty and stupidity lately.

She ran swiftly into the hallway and flung open the big door, slamming it behind her. She stood on the portico for a second and then ran down the steps, stopping in front of the lead man's horse, her head even with the rider's knees. Surprised, nervous laughter came from a couple of the riders. They clearly didn't know what to make of this, her ruffled white skirts flying behind her, black curls bouncing, her face furious.

She didn't wait for them to recover. She took a deep breath and put her hands on her hips.

"Listen here, hooded man. My name's Fiona Shanahan. I'm an orphan from Ireland where the English starved and killed my family because of evil thoughts just like the ones that must be churnin' in what brains you have underneath that bedsheet." Her stage voice projected loud and clear down the drive. She shook her head in disgust, hair swirling.

"At least the murderin' English bastards had the guts to come at us barefaced when they cut us down with their swords. But this is America, and I'd bet solid gold that some of you came from Ireland and Scotland too, for sanctuary from cruelty like that. Did you learn not a thing from listenin' to your grannies, you fools?"

Before the man had a chance to say a word, Fiona grabbed the white hood he wore and pulled it off his head and flung it to the ground. The man swore and tried to grab at it but nearly set his hair on fire with his torch in the process.

"Well, well. Didn't I see you on the showboat at our performance last night, mister? How do you think that showboat got to Natchez? The talented captain of that vessel is the gentleman you just called a gorilla, guidin' that boat to Natchez all so you and your wife could come to the show. Now, you say horrible things hidin' behind some mask?"

Startled, the bareheaded man began to back up his horse. None of the others said a word but they seemed confused, and two of the men turned their horses and left.

Cicely McClain strode out onto the portico, Julius and Abel beside her. Fiona was relieved to see she wasn't carrying a shotgun although she knew Julius probably held a pistol in his hand behind him, and likely Abel did too.

"Hiram Murphy," she said, addressing the bareheaded man. "I think your time as Sheriff of Adams County is coming to end. There's an election coming up and I wonder what the voters will think of your nighttime activities?" Cicely's voice was clear as a church bell. "Go on home, now."

Hiram Murphy's face was bright red and the color wasn't from the flames of the torches. He wheeled his horse around and as he did, so the rest followed down the drive, their torches still blazing. They watched them disappear into the night, taking their hate with them.

"For God's sake, Fiona, you frightened me out of five years of my life, you little Irish maniac. What where you thinking?" Julius said as she walked back up to the porch.

"That I can't put up with any more horrid nonsense from people who should know better, that's what I was I was thinkin'. There's been far too much of that and I just . . . had to go out there and try to stop it."

She began to shake a little then, thinking how easy it would have been for those men to have trampled her or worse. She'd been foolish, and lucky. Julius hustled her inside, Cicely and Abel following, shutting and locking the door firmly behind them. A bevy of servants, both white and black, stood in the hallway, eyes wide, and Cicely spoke softly to them, issuing reassurance and orders, and they quickly dispersed to their rooms and tasks. Cicely led them back into the library and poured more brandy, thrusting a glass into Fiona's hand.

"Drink this, darlin', you need it."

Fiona did, warmth flowing down her throat and spreading through her body. She smiled gratefully at Cicely. Julius didn't say a word. He simply gazed at her, his head cocked to one side, eyebrow raised inquiringly. Fiona swallowed the rest of her brandy.

"I hate people like that, people who think no one will stop them. I've been told before I've a bad temper once I'm riled and I didn't mean to cause you trouble." She held out her empty glass. Julius smiled and got her another, shaking his head.

Cicely patted her hand. "I'm grateful to you, Fiona. I was angry and not thinking clearly and this could've gone very badly tonight, except for you." She grimaced. "There's a lot of work to do in Natchez, more than I'd realized. I must thank you for tearing that hood from Hiram's face, now that was somethin', I swear. Now I know who's behind this latest surge in hatred, I can muster support to end their rule, at least locally on the legal level. Some of it will take much longer. There's no end to the roots of oppression, here or anywhere, I fear. We do what we can and what we must, and hope for the future." She smiled at Fiona. "That is true everywhere, is it not, my dear?"

Fiona nodded. Her thoughts were whirling but this was no time to share her own history. She glanced up at Julius and he nodded almost imperceptibly, the side of his mouth curling into a smile, quickly banished.

"It's been quite an evening, and I must say, a performance if I may term it that, I'd never expected from my star actress," he said. "I'm beginning to see why Lady MacBeth was such a success for you, Fiona."

Fiona had to grin at that. "I have hidden depths, Julius."

"Indeed."

Abel, who'd been unusually quiet, lifted his glass. "Thank you, Fiona."

Fiona felt the flush on her cheeks. That meant a lot, coming from Abel.

Shortly thereafter, they all went upstairs. Cicely had already had rooms made up for them anyway, expecting they'd spend the night and now there was no question of going through the dark streets of Natchez to the river.

They all paused at the landing before going to their rooms, looking at each other like survivors of a ship that had narrowly missed being a shipwreck and said their goodnights. Fiona leaned back against the door after she'd shut it when a soft knock prompted her to open it again. Cicely stood in the hallway, her candle in her hand.

"Let me show you another reason those men came here tonight, my dear," she said. Intrigued, Fiona tiptoed behind her up another staircase which led to the top floor, once a cavernous ballroom. Cicely put her finger to her lips and opened one of the double doors.

The huge room had been divided into three smaller rooms. The first room was set up as a schoolroom, with desks, chairs, and a teacher's area with a blackboard, bookcases lining the walls, filled top to bottom with everything from picture books to heavy tomes of history. Moonlight spilled into the room from the high clerestory windows, limning it in perfect detail.

Cicely opened another door onto what was clearly a dormitory, divided by a wall. On the left side were perhaps twenty beds, each filled with a boy, some looking as young as four, while others ranged up to adolescents. On a bed near the door, a young man sat reading by candlelight, and looked up and smiled at Cicely, who put her finger to her lips again, smiling back.

"All's quiet now, Miz McClain," he whispered softly and

turned back to his book. They continued on and in the next room, the beds were taken up with girls, again from very young to older girls, and all soundly asleep, even the girl closest to the door, a counterpart to the young man with the book. Moonlight gave a soft pearly luminescence to the motionless forms, adrift in dreams in a safe place. Perhaps two thirds of the children were black while the others were white.

They quietly descended the stairs, stopping in front of Fiona's door. She took Cicely's hand. "Thank you for trusting me. What you're doing here is incredible."

"I've had a lot of help. It's an everyday challenge, believe me. Julius and others have been a huge help."

That didn't surprise Fiona at all, not any more. They said their quiet goodnights and at last Fiona looked around her bedroom. It was as lovely as the rest of the house, the wooden floors gleaming under the Persian rug. No fire was laid in the marble fireplace, of course. Instead it was filled with a vase of fragrant branches of jasmine. Filmy white curtains wafted in the night breeze coming through the open windows.

Fiona fell back on the soft four-poster after donning the soft cotton nightgown that had been laid out on the bed. She stared at the ceiling, the plaster cherubs and angels frolicking above in the flickering candlelight, all of them without a care in the world.

America was a lot more than finding a safe haven, having enough to eat or even performing on a stage. She'd come here for refuge but she'd learned that accepting refuge had a responsibility. If she wanted to truly become a citizen of this land, it came with responsibilities. Being equal and free had its own price.

After tonight as well as the events of the last few days, she knew it wasn't going to be easy and she didn't quite know how to make it happen, but if thoughts could become actions, there was a pathway and she'd find it. She'd made mistakes but those mistakes had led her to where she was. Sometimes to do good, you had to be willing to do things others might condemn and she was finally in a place where she could make peace with that. She smiled to herself, falling asleep quickly even though she'd never thought she would, and slept dreamlessly.

CHAPTER 29

*R*amon grinned at Fiona, eyes flashing. He grabbed her hand and surrounded by the company, Romeo and Juliet took another bow amid the flowers being thrown onto the stage, the applause nearly deafening in the jewel box theater. Fiona laughed and blew kisses to the audience, and then, both of them momentarily back from the grave, hugged her Romeo to the shouts of approval from the seats in front of them. The curtains swept across the stage in front of them for the last time in Natchez, Mississippi.

Ramon lifted Fiona off her feet, his strong hands nearly spanning her waist, and swung her around and around while everyone clapped. Julius came onto the stage from the wings, smiling.

"Once more, another wonderful performance, everyone. You are all outstanding," he said. "I think this is one of the best Romeo and Juliets I've ever seen. New Orleans is going to be astounded, and that's not an easy feat."

Fiona had felt satisfied after a good performance before, but nothing like this. Doing this play with Ramon, a gifted actor with tremendous charisma, had elevated her own game past simply good to something that happened rarely in the theater: a performance that people would remember, even if it was Natchez, Mississippi on a warm summer night. She felt like her whole body was quivering with exhilaration when before it had been just a tired contentment, like New York or even on the boat when she'd done this play with James.

Julius leaned over and put an arm around her shoulder and Ramon's. "You made magic tonight, kids. This is what it feels like. We'll do it again, and not just with this one. You two are a team made in heaven, or in a play directed by me, of course. Close to the same thing."

They laughed, and Julius broke away to talk to the others. Ramon and Fiona walked backstage to the dressing rooms.

"Thank you, Ramon," Fiona said, kissing him on the cheek. "You made me look good, as always."

He laughed. "No, I think it was the other way around. Or maybe it's Julius, at least he thinks so. Good night, fair Juliet."

Maria Acaro waited for him in the hallway and gave Fiona a hug. "You two were enchanting. Sometimes it just takes the right actors to come together, you know?"

Fiona smiled. "Thanks, Maria. I think you're right. I return your Romeo and thank you again for the loan."

Maria and Ramon had been together for years, both of them beautiful and accomplished and while Fiona had no designs on Ramon beyond acting with him, she felt a pang when she watched them together, they were so in love with each other it was beautiful but hard to watch, especially when you were alone. On the other hand, she thought, it was nice to not have to think every minute about the welfare of someone else, especially someone who didn't give a fig about yours.

She said goodnight and closed the door to her tiny dressing room. She sat down at the mirror, wiping the stage makeup from her face. She didn't use a lot, unlike some of the actresses, but it was nice to get it off her face. She changed into a simple cotton dress and closed the dressing room door.

"If it isn't Little Miss Star," Mavis said, shoving her aside as she swept past in the narrow hallway. "Watch out. Think the world is all yours, do you?"

Fiona rubbed her elbow where Mavis had pushed her into the wall, resisting the urge to shove her back. Bide your time, she told herself, you'll get an opportunity. Julius had given Mavis the part of Nurse and she'd been forced to take it if she wanted to return to the boat so she'd been in a particularly foul mood. Fiona could only wonder what Julius was up to, letting that creature back on the boat but he must have a good reason besides the kindness of his heart.

The morning after he'd banished Mavis and James from the showboat, Mavis had shown up at dawn, sitting on her trunk beside the gangplank, distraught and crying. Julius had gone down and talked with her for a while, and taken her back onto the boat as far as New Orleans.

Having Mavis back on the boat was a small complication. Fiona still wanted her money from Sitwell and she still worried about Mavis and Sitwell thinking she had a stash of jewels from listening to James's drunken confessions, but she was biding her time and staying on her guard and she knew Julius was too, which meant Henley.

Just thinking his name made Fiona smile. There was something about Henley that just made Fiona feel safe and that all would be well in the world. If that wasn't sort of silly, she thought, she didn't know what would be, but there it was. It wasn't as though she cared about him in any other way, after all. She was pretty sure Henley was in love with Elena Acaro anyway. She'd watched them flirting since they'd started down the river.

She went out onto the deck, awash with moonlight. Tomorrow they would pull anchor and head downriver again to

Baton Rouge, their last stop before New Orleans, but tonight the showboat sat placidly, only the pull of the current slapping gently on its sturdy timbers. She leaned on the railing and looked across the river at the faint lights on the other side. She wondered about the lives of the people who lived over there, as she always did with the all the settlements and plantations they passed. People going about their lives, raising crops and children, going to their businesses every morning, to banks, stores, stables, things she'd never done, but the normalcy of it pulled at her in a way she couldn't name.

"Penny for your thoughts, Irish."

Henley. Fiona didn't turn but she smiled because no one but the river could see it. "They aren't worth that much."

He shook his head. "I doubt that. The play was quite a success, so I'm told."

"Yes. I loved it, to tell the truth." Fiona shifted to face him, surprised to find him so close that her nose nearly brushed his waistcoat. She backed up a half step, her back on the railing. In the light from the saloon windows, she saw the grin on his face, before he could hide it.

"Ready for Baton Rouge and then the big one, Fiona? Sometimes I worry about all the balls you're juggling, what with acting, visits ashore, and your plots and plans. Would you like to share your thoughts on any of that?"

Fiona snorted. For a minute she thought Henley was being romantic when all he was really doing was sticking his nose into her business. She wondered if it was his idea or Julius's. That she was disappointed made her angry, not only for the romantic part but that they didn't trust her for a minute, apparently. She thought they'd gotten past that after Natchez. And the romantic part, she had to admit, made her feel even worse, much as she'd like to ignore it altogether.

She shoved past Henley and strode off down the deck without a word. As she rounded the stern, she looked back to find him staring after her, a bemused look on his face, his hands on his hips. The hell with him, she thought. She was done with thinking any man could be trusted, at least not the ones you were tempted to let into your bed.

She stomped down the empty deck, darker on this side, too wound up to go to sleep. When someone grabbed her arm and pulled her into the stairway, she was too startled to even scream. She smelled cigars and cheap bay rum and knew beyond a doubt who it was.

"Don't yell, Fiona, or I'll have to hurt you."

"Take your hands off me, Sitwell," she snarled, "if I was going to scream I'd have done it before now. What the hell do you want?"

Surprisingly, he did so, but didn't move away. "Time we had a chat. I've been thinking about that money Ardrey lost. Maybe we can work something out, you and me."

Fiona was doubtful. "How would that be, Sitwell? You developed a conscience?"

He chuckled. "I don't think I have one, but you're a dear for thinking so. No, this is simply a business proposition that might benefit us both." He light up a cigar, the match illuminating his jowly face. Fiona swallowed her distaste.

"I'm listening."

"I think your boyfriend was telling the truth. About the jewels you've got stashed away. I also know something else, little miss not-so-innocent."

He was awfully pleased with himself, Fiona thought. Much too pleased.

"I know you likely killed those people you stole from back in New York. James was such a talkative fellow."

Fiona swallowed, waiting to hear what else he knew. He already knew what she feared, or at least he was good at bluffing. He took a deep puff on his cigar and blew smoke right at her. She coughed and waved her hand.

"Oh, I'm so sorry, Mrs. Gordon. Now what was I saying? Oh yes, the jewels."

"It's not what you think," Fiona managed. That was true enough. He couldn't possibly imagine that night of horrors, any more than James could, since he was passed out for most of it. But awake enough, it seemed, to have discovered what she'd taken with her. No wonder he'd spent the money so carelessly, because he'd always assumed there was a great deal more to come. Once again, she cursed herself for being so unaware.

Sitwell laughed. "Oh, I'm sure it's not quite what I think. It's likely much worse and I'm sure the authorities would agree."

Well, that was true enough. "Let's get this over with," Fiona said. "What do you want?"

He smiled and puffed on his cigar again. "I'll give you fifteen hundred dollars in cash, in exchange for the jewels. That sounds fair to me, since I'll be taking the risk of selling them, and I'm quite sure you don't have the faintest idea of how to go about that." He leaned down, his breath foul with cheap cigar. "Wouldn't want to get pinched by the Pinkertons, now would you?"

He was right. She didn't have any idea how to sell the jewels but if Sitwell had figured it out, it couldn't be that difficult. She did know they were worth at least ten times what he was offering her, but then again he didn't have any real idea what she had.

Fiona sighed heavily and put her hand on Sitwell's arm. "I think you make good sense. I am plagued by the thought of the things and wish them gone."

Sitwell chuckled. "Clear-headed thinking, young lady. I had a feeling we could do some business." He walked to the railing and tossed his cigar into the water. "What say I meet you here Thursday night at eleven? It's pretty quiet by then, and we'll have been docked in Baton Rouge for a couple of days but no performance until Saturday, so I hear."

"Eleven Thursday night, then. I'll bring the jewels, you bring the money."

"A bargain then." He walked away. "Don't disappoint me, now, Fiona."

Charlie Sitwell was a very bad liar, likely one of the reasons he'd found himself plying his trade on a showboat, trying to fleece the unlucky and unwary. Fiona thought Charlie was a very bad man as well, his lying and cheating just the top layer of nastiness he could employ.

This time, he was going to need something more. She smiled into the darkness. She didn't think any tools Charlie might have were going to be enough for him. People make choices and if Fiona had learned nothing else since leaving Ballyowen, she'd learned that choices could be fateful. Fate was a fickle mistress. Reading Greek philosophy in Julius's library hadn't been such an idle pursuit after all. Knowledge was power.

CHAPTER 30

By late October, Louisiana was cooling down from its sweltering humidity and temperatures, and Baton Rouge was a welcoming town, refreshed by its autumn weather. Tempers eased and dispositions improved among those who had some choler to begin with, say casual friends who disagreed with each other and even between normally tolerant husbands and wives who'd taken to quarreling for no real reason. A mercifully cool breeze wafted across them all and tensions abated, flowing away in the gulfstream, like it did every year.

For most, Fiona thought. Sadly, she didn't think it'd done a thing for Mavis or Charlie Sitwell. Fiona knew they were as close and ornery as ever, despite Mavis's quick departure and return, and she knew the reason why. The jewels. It was even possible James was lurking around somewhere but he'd seemed quite shattered by Julius's dismissal and Mavis's betrayal, so perhaps he'd decided on a future in Savannah. She hoped so.

For Baton Rouge, where they'd anchor for a week, Julius revived a bawdy version of The Taming of the Shrew, accompanied by the ever-popular French cancan dance and French chansons de amour, all in all a very European show. French was spoken as much as English from here on, not only New Orleans, but most of southern Louisiana, a blend called Creole, Cajun or some language all their own, made up from English, French, Cree and pirate, according to Henley. Julius had chosen wisely as always.

They'd been in rehearsals for two days, and would be for another. Merry and Ellen were even more exhausted than Fiona, and she was happy she'd chosen to act rather than dance. Tired, yes, but no aching muscles, although her nerves were fine-tuned, and all through the day her thoughts kept returning to her meeting with Sitwell tonight. Julius had been his usual tyrannical self during rehearsals but they all knew how that worked and she hadn't seen Henley at all. Likely busy with whatever business they were up to, and Fiona now knew that Julius's business enterprises involved a great deal more than a showboat and a theater in Chicago. For now, she had her own ventures to look to.

Merry held up her spoon, sighing regretfully at its shiny empty bowl. "That is some peach cobbler for the ages, that is. And I don't dare have one more bite or soon I'll be looking like some zoo animal lumbering about on stage."

Fiona laughed, thinking of Merry's slim athletic figure. "I agree with the cobbler part, but I'm quite certain you'll never lumber anywhere, Merry."

Ellen agreed. "Be quiet, Merry, you know what a little piggy you can be. Left to your own devices, you'd have seconds or worse." She rolled her eyes at Fiona. "This is called sisterly loyalty, Fiona, and I'm stuck with it."

Merry groaned, rubbing her calves. "I'm for a hot bath and bed, darlings. I think the worst is over for a bit, but Julius has a way of finding things to do over. My usual avenue is just disappear and he doesn't get any new choreography ideas. You coming, Ellen?"

"In a second, darling. You go first and I'll call for more hot water in half an hour." She smiled as her sister limped away and poured the last of the wine into her glass and Fiona's, holding up her glass. "To Baton Rouge and on, new sister."

Fiona walked Ellen to their stateroom and continued on to her own. After bolting the door, she dug out the carpetbag with the Lowells' jewelry. She hadn't really looked at the baubles since the night she'd dumped them in there, but now she spread them out on the counterpane, where they glittered like the embodiment of sin, temptation and power.

A diamond bracelet, a few golden ones, many earrings: ruby, emerald and diamond, rings from diamond to opal, necklaces pearl and emerald, and a tiara fit for a princess, at which she snorted, imagining Victoria as a virgin Spanish infanta. She'd likely relished that look.

Then, falling heavily into her hands, spilling onto the bed, there was a ruby necklace and matching earrings. She spread it out on the white cotton. Even she knew this wasn't just a ruby necklace. The thing must've weighed five pounds, the huge pigeon's egg rubies set in an intricate design of gold filigree, perhaps fifteen of the things, and two more dangling from the pendant earrings. Selling these rubies wouldn't be an easy task, Sitwell was right about that. Pieces this distinctive, likely from some famous European collection, would be noticed in a heartbeat. They'd have to be broken down first, and even then, it would be risky.

Fiona sighed. Being a jewel thief hadn't exactly been her plan when she and James had set out so long ago to confront the Lowells, but circumstances had intervened and now, she'd have to deal with it one way or another.

She put the rubies, some golden bracelets and the tiara into a smaller linen sack and dumped the rest back into the carpetbag, stashing it back in the wardrobe. She changed into a cotton shirtwaist and a walking skirt with pockets, ones big enough to hold the sack of jewelry. She laced up her boots and leaned back against the pillows, trying to control her breathing. Still an hour to go before meeting Sitwell. She needed the time to think.

She'd trade him the jewels in the sack for the money and be done with it, she thought. Even the rapacious Mavis should be happy with those rubies and the tiara, even if she was a bit long in the tooth for princess attire. Fiona smiled at the thought but sincerely hoped Sitwell was going to be alone, and not accompanied by the actress. This was a one on one operation, over neatly and quickly, and she didn't want any complications.

The little ormolu clock on the nightstand struck eleven and Fiona shot up, rubbing her eyes and angry at herself that she'd closed them for only a few minutes. This was no time to be foggy with sleep. She needed to be on her guard. She grabbed sack, stuffed it into a pocket of her skirt and left the stateroom, locking the door behind her.

The deck was deserted, no playgoers, no actors, no hands. All were in for the night. Fiona crept softly around the stern to the river side of the showboat, stepping soundlessly on the wooden deck to the spot near the stairwell where she'd met Sitwell the night before.

There was no one there. Filtered light from the docks and the pale half moon illuminated the deck but nothing but a lone moth fluttered past. Strange, she thought. A footfall sounded from the steps above her, and Sitwell appeared accompanied by the odor of cigar smoke and bay rum, foot by foot as he came down the risers, his plaid pant legs identifying him.

"Evening, Mrs. Gordon." He stepped down to stand beside her. "Do you have what we discussed?"

"Yes. And you?"

"Of course," he smirked, patting his pocket.

Fiona waited a moment. "Well? I can't see the money if it's in your pocket, Sitwell."

"Any more than I can see anything you have to offer, my dear."

"True enough," Fiona said. "But in this case it's ladies first to see what's on offer. Let's get on with this so show me the money."

Sitwell frowned but pulled an envelope from his waistcoat and opened the flap. In the dim light, Fiona could make out it was money, but not how much. She reached for it but Sitwell pulled it back.

"I don't think so," he said. "Let's see what you have, first."

Fiona reached into her left pocket and pulled out the linen sack. She reached inside and pulled out the ruby necklace, the links falling through her fingers, but enough of it visible that Sitwell caught his breath.

"Jesus, you really do have it," he breathed, his greedy fingers reaching for the red stones as Fiona dropped the necklace back into the bag.

"Of course I do. The money?"

He handed her the envelope and Fiona knew the minute her hands touched it there couldn't possibly be fifteen hundred dollars in the thin stack contained in the envelope, just as Sitwell grabbed the sack from her hand and shoved her into the stair railing, her head banging against the wrought iron filigree as she dropped the envelope onto the deck.

"Irish girls are so trusting," he hissed. "Too many potatoes and too much whiskey, just like their men, the whole country's fair rotten with it. You're just one more that won't be missed, I think."

She was limp as he pulled her towards the railing, grunting with the effort of her dead weight, propping her up against the rail as he bent down to pick up her feet and topple her over into the swift running river.

"Wait. There's more."

Surprised, Sitwell looked up. Fiona pulled the razor from her right pocket, flicked it open and slit his throat. The warm blood gushed over her hand and he gave a soft moan as he slid down to the planks, hands scrabbling at his throat. His feet drummed against the deck for a very few moments and then he lay still, while the blood pooled around him.

She stuffed the linen sack back in one pocket along with the envelope and threw the razor overboard. She stepped back daintily. It wasn't on her boots, but the dark green skirt was wet to the touch, even though she couldn't see the blood in the dim light. She sighed. She really hadn't wanted it to go this way, although she wasn't foolish enough to think it wouldn't.

She glanced around, but saw no one, and pulled Sitwell into a sitting position. This was going to be the hardest part, she knew. She didn't have the strength to push him over without some leverage. Earlier in the afternoon, she'd taken a chair from the saloon and put it behind the stairway, just in case. Now she retrieved it and with a mighty effort, positioned Sitwell on it, his waist next to the railing, head lolling on his chest. Even with that, Fiona knew, it was going to take all her strength to upend him.

She stood still, breathing deeply but still golden spangles were exploding behind her eyelids and she was already light-headed from her efforts. Don't give up now, girl, she told herself. You fail at this, you might as well toss yourself into that damned river. You just killed a man and the sheriff in Baton Rouge wasn't likely to dismiss that action no matter what you try to tell him.

"Irish." Strong hands fell on her shoulders but his voice was just a whisper. "This is a fine mess you've gotten yourself into, isn't it?"

A hysterical giggle rose in her throat but before it erupted, Henley spun her around and clasped her to his chest, the buttons on his waistcoat biting into her face but she didn't mind at all.

"Hush, now, Fiona. I'm damned sorry I didn't get here sooner, but I'm here now."

A precious moment passed, one they couldn't afford. Fiona pulled back and grabbed Henley's lapels, breathless with exertion as well as tamping down hysterics. She didn't have the time for niceties.

"A little late, but now that you're here, my fine man, let's dump this bastard into the river, before someone comes strollin' by, what say you?"

For a minute Henley didn't move. Then he shook his head. "Jesus God, Fiona, you are truly something."

Then he picked up Sitwell's body as though he was light as a feather and pitched him into the dark water. Fiona saw his head bob up once in the swiftly moving current and then he was gone as though he'd never existed at all. If he didn't get caught up in a snag, he'd either float clear down to the ocean or be fishes' dinner, never to bother her again.

She turned to Henley. "Lovely. I was worried about getting him over that railing. He's a hefty one, you know." She looked down at the deck. It didn't look so bad in the dark, but in the morning light, there was going to be no mistaking the blood.

"I need some water and a mop." She was really dizzy now but she knew she had to take care of that.

Henley took her arm and gently steered her down the deck. "I think you've done enough for the night, Fiona. I'll have Sean come up and take care of that bottle of Bordeaux we spilt. He won't mind."

They went to Julius's office, the closest haven. Fiona sat down on one of the chairs in front of the desk. The back of her head hurt and her fingers came away with blood when she touched her hair. Henley put his handkerchief to the wound, dabbing here and there, taking a closer look.

Fiona winced. "How bad?"

"Not so much, don't think you'll need stitches which is good." He put down the hankerchief and poured water into a basin, handing her a small towel and some soap. "For now, take off that skirt and give me your keys, I'll find a replacement. You can't go out wearing that one. I'll be back shortly."

Fiona cleaned all the blood away, Sitwell's and her own. Henley was as good as his word but he wasn't alone when he came back, tossing her a black skirt which she hastily pulled on. Julius stood in the doorway, and for the first time since she'd known him, he looked furious. He shut the door and sat down behind the desk, glaring at Fiona.

"Fiona, what am I to do with you?"

It didn't seem a question she ought to answer. She stared down at her clenched hands.

"For the love of god, girl. I let Mavis back on the boat because I had a feeling Sitwell might run into trouble, namely you. Fiona, you can't go around killing people you disagree with. Besides, I needed him for a bit longer and now I've only got Mavis to work with." He rolled his eyes and leaned back in his chair. "So, tell me how this came about, would you?"

"It's pretty simple, really. Sitwell said he wanted to make a deal, give me back half the money James lost in exchange for some jewels I have. I met him in good faith." She looked up at Julius. "Well, on my part but not his, which I was expecting. So, I brought the razor, never thinking I'd use it, but when he tried to kill me, I didn't have any choice but to try and defend myself."

"She's telling the truth, from what I saw," Henley said. "I overheard them agree to meet the other night but I got delayed and wish I'd gotten there sooner. Things happened very fast."

Julius sighed. "They certainly did. I wish both of you had enlightened me about this situation. I knew that Fiona wasn't going to let things lie with Sitwell, although I never imaged he'd be taking a river swim, at least not so soon." He gazed at Henley, then at her. "So I've got Sir Lancelot saving the damsel, who turns out to be more adept with sharp objects than he is, plus a man goes into the river. Quite a homicidal pair. That about right?"

This didn't seem like a question Fiona should answer either but Henley apparently had different thoughts on the matter.

"Yes, that's about right."

"I'm sorry," Fiona managed and much to her surprise, like a dam that crumbled under pressure, she began to sob. "Not for Sitwell but for endangering you and the showboat and Henley and everyone. I never meant to, please believe me." She rarely cried, having learned the futility of that as a child, and she wasn't a pretty crier. Her nose ran and she couldn't breathe.

Julius tossed her a clean handkerchief. "Blow."

She did, noisily and felt a complete fool. She should have never gone to Sitwell and tried to get the money back. As for the jewels, if she never saw that damned ruby necklace again it'd be a blessing. She crushed the handkerchief in her fist and gazed bleakly at Julius. Now her temper was going to land her in the backwoods of Louisiana and she'd have to trade the rubies for dinner and a ride in a wagon.

"I'll pack my things. I'm sure you've got someone who can fill in tomorrow night," Fiona said, and stood up. A hand on her shoulder pushed her gently back down. Henley.

"You're not going anywhere," Julius said. "Unless you want to, of course. And no, I don't have anyone who could play Kate but you, so there's that." He leaned over the desk, pinning her to the chair seat with his eyes. "Part of this mess is my fault for letting those thieves onto this boat to start with." He ran his hand through his hair as though distracted, but he was far from that. "Most of all, Fiona, there's you."

"I don't know what you mean," she stammered. Truly she did not, unless he was talking about how she looked. She knew she was pretty and men were attracted to her but that had been more of a curse than anything special.

Julius came around the desk and took her hands in his. "You're beautiful, but that's not what I meant, Fiona. From the first night we met, I saw something in you, an outlook on life that takes no prisoners, molded from want and injustice into something very fine. I've watched you grow as we've gone down this river, and while you've been ruthless both now and in the past, it's been in your own defense, or the defense of others. When James betrayed you, you took it in stride like you have dealt with adversity every time, from what I have observed."

She was speechless. She'd made her way, with plentiful mistakes, doing what she had to and what she could. She'd killed people and no matter that she'd done it because she had to save her own life, it was still the worst sin, one that any God would condemn her for. That this man, whom she admired so much, not only did not condemn her, but believed in her, was nearly beyond comprehension. She wanted to cry again, but looking into Julius's eyes, she took a deep breath and swallowed the lump in her throat. She thought about Ewan Delaney and Joel Prescott for a second, kind men who'd believed in her, too. The warmth of Henley's hand on her shoulder comforted her. Maybe there was another, at least she wished it so.

"Stay. Work with us. We try to make the world a better place for those who deserve it, and sometimes a very bad place for those who do evil to others. Sometimes our methods are a bit unorthodox, but you're no stranger to that, as we both know. What do you say?"

"I say yes, please." Her voice was very faint but the sentiment behind it was not. Julius squeezed her hands.

"Good. Now, go with Henley and get some sleep. We've got a problem to take care of and you may be able to help with that."

Fiona stood up and wafted sideways until Henley took her arm, righting her.

"Take it easy, Irish. You've had a little concussion, I think." He glanced over at Julius who nodded. "We'll get you to bed."

And so he did, as gently and professionally as a ladies' maid putting her mistress to rest, a role she knew only too well. Fiona lay back on the soft pillows and saw Henley settle himself in the chair beside the bed, the lamp turned down but illuminating his face, the hawklike cheekbones in shadow, and his long legs stretched out way past the cushioning chair.

"Goodnight, Irish."

Fiona closed her eyes.

CHAPTER 31

*L*ight filtered into the cabin and Fiona blinked and turned her head. *Mistake,* she thought, as the pain sliced into her skull. Mother of god. She closed her eyes, but not before glimpsing Henley's boots and then the rest of him, snoring softly in the chair. She groaned and fell back asleep.

A long time later, the smell of coffee and cinnamon woke her. Her head hurt, but not quite as badly as before. She sat up slowly. Henley was gone, but a tray with coffee and buns sat on the bedside table. She poured coffee into the cup, the pot still warm and her hand didn't shake. *All right so far,* she thought, and when she swallowed the creamy mix Andre knew she liked, she nearly moaned with pleasure. Such a simple thing, but what a difference.

Within minutes, she demolished both the buns and most of the coffee, beginning to believe she would live another day. Memories of the night before surfaced, foggy but she remembered everything Julius had said. Perhaps some would think she'd landed in the midst of a den of cutthroats, but Fiona knew better. These were people like her, people she could trust.

She washed and dressed simply, a cotton shirtwaist and skirt. There was no time for a full bath or to wash her hair but she fluffed it out, hopefully covering the cut and grateful for that Black Irish blood. She found Henley standing outside, dangling her keys from a finger.

"Morning." He grinned and handed her the keys. "I didn't want to disturb your ablutions."

She locked the door behind her and turned to face him. "Thank you for all you did last night. I appreciate it."

"You're very welcome, Irish. Happy to be of service."

He looked refreshed, especially since she knew he'd slept on her chair. She wasn't ready to talk to him about Sitwell, the night before, and especially not about sleeping in her room. He didn't seem surprised, just raised an eyebrow. Fiona set off for the theater since she knew there was a rehearsal and she'd slept way past noon. He followed and walked her to the door, bowed and left without another word.

The troupe was assembling on stage as she walked in and Julius was sitting in the front row of seats, issuing orders as usual, as though it was any other day, and really, Fiona's nighttime escapades aside, it was. The show must go on.

They did two run-throughs of the Shrew, Julius's annotated version, of course, which he tailored to the showboat audiences. Mostly it was highlights of the original play, heavy on the interplay between Kate and Petrucchio, leaving the side plots out. Ramon was a wonderful partner, and Fiona was looking forward to the evening's show, even though her head throbbed occasionally. It was a very physical play, but Ramon was very gentle and Fiona knew that Julius had alerted him that she wasn't feeling her best. As everyone drifted away, Ramon gave her a quick kiss on the cheek.

"See you at seven, Kate, don't run too far away." He jumped down from the stage and away down the aisle, following Maria Acaro.

Fiona blew him a kiss. Julius was still sitting in the front row and she made her way carefully down the few steps to the aisle.

"How's the head, Fiona?" He tucked some papers into the leather satchel he always carried, his eyes assessing.

"Sore, but I'm good otherwise."

"Excellent," he said. "I never had a doubt. When we get to New Orleans, we'll take a couple of weeks to plan our winter repertoire. The city offers a more sophisticated clientele than we've been playing to on most of the river. You're going to be very busy, and I'm going to have to hire a couple more actors."

Fiona was relieved. Even though he'd said he was keeping her on after last night's debacle, it had been a long time since she'd made that big a mistake and trusted someone who knew it to support her. She bent down and impulsively kissed his cheek, as Ramon had done with her.

"Thank you, Julius."

He seemed pleased but not surprised and continued to fill the satchel. "You're very welcome, Fiona. At seven, then."

She stopped into the restaurant where desserts and sandwiches were always available in the afternoon, Andre's idea of high tea, or sustenance for the Queen's workers, from deckhand to captain to actor. She hadn't had much of an appetite earlier, but now she was starving. Fiona devoured two of Andre's marvelous chicken salad sandwiches and stuffed some macarons in her pocket for later. She didn't chat with anyone in the restaurant, or stop on the way back to her stateroom. She wasn't quite ready for casual conversation, rehearsal had been all she could manage.

She'd stopped one of the stewards on her way to the restaurant and asked for hot water for the bathing tub. By the time she got back to the room, she figured the bath should be ready. The stewards all had skeleton keys and she was greatly looking forward to pleasure of that steaming tub. She pulled her own key from her pocket and bent to fit it into the lock when Mavis Thornton's voice hissed in her ear.

"Where the hell is Charlie?"

Startled, Fiona dropped the key and bent down to retrieve it, thus missing the slap from Mavis's hand. She hadn't been expecting the woman's attack and backed up rapidly, out onto the deck.

"Get away from me," Fiona said, looking around for anyone passing by but the deck was empty in mid-afternoon. "How would I know where that crook is?"

The woman looked half-mad, her usually carefully arranged blonde hair frizzing about her head like a stage version of a drowned Ophelia. "Don't hand me that nonsense, you little bitch," she snarled. "He told me he was meeting you last night."

Well, Fiona thought calmly, that wasn't good, but not entirely unexpected. She knew they were partners in their nasty little ventures and this one was apparently no exception.

"Mavis, I haven't seen your friend Charlie. He's not exactly my sort, you know? As for last night, I was with a friend all evening and certainly didn't see Charlie at any time."

Fiona could see the rage growing in Mavis's eyes but she couldn't resist. "Perhaps you have confused me with some other woman Sitwell has cheated out of their money? I'm sure there's quite a few. A natural mistake, what?"

Mavis snarled and grabbed at Fiona, who sidestepped and pushed the woman's face into the wall beside the door as the momentum carried her by. Momentarily stunned, Mavis fell to the deck. Fiona took the opportunity to fit her key into the lock, step over Mavis and lock the door behind her. Sometimes people underestimated her because she was only five feet four inches tall and delicately built, but Fiona had found it to be quite an advantage. Poor Mavis. She'd clearly lost whatever subtlety or ability to dissemble she'd had, and now had resorted to heavy-handed and hysterical physical attacks. Just the sort of thing that led to an unfortunate demise if people weren't very careful.

Just as Fiona had hoped, the bathing tub was full of water, steaming into the already warm room, but as far as Fiona was concerned, that was just what she needed. She threw rose petals and crushed lavender into the water and reveled in the delightful aroma that filled the stateroom. She peeled off her clothes and stepped into the water, sinking down into the warmth, feeling truly comforted and at peace for the first time in the last two days. She arched her neck back and the warm water caressed her head with gentle fingers, the slight sting when it touched the cut on the back of her head even therapeutic.

Unfortunately, Fiona thought, people like Mavis were a fact of life, just like so many other unpleasant people she'd encountered. Her thoughts turned in a more pleasant direction and she pictured Henley's face.

She owed him a great deal of gratitude for his assistance in her encounter with Charlie Sitwell, but that wasn't the most pressing reason. She certainly hadn't planned on it, but Fiona was becoming attracted to the usually stoic Mr. Henley. She could still feel his hands on her waist pulling her towards him. She would most definitely like to feel those hands on her again, a feeling that had been building for some time as much as she'd like to deny it. The thought of him sleeping so close to her last night made more than her toes tingle, as much as she'd like to deny that, too.

* * *

Baton Rouge's debut performance was a resounding success, especially the can-can dancers. They all got standing ovations, and Julius was beaming as he wished them a good night. Everyone had left the theater and Fiona was carefully removing the extra cascade of black curls from her hair when a gentle knock came on the dressing room door.

"Yes?"

"It's Julius, may I come in?"

He was such a gentleman, Fiona thought, thinking back to the days of Augustin Drewry in New York. He'd walked in on her half naked after a show without asking many times until she came to not even care and assumed that was the way of theater folk. Not really so.

"Of course."

He did so, settling himself on a chair beside her. "How's the head?"

Fiona smiled a little and shrugged.

Julius patted her shoulder. So, I've an idea. Well, more of a proposition." He saw her stiffen and stared up at the ceiling. "Hmm. Not a good choice of words. Let's say I could use your assistance."

Fiona gazed at him. "I'm really not quite that skittish, Julius, but thank you for considering my delicate ladylike sensibilities, not that I've ever had any. I am, however, a damn good actress."

Julius laughed. "Christ Jesus, Henley tried to warn me. I'm starting to think your real parents were Brian Boru and the Morrigan, with a dash of faery dust. Would you tell me if you knew?"

Fiona fluffed her hair and clasped her hands together piously in her lap. "I'm just a poor girl makin' her way. For the love of God, don't be bringin' the faeries into it or we may not be here come sunrise, man. I'm feelin' a bit misunderstood, but eager to help you in any way I may be of service."

"I haven't seen a performance like that since Sarah Bernhardt debuted. I may to have to rethink my play selection."

Fiona grinned. "Don't do it on my account. As you know, I'm ill-educated but a quick learner when it comes to scripts. On the other hand, I am beginning to think I could use my talent for drama just as well off the stage as on it. What do you think?"

"Gather your things. We'll meet Henley in my office." He waited while she did so, and they left the theater together.

The showboat was relatively quiet by the time they were ensconced in Julius's office. Henley poured three glasses of whiskey after locking the door and they settled themselves in the rather uncomfortable chairs around Julius's desk.

"You," Julius said, gesturing in Fiona's direction, "have proved to be a complication to my dealing with a larger problem." He looked pointedly at Henley, who stared into his glass. "You've got an audaciousness and a taste for justice that's been evident with those jewels and your former paramour's indiscretions. You are not responsible for his stupidity and in fact, have been left to deal with the consequences of it and of course your own actions. Which brings us back to the larger problem."

Fiona finished her whiskey and held up her glass, which Henley refilled. She was eager to hear Julius talk about the other matter, some of which she'd already figured out.

"I'm pretty sure Mavis Thornton and her late colleague have stumbled across one of my major sources of revenue, as well as the recipients of some of that venture. That must be dealt with, starting with how they found out about it in the first place, which worries me."

"You're a smuggler," Fiona interrupted, but neither man reacted, their faces blank. "You weren't terribly interested in hiding that from me, I hope because you trusted me even then, back at Amaro and Abel's plantation." She stared at Henley and Julius and didn't see anything that dissuaded her so she plunged on. "I know you smuggle guns downriver but if you've got an upriver, I'm just as curious as I am wanting to help. Apparently that's why you let Mavis and Sitwell on board in the first place, to have them close so you could find them out. I'll do whatever it takes."

She took a large swallow of whiskey. They were either going to send her to Sitwell's resting place or let her in all the way, which of course was what she wanted. That they knew she was a thief, a liar and a murderer didn't go a long way to establishing trust. She looked up at Julius because it was he, she knew, who would decide, no matter what Henley wanted. Fiona knew better than to say a word. She'd already said what she needed to and she was pretty certain that Julius, likely with Mama Rosa's help, had already made up his mind anyway.

"Well, that saves some time," Julius said. "Let's get down to details." He put on his gold-rimmed spectacles and that was the end of it. Henley spread a map out on the table. Fiona let out a breath she didn't realize she'd been holding and pulled her chair closer.

"They picked us up in Memphis," Julius said, stabbing a point on the map with his finger, "only a week after Sy Higley, my man in Cincinnati, was killed. Tortured first." His mouth was set in a grim line. "Nasty as she is, I don't think Mavis is up for that sort of thing, and that idiot Sitwell doesn't figure either. There's at least one, perhaps two, other people waiting for us here in Baton Rouge." He looked up at Fiona. "Because Baton Rouge, not New Orleans, is our usual delivery point. New Orleans is much too obvious and I detest being obvious."

"Unfortunately, Mavis is all you've got left to work with," Fiona said.

"Exactly, and she's panicking because Sitwell's gone. And, she's been distracted from that endeavor by the thought of the jewels she thinks you have. Mavis is like a bird feathering her nest, attracted by the nearest shiny things rather than keeping her eye on the prize, a dangerous habit."

Henley nodded. "That's where you come in, Fiona. No matter what her cohorts think they may get from us, Mavis thinks there is even better pickings right here. You are going to make a deal with her, in exchange for the names of the people she's working with who are planning a little coup here in Baton Rouge."

Fiona looked up at him. "Assuming of course that I have the jewels. James was such a silly man."

"Let's not be ridiculous," Julius said. "Unless you threw them overboard with Sitwell, stop pretending. No one here gives a damn how you got them, so let's put that behind us. I think the question is, how many and which ones you're willing to part with. I'd suggest the rubies because they need to go. They're much too well known. Do we understand each other?"

Fiona felt like a fool. Of course they had to go, she'd known that for a while. And it was way past time to profess any innocence in their acquisition. She nodded.

"Yes. Sorry."

"Good." Julius stood up and stretched. "We're in Baton Rouge for another four days. I'm supposed to meet my associate two nights from now. Plenty of time for you to lay a trap for Mavis. Tell her you want to make a deal and have her come to your room after the show tomorrow. We need to know where and when her friends will come for us, and how much they know. With any luck, it should go quite smoothly and then this business will be over." He raised an eyebrow, gazing at her. "You're an actress, Fiona, and keep in mind in this new role there's nothing in the part description about volatile temperament. Keep that razor in your stateroom."

Henley walked her back to her room, their footsteps the only sound besides that of the water lapping at the hull. It was late and it seemed everyone was asleep, or at least quietly occupied.

Fiona fit her key into the lock and turned to thank Henley for his attentiveness. She was only mildly surprised when he gathered her in his arms and kissed her. It was a long kiss and quite thorough and she returned it with enthusiasm. She'd been anticipating it for quite a while and when it ended, Fiona found it wasn't enough. She slid her arms up around his neck and bent his head down to hers again, pressing her body into his. With a soft moan, he clasped her closer, his lips only leaving hers to find their way to her neck and back again, both of them leaning now against the doorframe. She felt like her entire body was on fire and she kicked the door open, drawing him inside.

"Last night you slept beside my bed. Tonight I'd rather you were in it."

Henley drew her inside, kicked the door shut and shot the bolt. He picked her up as though she weighed next to nothing and very gently deposited her on the bed. "Your every wish is my command, lady. I've only waited for your invitation as I do live to serve."

CHAPTER 32

*I*t was before dawn, but light enough Fiona could see his face beside her. She propped herself up on an elbow and watched him breathing shallowly, his face in repose no longer so commanding, but softer, perhaps what he was like as a child, the long lashes closed and nearly brushing the top of those hawklike cheekbones. She couldn't resist, and ran a finger as gentle as a feather down the side of his face.

His fingers circled her wrist in an iron grip and his blue eyes flew open, staring at her without recognition. She didn't resist and waited as he blinked a few times, and then smiled lazily.

"Sorry. Force of habit, I fear." He released her arm and turned his body towards her. "Sleep well?"

"I think you know well I did," she said, "what little there was of it."

"Hmm." He pushed her hair from her face, his fingers trailing down her neck and onto her belly. "It's not a decent hour for gentle folk to be awake. We should stay abed for a time, don't you think?"

Fiona lay back on the pillows and looked at the ceiling. "I've no chickens to feed, 'tis true. There must be something I could do to pass the time and weary myself to sleep a bit more."

She ran her hands over his chest and then further. "Well, there it is, then. Seek and ye shall find, mother superior always said. She had no idea how right she was." She grinned wickedly. "A good Catholic education is a boon, I've always said so."

Henley made a sound somewhere between a moan and a sigh and and there was no more discussion of Catholicism or education, a blessing since Fiona was not very interested in either one.

HENLEY HAD KISSED her on the forehead before he left, along with calling for a bath and Fiona was grateful for both, especially the bath. She lay back in the cooling scented water and smiled, running her fingers lightly over her body, reminiscing over the night past. Michael Henley was quite a discovery, one she'd been curious about for some time. She'd had only two other experiences, one bad and one very good, but this was one she intended to keep, if circumstances allowed and she was determined that they would.

She couldn't help but wonder how James was faring. She hoped he'd have Savannah eating out of his hand in no time. He was a charming manipulator and very capable of it. She'd loved him, and he'd been a thoughtful and gentle teacher of the arts of love, showing her that not all men were of the Sean Dooley variety, when she'd been fairly convinced they were. He'd taught her more than the ways of the bedroom and the stage. His sense of style, manners and everything she'd needed to transform herself from an Irish ladies' maid into a woman of style and substance were gifts he'd freely given and ones she'd taken full advantage of from the beginning.

She had to say, though, from the first moment she'd laid

eyes on Michael Henley, she'd been fascinated by the man's brooding intensity, his violent capabilities tempered by gentleness and intelligence. Here was a man to match her and she had no intention of letting this one go. If Julius was the king in this venture, Henley was the crown prince, having learned well from his mentor. Fiona didn't know what role she might fill, but today would be the first act in this play and she was prepared to jump in, rehearsal not necessary. Her wits would be her only guide and she was as ready as she could possibly be.

She dressed in a pale blue muslin summer gown and locking the door behind her, set off to find Mavis. It didn't take long. Mavis sat at a table by herself in the restaurant and scowled when Fiona pulled out an empty chair and sat down.

"Good morning, Mavis. Having breakfast? I think it's time we had a chat, don't you?" Fiona took a sip of the coffee she'd brought with her. "My goodness, that's rather a nasty bump on your forehead. I'm terribly sorry that had to happen."

Mavis's hand tightened on her fork. Fiona was glad she had a cup of hot coffee in her hand and then Mavis put the fork down on her plate.

"You are really something," Mavis said. "For someone I know is a thieving slut, you've got the innocent act down very well. After our last meeting, what could you possibly have to say to me that might be of interest?"

"Rubies."

Mavis leaned back in her chair. "So. Coming clean, finally?"

Fiona gazed around the restaurant and after a few seconds, met Mavis's eyes. "I wouldn't term it that, exactly, but yes, I have rubies, if you're interested. I would expect a payment in equal measure, of course."

Mavis snorted in disdain. "Not getting taken away by Pinkertons would be my best offer, sweetie. You've got no bargaining room left."

"Pinkertons is it? I would think they might be just as interested in you, Mavis."

"Ha, I don't think so, my dear," she sneered. "You've been playing a dangerous game for a novice, my little Irish colleen." She picked up her neglected fork and shoved a large bite of eggs into her mouth. "You're way out of your depth and right now, I'm the only one who can help you."

"I think I'm the one who's giving you something of value, Mavis, and it isn't Pinkertons you should be worried about."

Mavis stared at her. "What do you mean, Fiona?"

Fiona glanced around, as if to satisfy there was no one within earshot again. "I overheard an interesting conversation between Julius and Henley. There's a lot going on besides theater on this boat, and they are fairly certain you are aware of it. You're the one playing a dangerous game and it's a very deep river out there. Maybe there's a reason you haven't seen your friend Charlie lately and an even bigger one as to why Julius let you come back."

Mavis put down her fork, her face paling. "What?"

"Time for you to come clean, as you put it. You can have the damn rubies, they've been nothing but bad luck to me. I also just gave you something worth far more and it's called a warning. I can help you and what I want in return is to know who else is in on the plot to steal from Julius. Be smart and make the right decision."

Mavis looked as though she was going to be sick, all her bravado vanished. She was a good actress but this was no act, and for half a second Fiona even felt a twinge of sympathy.

"Mavis, look at me."

The woman looked back at her across the table, on her guard now. Fiona was surprised that Mavis could be naïve enough to think that someone like Julius wouldn't have suspected she and her pals were up to no good, but people could be masters of self-delusion.

"Let me put it this way," Fiona said, her tone business-like. "Since Charlie is out, who's left besides you? When were you planning to do the job and who else is in on this? There has to be at least one more, if you'd planned on taking on Julius and Henley. It'd be suicidal to go it alone and I don't think good old Charlie was up to that task on his own anyway." She poured a little more coffee into her cup and took a sip. She set the cup down carefully and smiled sweetly at Mavis.

"Jesus Christ," Mavis said. "You are quite something, aren't you?" Clearly she was starting to recover. "What makes you think any of this is real, based on some some spying? I'd be a fool to trust you."

Fiona reached over and grasped Mavis's wrist. "Don't be an idiot, Mavis. You're about to be in really big trouble. Once that happens, I'll keep my rubies and watch you go down. If you listen to me, you might make it off this boat with them and your life."

Mavis peered at her suspiciously. "Hmmm. Let me think about it. Let go of my arm."

Fiona shrugged and released her grip. "You don't have time to think about it, Mavis. Tell me the plan now."

They sat there for a few minutes while Mavis was weighing her options and deciding what to do. Fiona was patient, sipping her coffee and nodding hello as people went past but internally her nerves were jangling, waiting for the odious woman to come to a decision. Finally Mavis clasped her hands together and sighed. She stared at Fiona and the ill will was palpable, a cloud of hate that wafted across the small table.

"All right, you little bitch, I'll do it." She nearly spit out the words. "Tomorrow night, there's supposed to be a delivery and the safe will be open. We've been working on this for months. That goddamned Julius thinks he's so clever, but there's always somebody who's hungry and I found him, a ripe peach just waiting to be picked. A man who gambles with Charlie Sitwell is a man who needs money no matter how much Julius pays him."

Fiona didn't dare say a word, just stared at Mavis, waiting for her to say the name.

"George Harper is our inside man. That what you wanted?"

Fiona felt sick. George Harper? A gambler? He'd always been so solid, so safe, so trustworthy. She would never have suspected him, or anyone else in the troupe, for that matter. People could certainly fool you.

"Thank you, Mavis. That's exactly what I wanted."

Mavis stood up. "What about the rubies? You owe me."

Some people certainly had a skewed sense of right and wrong. "Tomorrow night, after the performance, come to my dressing room."

Fiona breathed a sigh of relief as she watched Mavis leave the dining room. That was not a confrontation she ever wanted to repeat, but she'd got what they needed. George Harper. She'd never have thought of him for a minute, and likely Julius had not, either.

CHAPTER 33

"I'll be damned," said Julius, staring out at the river. "George, eh? Now of the two, I would've thought Sean, maybe. He's much more adventurous, that one." He shook his head and his eyes were sad when he looked up at Fiona. Sad perhaps, but Fiona felt the tightly controlled anger that crackled around him like heat lightning. Henley hadn't said a word but he stood stiffly beside the desk, shocked and angry.

She'd wasted no time in discreetly coming to Julius's office after her conversation with Mavis. This wasn't information that could wait, and she wanted to unburden herself of the knowledge as fast as possible. She had no idea what Julius would do with it, only that she didn't want to be the only one who knew it. Unfortunately, the telling hadn't helped alleviate her own anxiety.

"Well." Julius sat down at his desk. "What to do. 'The better part of valor is discretion', the man said and I should heed that, rather than follow my base instincts which would be similar to MacBeth's. I am no stranger to betrayal, but this one took me by surprise." He laughed dryly and glanced at Henley. "Your thoughts?"

"I'd like to dump him in the fucking river, sir." Henley cleared his throat. "Then again, he's been a good friend for five years now so perhaps there's a better way. One thing I know for sure is we don't wait for tomorrow night."

"Most assuredly."

That said, silence reigned in the small office. Fiona smoothed her hands on her skirt, her palms sweaty, and not from the heat. She looked out at the afternoon sun setting earlier now than in the high summer when their voyage had begun. She never imagined when she set foot on the Queen of Dreams that she'd be standing here now with the events that had transpired in the last few weeks. She glanced at Julius and then Henley, both mired in their own thoughts and waited to see what would happen next. It didn't take long.

"Go get Sean and George," Julius said to Henley. "Let's get at least part of this over with. I cannot fathom what chaos could erupt from waiting to catch George and maybe even Mavis in the act, so to speak. God knows what they had in mind, guns, swords at midnight? Good Christ." He turned to Fiona. "There is no need for you to be here, Fiona. You've done your part and very well, convincing Mavis to trust you."

He was right about that, Fiona thought, and turned to go along with Henley. Then she stopped. "You know, Julius, if you don't mind, I'd like to see this out. I'll stay out of the way, I promise."

Julius shook his head. "It could get messy, darling. I'd prefer you to be out of the way."

"Messy doesn't bother me," Fiona said. "I've been there before, Julius."

Julius threw up his hands. "True enough." He looked at Henley. "What do you think?"

"She knows her own mind," Henley said with a small grin. "Besides, she's likely to be lurking around anyway. Better to know where, like here in the corner, so we don't run her over accidentally."

"The corner it is. And it's a corner you'd better stay in, Fiona," Julius sat back. "This is against my better judgment, just so we're all aware of this." He glared at her. "We'll be here, apparently."

Henley left and Fiona sat down beside the desk. "What corner did you have in mind?" She pointed to the back of the room, beside the bookshelves. "That one looks comfortable."

Julius took a revolver from the desk drawer, checked that it was fully loaded and set it down on the desk. "It shouldn't be necessary, but one should always be prepared, I find. And yes, that corner will be fine, Fiona, even though I prefer you to be out of the room altogether. You're such a feisty little thing, you constantly surprise me. That orphanage certainly taught you defiance along with Jesus and the saints. What a breeding ground."

Fiona smiled benignly. "It taught me well that Jesus and those saints can't help me or anyone else. I had to learn survival but what I need to refine is discretion, as you mentioned. I can't think of a better teacher than you."

"Ah." He stared at her. "I hope I've been of some service, then." He poured them both a small glass of brandy. "This could go badly, but I hope things will remain civil. As a lesson in discretion, of course." He handed her a glass and picked up his own. "To civility, and of course, justice."

They drank in companionable silence until there was a discreet knock on the door and everything went to hell.

Henley held open the door, and Sean McKean and then George Harper came into the room. Henley followed them in and shut the door. They were all large men and it seemed crowded now, even though it was a spacious area and Fiona shrank back into her designated corner, immediately regretting her decision to stay.

"Thanks for coming," Julius said, standing up. "We've got a little situation that I hope you can help with, as you so often do. Please, have a seat, gentlemen."

Sean McKean sat down, smiling, and George Harper made to do the same when he spied Fiona standing by the bookshelves. He stood up and backed towards the door. Clearly Mavis had warned him. Henley moved to stop him, but Harper landed a surprise roundhouse punch to Henley's jaw and he fell to the floor, momentarily stunned. Harper threw open the door but Julius's voice stopped him in his tracks.

"I will shoot you in the back, Harper. I've no compulsion about that old saw when it comes to thieves, since they're usually running away."

Harper turned, saw the pistol in Julius's hand and shut the door. "Goddamnit, DeMonte, I know you would." He leaned back against the door, his face a mask of anger and desperation. Henley picked himself off the floor and shoved Harper into the other chair in front of Julius's desk, his hand searching none too gently for a weapon in Harper's clothing and boots. Satisfied, he stood back.

Fiona stood as still as a statue. She was as superfluous in this situation as a flea and she fervently wished she'd left when she had the opportunity. Harper stared at her and shook his head quickly.

"I see your little informant here. Mavis just can't keep her mouth shut, can she?"

"No," Julius said. "But, George, Mavis isn't really our main concern right now. I've known and trusted you for a long time. Tell me, if you would, why has it come to this?"

"Oh, Christ, Julius, it's a long story," Harper said, running his hands over his face, aiming for contrite. "I never planned for it to go this far, I swear. I needed the damn money. It's not just the gambling debts. My sister's sick and the doctor's bills are piling up, and she's got five kids to support and her no-good husband's in jail again. I just didn't see any way out."

He ran his hands over his forehead again, the sweat breaking out. They waited.

"Stupid, I know that now but back in Cinncinnati when Charlie and Mavis started talking about you and the Queen, and when I found out about Hamilton's darkies and the guns and all that, well, that's not been the best idea you've ever had, there's a lot of people down here who take offense at that, in case you didn't know, but you're making a lot of money. I been part of this operation a long time and I know how things operate with you…"

"Unfortunately, you do," Julius interrupted. He sighed softly and shot George Harper in the heart. "And you don't have a sister."

The impact of the shot sent Harper's chair abruptly backward, and both Harper and his chair fell at Fiona's feet, his dead eyes staring blankly at the ceiling.

For a moment or two, silence, as befitting the dead, reigned in the office, the smell of cordite thick amid the curls of gunsmoke circling lazily around the room.

"I apologize for my precipitousness," Julius said, setting the Colt on the desk. "While there never was much choice, my temper got the best of me. Too many lives have been endangered by this foolish greed and that I cannot countenance." He looked up at Henley. "Perhaps a tarpaulin?"

In short order, George Harper was wrapped in canvas and rolled over beside the bookshelves to await darkness and further disposal. Sean McKean, loyal and unflappable, left to attend to any curiosity generated by the gunshot. Julius poured more brandy and he, Fiona and Henley watched the sun set over the river, studiously ignoring the canvas bundle behind them. Fiona hadn't said a word since the men had entered the room and was surprised at herself, she who was usually so voluble.

She'd seen her share of death, more than most ever would, and she felt no regret at Harper's abrupt passing.

In another time, perhaps a few years before or even centuries past, when retribution would have been equally as swift as it had been here.There was a part of her, some dark specter, who termed it fitting now.

"Are you all right, Fiona?" Julius asked, eyeing her carefully. "You've been very quiet."

She sipped her brandy. "Rough justice, Julius, but deserved." She felt Henley's eyes on her as well and turned to him. "It's not the first righteous blood I've seen spilled. Have no fear for my delicate sensibilities."

"Jesus, Fiona," he whispered. "I will not." But his hand traced the contours of her face. "I hope I never disappoint you, Irish."

Fiona smiled and so did Julius, as his eyes met hers. Kindred spirits, she thought, and not for the first time. That, she thought, was a sure sign that Mother Superior would say she was destined for the fires of hell. Still, she was thinking she might have good company.

"What," Fiona said, "do we do about Mavis?"

THAT EVENING'S performance of the Taming of the Shrew went spectacularly well but Fiona was tired to her bones as the curtain fell for the evening on Kate and Petrucchio and she made a hasty exit to her dressing room. She plopped down on her stool and took off her makeup as fast as she could. It had not been a day she would wish repeated and all she wanted right now was her bed. She began to unlace the tight corset of Kate's costume when the door flew open. Mavis stormed in, her blue taffeta skirts rustling like a brush fire.

"I've come for the rubies. And where is hell is George Harper? I haven't seen him since noon."

"Mavis, I don't know." That at least was true. George was well and truly gone by now.

Mavis threw herself into the chair beside the dressing table, fuming. Fiona continued to work on the corset and turned to face Mavis. "How did you ever get involved in this scheme in the first place?"

The question clearly took Mavis by surprise. "A girl's got to look out for herself, Fiona. A concept you should know well by this point, if anything I've heard from James is close to the truth."

"You're an actress, Mavis, and a pretty good one," Fiona said. "Surely you've managed."

Mavis laughed harshly. "Oh, I've managed all right, running from two husbands who thought to live off my talents. I'm pushing fifty, and that means an end to the stage pretty soon now. Even you must have noticed I'm relegated to parts I never thought I'd be forced to play. Nurse? Mrs. Dreadlow? God knows what'll be next, the MacBeth witches?"

It was true. Mavis looked amazing for her age, but it was catching up quickly. Perhaps stealing was a good option, at least she could see why Mavis thought so.

"So what are planning to do?"

"What the hell do you care? I could ask you the same question."

Fiona shrugged. "Be my own person, I suppose, without having to depend upon anyone."

Mavis sat back in her chair. "Exactly. You've figured this out pretty fast for somebody as young as you are. Life in the peat bog must've been quite the carnival."

Now it was Fiona's turn to laugh, and not in a happy way. "Orphanages and life as a bought and paid for crofter's wife at fourteen are good training grounds for cynical, Mavis."

"Jesus."

"Exactly," Fiona echoed Mavis's own words. This conversation was becoming uncomfortable and it was time to bring it to an end.

"Listen to me, Mavis," Fiona said. She took out the last lace on the corset and put it aside, smoothing her underdress. "You're on your own."

Mavis's eyes were frantic and she stood up. "You've got those rubies, right?"

"No."

"What?"

"I never did. James was a liar."

Mavis wasn't just afraid now, she was angry. She glared at Fiona. "Well, he learned from the best. You're really something, you Irish brat. I'm getting out of here before they come for me."

She threw open the door and gasped. Henley was leaning leisurely against the doorframe, arms crossed.

"Evening, Mavis. Let's take a walk." He cocked an elbow. Any attempt at bravado fled and Mavis's shoulders slumped as she took Henley's arm. She glanced fearfully back at Fiona who hadn't moved a muscle. The taffeta skirts rustled as they disappeared down the hallway and Fiona turned back to the mirror. She stared glumly at her reflection. Yes, she was very likely going to hell. Maybe it was time to think about redemption.

CHAPTER 34

The Queen of Dreams's engines throbbed and the great paddlewheel churned the river water, the droplets glistening in the rising sun. Fiona stood on the third deck, her usual custom, feeling the power beneath her feet as the great boat readied itself for the last leg of its journey to New Orleans. This morning, she was on the dockside rather than the river, looking for something and it didn't take her long to find the object of her search.

Mavis Thornton sat forlornly on a sizeable trunk, dressed in black, her fist propping up her chin as she watched the boat move slowly away from its berth. Fiona gave a great sigh of relief. For all the woman had tried to do to all of them, she hadn't wished doom upon her, although perhaps to Mavis, stranded in Baton Rouge came pretty close.

"My dear," Julius said, noiselessly coming to stand beside her. He was elegant as usual, dressed in a black waistcoat even at the early hour, his pale hair brushing his shoulders. "You didn't really think I was going to throw the poor silly bitch into the mercies of the current, did you?"

Fiona turned to him and he chuckled at the look at her face.

"Yes, by god, you rather did, I think." He shook his head. "I know the Harper incident was a bit of a shock, but believe me when I say that was a dangerous man who betrayed and endangered others, but that's not my usual method of dealing with adversity. Now, Mavis, on the other hand, is an entirely different kettle of fish. Down on their luck actresses have a tendency to make poor decisions of all sorts, say in men, or money-making schemes. But I'm a forgiving man when it comes to those sorts of peccadilloes, especially in women. Most are misguided or frightened and not malicious by nature."

Fiona listened quietly and then couldn't help but smile. "And then there's me, Julius. I'm a little different than your generalization of the female persuasion, I think. I'm not down on my luck as an actress yet, but the days are passing." She gazed at the trees passing by as they gathered power and Mavis was but a black dot quickly disappearing from view.

"Christ Jesus, Fiona," he laughed. "I'm going to have to have a think on that one."

Indeed you might, Fiona thought. *Dear Julius, I'm not yet certain how I fit in, but fit in I shall.* She took his arm. "Let's have a stroll, shall we?" And down around the deck they went. It was a lovely morning, after all.

She didn't see Henley until late afternoon when he knocked at her door. She opened it and stood looking up at him.

"Hello, Michael."

He stepped in and closed the door behind him, gathering her up as though she was weightless, kissing her like a starving man. She returned his kisses avidly and before she knew it they were on her bed, clothes strewn here and there, to which she hadn't the slightest objection.

Before things went any further, Fiona demanded answers, her hand insistent on his chest. "What happened with Mavis? When you left, I didn't know what was going to happen. What did she say?"

Henley grimaced. "She cried. A lot. In the end, she confessed all, blamed most of on Harper, which might be true. She's a shrewd one, she is. There very well might be another conspirator or two out there, but we'll deal with that when the time comes. Still, I agree with Julius. He gave her some money and leaving her in Baton Rouge was a gift, in my opinion. She'll make out. Her sort always does." He bent down to her, his lips traveling from her neck down her body. "We have better concerns, I think."

Quite some time later, they lay spent, Fiona trailing her fingers down his stomach, grinning as he twitched now and then. He grabbed her hand.

"No more, Irish. A man needs recovery time."

Wide-eyed, she batted her eyelashes. "Oh my mistake. Thought I had me a New York stud. How wrong a poor crofter girl can be."

"Wench." He rolled her over and straddled her hips while she grinned up at him. "It's not a long voyage to New Orleans, but we'll pass the time, if you're amenable."

"Maybe." Fiona gently pulled his head down. "Show me some magic and we'll see. It's long enough trip, I'm thinkin'."

And so it proved to be.

Henley was still snoring softly when she dressed in the pre-dawn darkness, but her hands were steady on the simple skirt and blouse she put on. They were equally as steady when she pulled the carpetbag from its hiding place behind the wardrobe and pulled out Victoria Lowell's necklace, her fingers moving surely through the baubles until they found the rubies. Fiona put the cursed thing in her pocket and tiptoed to the door, opening it soundlessly and slipping outside. The deck lights still glowed, one at each end and two in the middle, but she found a pool of darkness in between them. She stood at the rail, watching the water curl at the Queen's passage and pulled out the rubies, holding them over the river. She tossed them in, never seeing when they sank to the depths, sighing audibly in relief.

Her hands gripped the railing. It was as though every bad thing she'd ever done sunk with the necklace, and although she knew that wasn't really true, it still felt like something foul had fallen into the river with the rubies, never to rise. Maybe now she really could begin again.

* * *

HER FIRST GLIMPSE of New Orleans came with the dawn, as Fiona, Henley and Julius stood on deck, as Captain Hamilton and his pilot deftly maneuvered the Queen into her berth.

"It's a big city," Fiona breathed, looking over the rooftops of New Orleans. She'd seen New York and Chicago, but this seemed different somehow.

"Yes, it is." Julius smiled. "And it's unique to itself, sort of a slice of Paris mixed with American blood of all kinds. I love this place, especially the French Quarter, which is where I always dock. Just like Jean Lafitte in his day, when he brought his ill-gotten wares to the market where the elite of the city swarmed to be the first to snag his silks and brandy." He laughed. "I'm a hopeless romantic and I do love entrepreneurship."

The sun glinted upon the towers of a cream-colored building not far away like a beckoning light calling them forward.

"What is that?" Fiona said, pointing.

"Ah. Jackson Square, and St. Louis Cathedral," Julius said. He turned to Henley. "Your services as a tour guide are about to be on order, young man. She's got a lot to discover and you're just the man to acquaint her with the place."

Henley grinned. "I've got no agenda, at least that I know of, for a few days," he directed his words at Julius, who nodded. "So, if you're of a mind, Irish, we have excursions ahead."

Fiona couldn't have agreed more. She gazed out at the buildings and sighed with pleasure. "New Orleans looks wonderful."

It was as though a deadening weight had been lifted from not just them, but everyone on the boat, even those who hadn't been aware there was a threat to their safety and serenity. Or maybe, Fiona mused, it was simply arriving at their final destination, a fabled city that she could hardly wait to see, smell and touch, a haven they'd all been anticipating even if it was one they'd never seen before. She could hardly wait to step foot on those enticing streets.

Henley smiled. "Gather whatever you may need, Fiona. As soon as the gangplank's down we're into the French Quarter."

She looked at him quizzically. "The French Quarter? Is that New Orleans?"

Julius laughed. "Oh my dear, the very best and oldest part of it. Trust me, you're going to love it." He looked at Henley. "I suggest Café du Monde as a first stop, and who knows what thereafter, eh?"

Henley nodded. "I think Mademoiselle needs a new dress, maybe a hat and I know just the place."

For the next three days, Fiona and Henley left at dawn and returned at midnight, tired and happy. From her first explosive bite of a beignet that showered her with powdered sugar to a late dinner of etouffee at Antoine's, she felt as though she were in a fantasyland. The shadowed interior of St. Louis Cathedral spoke to her, its shadowy recesses and soaring ceilings like her soul, the dark and light merging into a serenity she longed for. She began to replace the dismal memories of St. Hilda's version of god, and to make a new version, one with sunlight and mercy.

New Orleans was a melee, its citizens sharing the city together, whether white, black, Creole, Cajun, or an array of mixed bloods, all treating each with equality and respect, or so it seemed on the surface. Occasionally, though, Fiona noticed an incident here and there which let her know that not all racial tensions had evaporated, and there were beggars, hucksters and plenty of streetwalkers just as there were in every major city she'd been to. They didn't venture further afield into the Irish channel neighborhoods or other depths of the city, even though she was curious, because she didn't want to mar this time they had together, as though they were any normal couple on a holiday.

After a day of exploring, she and Henley would return to the boat, footsore but happy. The nights were magical too, as they discovered more about each other, both in body and mind.

On the third morning, Henley took her arm and steered her into Madame de Chantilly's hat shop, where Colette, the lovely French owner, designed the most beautiful hat Fiona could've imagined. A pale cream, the felt hat fell gracefully over her left brow, and the brim swooped up to the crown, festooned with soft egret feathers dyed a pale pink, while a cream velvet ribbon circled the crown of the hat and left streamers that ran down her back.

When she peered at herself in the mirror, she laughed and clapped her hands in delight.

"Oh, Henley, have you ever seen anything like this in your sweet life?"

He chuckled. "Never, Fiona. But it's not simply the hat, it's the wearer that truly makes it wonderful."

Colette nodded sagely. "*Exactemente, monsieur*. This is what I do, make the hat reflect the person who will wear it." She crossed her arms in satisfaction. "This one," she nodded at Fiona, "was a joy to design for. This is just the first, I hope, *mademoiselle*. Life gives us many moments that must be treasured and I always say, the right hat makes them extra special forever. You will be back, I know. You are a woman who is destined for special moments."

"Thank you so much," Fiona said, taking Colette's hands in

hers. "Your skills and your hat make me feel special. I hope to come back many times."

She meant it, too. Not just the hat shop, but the dress shops, the French shoemaker and especially the perfumerie Honore, where they made her a perfume that blended orange blossoms, roses and an ingredient that Mr. St. Clair, the blender, said was his secret. Whatever it was, Fiona loved it and bought three bottles, clutching them greedily before she stashed them in her bag while Henley chuckled and shook his head.

"Now there will never be a mistake in the dark about who is next to you," Fiona said, as they stood on Chartres Street outside Honore. "It is my scent and no one else's."

Henley kissed her, the scent washing over him. "There won't be any mistakes, Irish, perfume or no."

The three days respite were over too soon. The next morning the troupe sat in the theater with Julius, working through the performance schedule for New Orleans, where they would be until the northern part of the river was free from any ice, likely late April. They would be doing many Shakespeare variations, occasionally a full length version, interspersed with more modern plays and a variety show of dancers, singers and performers that changed and reinvented itself weekly. Julius hired six new actors from New Orleans, to bolster their numbers and fill the roles in the bigger productions.

Not only were there to be performances on the boat itself, but some were planned for the magnificent French Opera House on Bourbon Street. Julius had connections, of course and many days while they rehearsed, he was away into the city doing other business, and Henley and Sean with him. Fiona didn't mind because she had new roles to learn and needed to concentrate solely on that many days, but the atmosphere changed somewhat, at least for her. When Captain Hamilton left to spend the winter at Heart's Ease, it cemented her feeling that a new phase had arrived for the people on the Queen.

Clearly, the entertainment portion of DeMonte Enterprises was only one part of all the things Julius had an interest in. Darker things roiled beneath the outwardly placid surface of their lives.

Still, the week before Christmas, they staged Dickens' A Christmas Carol, and Julius himself took on the role of Ebenezer Scrooge. He was magnificent, and Fiona suspected he'd played the part many times before, and even though the play was new to her, she loved it, playing the Ghost of Christmas Past. After that, they were firmly established in New Orleans as the place to go for the upcoming season, and tickets to all their performances were in great demand.

The weeks passed, and Fiona grew contented but restless at the same time. She spent her days busily learning and rehearsing, the evenings often performing, and nights with Henley, when he was around. They drove upriver to some of the plantations and spent the night with an old friend of Julius's at a lovely place called River Run. The war had not been kind but the family was restoring the place to some of its former glory year by year, as so many of the old places on the river were doing.

On her evenings off, they wandered the city as they did their first days in it, visiting Fiona's favorite restaurants and listening to music at the various establishments they passed by. She hadn't had such a placid time in her life since working for Audrey Prescott but it was as though she was waiting for something and she didn't know quite what.

Then came the night when Julius was shot and everything changed.

CHAPTER 35

Merry St. John looked up when Fiona tiptoed into the room. She put a finger to her lips and finished wringing out the washcloth in the basin of cool water, placing it gently upon Julius's forehead. He slept on, in the arms of Morpheus. The small dose of laudanum was doing its work.

Merry stood up from the chair beside the bed, and Fiona took her seat. "Any change?" she whispered.

Merry shook her head, the lines of worry deepening. She patted Fiona on the shoulder and left. They'd been nursing in shifts for two days now, with an occasional check-in from Dr. Miller, the boat's surgeon. The gunshot wound in Julius's shoulder was healing, but the broken ribs and the blow to the head were the worrisome issues. Although he'd woken up twice, he'd groaned and lapsed back into sleep. Fiona smoothed Julius's hair from his forehead, her hand lingering. She loved this man like the father she'd never had and the thought of losing him so soon after he'd come into her life was devastating. She shook her thoughts away. No, she wouldn't allow anything like that to even cross her mind for fear it could become reality.

Two nights ago, she'd been ready for bed when Henley knocked on her door.

"Come with me, Fiona. I need your help."

She'd thrown on some clothes and they'd run down the deck to Julius's cabin. He was on the bed and Dr. Miller was cutting his shirt off, blood pooling on the sheet beneath him. He'd been shot in the shoulder, and when the shirt came off, Fiona gasped. It looked as though someone had taken an oar to his side, the skin already purpling, as well as his head, a makeshift bandage around his forehead absorbing a good deal of blood there as well.

"I need hot water and bandages, Henley," Dr. Miller rasped. "You," he gestured to Fiona, "help me get this shirt off so I can see how bad it is."

It was bad. An hour later, Julius lay still, his eyes closed, an occasional low moan escaping from his lips. Dr. Miller had taken out the bullet and cleaned the shoulder wound, now wrapped in white bandages, as was Julius's head, after ten stitches to close the wound. His ribs were wrapped in even more, and the doctor estimated at least three were broken.

"All we can do now is wait," Dr. Miller said, gathering up his bag and a basin full of bloody instruments and rags. "He won't be moving around for a while, so somebody will have to watch him constantly."

Fiona nodded. "I'll be here."

Henley shut the door as the doctor left and sat down beside her. He looked a little the worse for wear himself, a nasty bruise on his cheek and he was moving carefully, as though something hurt.

"What happened?"

Henley sighed. "We were down at the new warehouse on Decatur, overseeing the shipment from France that came in tonight, me, Julius and Sean. Two of our men were unloading down at the dock when out of nowhere these three guys came in and attacked us. I was in front and got smacked in the back and head with a pipe or something and was out for a minute or two. I heard a shot, then two more. Julius fell, and Sean shot one of them. The other two got away. Christ what a mess."

Fiona put her hand on his arm and he stared bleakly at her. "It's my fault, I should be the one lying there, not him."

"Don't be an idiot, Michael," she said and he started, knocking her hand away. "It's not your fault. Is Sean all right?"

"He's fine. He's down in the cargo hold with the man he shot. We brought him back with us. So, you see, I have to take care of some garbage."

Fiona raised an eyebrow. "Oh?"

"Let's just say he was very helpful identifying his pals. Unfortunately it took too much persuasion and I wasn't in a patient frame of mind." He brushed his hand over his eyes. "However, good old George Harper managed to do some damage, even from hell."

She wasn't surprised. She'd been expecting they'd find that he had, as she was sure Julius had known as well.

He stood up and kissed the top of her head. "You take care of him. I'll take care of the rest." She hadn't seen him since, and three days had passed.

* * *

SHE MUST'VE DOZED off but her eyes flew open, her wrist gripped in an iron hand. Julius stared at her.

"What happened to me, Fiona?"

She told him.

Fiona put the spoon down in the bowl of chicken soup she'd been feeding Julius. He smiled ruefully, dabbing his lips on the napkin with his left hand, the right encased in the sling Dr. Miller had insisted upon. He put it down and snatched up the piece of fresh-baked bread instead, chewing thoughtfully, eyes still resting upon her.

"Tell Andre tonight I think I need a steak, with mushrooms, béarnaise sauce and butter. A nice Bordeaux, say an 1845 would be excellent as well, builds up the blood. I seem to have lost some, according to the doctor."

Fiona laughed. "Damn. I'll have to do the cutting. Perhaps a beef bourguignon instead? As for the wine, I do agree." She put the tray aside and handed him a glass of water but he shook his head. "Ah, the patient grows restless."

"Come on, Fiona." Julius threw the covers away and swung his legs over the side of the bed. "Help me stand up, will you? Another day of laying in this bed will kill me surer than any bullet. To say nothing of that noxious chicken soup."

She wasn't sure that was the best idea, but she knew there was no stopping him. He was unsteady and she let him lean on her. After four days in bed, no one would be ready to walk freely, especially somebody that'd been injured as he'd been. They took tentative steps around the small room, over to the window, streaked with rain, which had been falling steadily for days now.

"You see, Julius, even the heavens weep when you're not well," Fiona said. "Trust me, I grew up in a convent. I know these things."

She was gratified at his small chuckle. "Those nuns didn't do much for your temper, little one, rain or no rain."

"That could be true," she said, guiding him back to the bed as he was leaning more heavily on her and she could tell his strength was waning. "But I'm a force to be reckoned with now, thanks to their kind guidance."

"Indeed," murmured Julius, laying back on his pillows. "We're going to have to do that a lot more often if I'm ever to get out of this room."

"Sssh. You'll be right as rain in no time, man," Fiona said.

"Taking on the world as usual. Don't despair." She sat down in her bedside chair.

"Where's Henley?" Julius said. "I need to talk with him."

As if on cue, Henley knocked and then entered unceremoniously, dressed in his usual black suit and crisp white shirt and cravat. Fiona was grateful, having been on duty since dawn. Her back ached and so did her head. Contending with Julius was no mean task, especially when he was decidedly cranky. She stood up but Henley's hand on her shoulder sat her back down emphatically in her chair.

He looked well, clean-shaven and smelling of some spice. She hadn't seen him in three days but apparently things had gone well, since he wasn't dead. Relief flooded through her, tinged with annoyance. He could've sent a message at least but that wasn't Henley's style, she'd learned, so there was little point in being annoyed with the man.

He pulled up another chair. "It's taken care of, at least for now. We tracked the other two and talked to them. Harper was their contact. The dumb bastard did some damage, as we feared. They told me no one else knew and we questioned them well, but I have some doubts, nonetheless. Criminals always have friends who pick up on their activities, so we'll have to be vigilant. More vigilant than ever."

Julius nodded. "Of course. Are they…forgive me, of course not, you know your business." His smile was quite terrible but Fiona didn't mind in the least. She knew they were dead and she hoped that was just as fitting, glancing at Julius's pale face. She had a surge of regret that she hadn't been there herself. Her thoughts of eternal damnation had diminished a great deal in the last few days.

"You have a lot to discuss. Perhaps I should leave," she said. Julius put a hand on her arm and was firm.

"No," Julius said. "I've had nothing to do but think, laying here, and it's not laudanum clouding my thoughts, trust me. I've decided we need to maintain more of a presence here in New Orleans, not just an occasional trip to check the warehouse, or rely upon the men I hire here to make sure things are running smoothly. Much as I like New Orleans, it's not the place where I can spend most of my time. There's the financial firms, theaters and contacts in Chicago and of course, Angel, even now that she's at school."

Henley gazed at him. "What are you thinking, Julius?"

Julius sat up straighter on his pillows and he gazed thoughtfully at Fiona and Henley, looking nearly like his usual self, his dark eyes boring into theirs. "I've been thinking about this for some time, even before that debacle at the warehouse. Things are going to get worse for many of our friends before they better and I think we're going to be very busy with hard goods and oversight, along with the usual tax-free luxury items."

He coughed and cursed softly, holding his ribs. "It'll take some time to set up, but I've an idea if the two of you are interested. You seem to be getting along well so that's one hurdle we don't need to jump."

Henley and Fiona exchanged glances. She could tell he was as surprised as she was, but she saw the spark of interest in his eyes.

"Before we sail up the river at the end of April, six weeks from now, I want to set up an office in the Quarter to handle all the southern business. Maybe combine it with something else, an art gallery, say, or a clotherie, as a legitimate business but also a front for mine. What do you think, Fiona? Perhaps a milliner since you're so fond of those lovely hats you've been wearing lately." He smiled, Julius's old sly smile and Fiona knew, even with the pain, he was on the mend.

Still, she was speechless, a rarity for her, but she was thinking fast. She loved New Orleans, all of it, the Quarter, the Irish Channel, the Garden District, and the people, so varied and so accepting, their sweet slow rhythm of life the epitome of the southern charm she'd come to love, and even the problems she could see now and then and even those that she knew lurked beneath the surface. If she had the time to spend here, she'd find them out and she loved nothing more than ferreting out trouble and making things right, especially for those that couldn't do it for themselves. She'd been thinking about this for some time and she suspected Julius might have an inkling where her thoughts might lie.

She looked up at Henley, who raised his eyebrows and shrugged almost imperceptibly. That was all she needed.

"Hats be damned, Julius," she said. "I've got a better idea, one I've been thinking about for a while myself. Acting's been an excellent steppingstone, teaching me how to react and find out how others do as well. I'm quite good at discovery. It's a skill that serves a person well, along with not being afraid to implement solutions to the problems I find. A great many people, as you've found throughout your life, need help now and then. I know I did. You've given that help and I'd like to follow your example."

She took a deep breath. "What about a detective agency?"

She didn't think she'd ever seen Julius truly amazed before or at least acting like that, and Henley burst out laughing. Julius began to cough, holding his ribs. She waited, while both of them finally quieted and stared at her.

"Christ Jesus, Fiona," Julius winced. He peered at her intently. "I think you're serious, aren't you?"

"Yes." She stood up, hands on her hips. "You know I am. I can do this, and what's more, I want to do this." She glanced at Henley. "Be right nice if I had a partner with some muscle and some grit to back me up when my wits aren't enough. One never knows. Maybe we should talk to Sean."

Julius chuckled softly. "Fiona, Fiona. 'Find though she be but little, she is fierce', eh Henley?"

He looked at Henley expectantly, who threw up his hands. He grabbed Fiona around the waist and turned her to face him.

"We won't be needing Sean, Irish." He kissed her soundly and turned to Julius. "I've always liked New Orleans, you know? Especially in the spring when the jacaranda and lilies bloom. And of course there's beignets...and hats...and detectives."

Fiona held out her hand to Julius, who smiled like a cat at a dish of cream. The wily old fox had led them well, but she'd been the one who'd thought to put out the dish, weeks ago. Some people just knew each other's thoughts, and she really had indeed become good at discovery. She'd had an excellent teacher, after all. The Irish and the English had found common ground in the most unlikely place but one that would serve them both very well.

He squeezed her hand, eyes twinkling, and pulled her closer, whispering in her ear. "I'm going to miss seeing you both every day but I'll be around now and then. Take good care of Henley, my dear."

Julius gave a dramatic sigh and lay back on his pillows. "Now let a man get some rest, will you? I believe you have plans to make. Remember, 'To do a great right, do a little wrong.'"

"Surely our motto," Fiona whispered and saw the smile on Julius's face as she gently closed the door and took Henley's hand.

EPILOGUE

On any given morning, whether the sun is shining, or the rain is falling, if you walk down Royal Street to No. 416, Jean-Claude St. Clair's Art Gallery whose large windows are filled with glorious paintings, sometimes an old master or sometimes a modern and exciting new artist, you will find beside them a black door with a discreet but polished bronze sign that simply says "S&H Investigations".

If you open that black door, as you might have a need to, you will enter an elegantly furnished anteroom with a walnut desk, behind which sits a charming young man, who will greet you with a smile and the words, "How may we help you?" in charmingly French-accented English. He will offer you coffee and perhaps a plate of beignets while you explain your needs.

After a few minutes, he will escort you down a softly lit hallway to an office and introduce you to Miss Shanahan, a lovely petite young woman, her black hair pulled into a tight chignon, who shakes your hand and offers you a seat to further explain your problem.

Sometimes Miss Shanahan will call in an associate, Mr.

Henley, a tall man with a hard face but a kind smile, who will listen to what you have to say as well.

Before you leave No. 416 Royal Street, you feel reassured. You know that you have placed your troubles in hands that will take good care of you. The coffee and beignets were delicious as well, and the visit was well worth your time.

ABOUT THE AUTHOR

Kathleen Morris loves American and Western history, is a graduate of Prescott College in Arizona and lives and writes in the desert Southwest. She loves being able to immerse herself in the lives of her characters, especially bringing to life the charismatic women of the past, both real and imaginary. Meticulous research and dedication to detail are the hallmarks of her work. Her debut novel, **The Lily of the West**, the story of "Big Nose Kate" Haroney, was published in 2019 to critical acclaim and won the Peacemaker award for "Best First Western Novel" from Western Fictioneers. **The Transformation of Chastity James** followed in 2021, and was designated a SPUR award finalist from Western Writers of America. In 2022, she won the Peacemaker award from Western Fictioneers for Best Short Story, **"Mary, Mary Quite Contrary"**. She is a member of Western Writers of America and Western Fictioneers. Visit her website at www.KathleenMorrisauthor.com.

www.ingramcontent.com/pod-product-compliance
Lightning Source LLC
LaVergne TN
LVHW021233080526
838199LV00088B/4328